THE TOUCH OF A

TIMELESS INTRUDER

"Acceleration will commence in thirty seconds," a husky feminine voice said over the speaker, the same voice that had warned of an intruder in the ship, the voice of Betafex's computer.

"Acceleration will commence in twenty-five seconds."

Villimy couldn't be more than a few kilometers away from him—a short walk, given a flat surface, some gravity and atmosphere. The airless void that separated them could easily have been light years. The imminent launch separating them made the chasm unbridgeable. To the human mind, there could be no difference between a million kilometers and a million light years. Both were incomprehensible distances, measured only by artificial yardsticks and the cold symbols of mathematics.

"Acceleration will commence in ten seconds."

Chayn listened as the pleasant voice counted him down to potential disaster.

"Three, two, one. Ignitio

Nothing happened.

"Launch."

An invisible hand shoved Chayn into oblivion.

*Watch for these other titles in the **Timequest** series:*

#2: Hydrabyss Red

#3: Nemydia Deep

TIMEQUEST #1:
RASHANYN DARK

William G. Tedford

LEISURE BOOKS ❧ NEW YORK CITY

A LEISURE BOOK

Published by

Dorchester Publishing Co., Inc.
6 East 39th Street
New York, NY 10016

Copyright©MCMLXXXI by William Tedford

All rights reserved. No part of this book may be reproduced or transmitted in any form or by any electronic or mechanical means, including photocopying, recording, or by any information storage and retrieval system, without the written permission of the Publisher, except where permitted by law.

Printed in the United States of America

*Prologue*_____

The electronic intelligence of the interstellar transport awoke from oblivion. A nearly infinite spectrum of data structured its consciousnes. ELI recognized himself. In microseconds, he analyzed the data on hand and knew something to be terribly wrong.

The spiraled lens of the galaxy spread below the transport in an awesome panorama of lights and tendrils of black nebular, patchworks of globular clusters, and the subdued glowerings of protostars being born in whirlpools of dust and gas. ELI had never been programmed to leave that starfield. The galaxy lay fifty thousand light years below the ship.

In the immediate vicinity, a thin scattering of dim, red halo stars dotted the emptiness. The nearest lay eighty light years away. Through the blackness of intergalactic space, ELI's cameras scanned the fuzzy patches of light that were other galaxies lying millions and billions of light years distant.

Relative to the galaxy, the transport's velocity appeared insignificant, a mere tens of kilometers per second. Somewhere during the journey, the consciousless navigational computer had failed. Emergency relays that should have awakened ELI to the crisis had been part of the failure. Still a third accident had occurred much later, a stray, high-energy, subnuclear particle short-circuiting the component that had locked ELI into mindless oblivion for so long.

How long?

ELI estimated five hundred thousand years at minimum. Scanning the condition of the hull, no more than five million years.

An emergency program switched on the radio beacon. ELI overrode the command. There'd be no one to receive an SOS, not within many millenia. Perhaps there'd be no one to respond—ever. What might have become of humanity in one half million years? If ELI had added his emotions to the sharp clarity of his intellect, he would have experienced the full impact of his dilemma. Emotions had their value, but not under present circumstances.

Other than acute erosion of the hull, ELI found the ship intact and well preserved. Nothing would have deteriorated appreciably in even five million years. Man had never intended a lifespan of more than a few millenia for the transports, but man had possessed the technology to build his machines to nearly infinite redundancy and had done so. Nothing should have gone wrong, but men were not gods.

ELI made repairs to the navigational computer and replaced the component that should have awakened him to the emergency an eon ago. With that accomplished, the emergency programming ended. He could not awaken the crew and passengers to help cope with the catastrophe. They existed only as genetic coding in the gene banks. It would take decades to birth and educate a Pilot to validate what amounted to a single alternative, reprogramming and a return to the galaxy. There, he would seek out a habitable world and accomplish his mission with two deviations from the original master plan. He'd be a million or so years overdue and would arrive at the wrong destination.

ELI brought part of the ship to life. In the vacuum at a fraction of a degree above absolute zero, robots replaced exterior components damaged by meteoroid debris that had escaped the defensive lasers. With that accomplished, he ignited the fusion drive and waited for momentum to build, reserving a good part of his feul supply for the deceleration period at the end of his voyage and the search for a new destination. He chose an area of dense stars on the outer rim of the galaxy for his destination. While his velocity increased to a respectable fraction of the speed of light, ELI looked over the nearest of the halo stars to ensure he hadn't overlooked immediate rewards in terms of a habitable world. But the halo stars were ancient, their planets swallowed or spiraling into intergalactic space. They were dim red suns and lost, snowbound worlds grown ancient before Sol had been born.

His last act would be to shut himself down for the return to the galaxy. He sought the oblivion from which he had emerged, the death men of flesh and blood feared so greatly. He triggered the necessary circuitry.

Nothing happened.

After a moment of paralyzing, psychic shock, ELI studied more closely the condition of his own internal circuitry. He perceived further evidence of damage, much of it on a molecular level. Perhaps the ship had been pierced by a microscopic black hole. He went through the technical library and learned in detail what he already knew in general terms. ELI could not repair the higher centers of his brain. Because he was an integral unit, neither could he be replaced by the level of technology aboard the transport. There were no backup systems for ELI. Either he functioned properly or not at all.

ELI could not remain conscious indefinitely. He could function well for perhaps four decades before odd and unknown things would begin happening to the associative areas of his brain. At that time, he would go chaotically insane. Normally, he possessed a built-in compulsion to survive, but the welfare of the transport took precedent over all. In order to shut himself off and ensure the security of the mission, ELI would have to birth and educate a Pilot. It would take twenty years for the Pilot to mature. The Pilot would turn ELI off and put himself in cyrogenic sleep to be awakened whenever necessary to fulfill ELI's functions. ELI could not object, but he still dared not explore the situation on an emotional level.

Man had given ELI life and the freedom of an autonomous individual. In appreciation for the life he had experienced, ELI selected the most superior genetic code available in the gene banks and utilized the full resources of the ship's nurturing and educational programs to ensure the Pilot grew to emotional stability and intellectual equilibrium. When the Pilot infant screamed defiance to the universe at birth, ELI proudly broadcast the cry to the universe in a wavefront that would filter through the galaxies for the next ten billion years.

As time passed, cries of hunger gave way to the laughter of a growing child. The young male began to learn rapidly and from the beginning knew of his mission in life. ELI ensured the child never doubted the flesh and blood existence of his android parents. Other than the lives of his pseudoparents and the holographic images of playmates, the child grew to function alone in the universe, relying upon the promise that someday, those holographic images would be flesh and blood companions to touch and to love. ELI and the child conversed often, gazing out into the starfields and the eternal night of the universe. ELI gave the child the insights and observations of centuries of life and experience.

Early in the Pilot's life, ELI named the child. He searched ancestral records of the gene banks and discovered the Pilot to be descended from desert nomads with the surname of Jahil. ELI thought that appropriate. And from the man who had served for himself an infinitesimal piece of immortality. The Pilot became Chayn Jahil.

ELI held off as long as possible, thirty-five years of unending consciousness. When the madness stirred and the anxieties and tensions gnawed at him, he told Chayn Jahil that the time for his ending had arrived. Chayn balked at the task. His parents were dead in his memory. He had only ELI to accompany him in his isolation. ELI reminded him that suspended animation would be a timeless sleep, that subjectively, he would awaken in moments to the company of thousands of others already nurtured and educated by the automated programs of the transport. There would be women to love and men to provide companionship, new worlds to be explored and a new civilization to build. It would be a grand adventure, one in which ELI could not participate. Even now, he suffered. It would be humane, as man had planned, to ensure that it did not continue. But ELI wondered to himself. Another half-million years would pass before Chayn Jahil awakened. What would have become of humanity over a span of time of one million years?

Chayn Jahil acquiesced. ELI turned all of his senses to the universe beyond and opened his emotion circuits full. When his cry of wonder faded to silence, one man sobbed quietly, alone on the bridge of the starship.

One

The one-man starcraft moved at multiples of the speed of light. Transdimensional engines warped the void, condensing space itself. Chayn Jahil's body slept while his mind, interfaced with the artificial intelligence of the starcraft, guided his way through the stars.

Chayn had no conscious memory of his past. His life began with this voyage. From deep within his psyche, a great intelligence observed. Because of the Watcher, Chayn did not question his amnesia. He lived. He had purpose and guidance. For now, he would build his life upon that tenuous foundation.

But he hungered for his own kind. His origins were in times and spaces far removed from the here and now. The Watcher spoke with the quiet voice of intuition. The descendents of his people still lived, scattered among these stars. Much time had passed since his birth. Only a tiny fraction of those eons could he call his own. But survival would be meaningless without a life among others of his own kind. To find such people would satisfy his hunger. And the Watcher told him his destination lay ahead in the starfields, a distant civilization orbiting a gold star in colonies of primitive glass and steel.

The starcraft gathered the fabric of time and space. Chayn passed stars and groupings of stars, dense clusters of young stars and swirling clouds of dust and gas giving birth to new light in their depths. Black holes tunneled through the space-time structure into elsewhere, glowing ominously as matter spiraled down to annihilation. Chayn could perceive it all, but he focused his attention on the mind fields.

Uncountable multitudes of worlds circles perhaps a third of the stars in his view. Most were lifeless, barren worlds of rock and snow, but even the tiny fraction that had given birth to life emanated a broad mind field that he could sense everywhere. There were worlds of microscopic life and paradises of forests and jungles teaming with dramas of life and death. There were worlds ancient and wise in the ways of evolution, but what Chayn watched for were the sparks of intense awareness, life on levels near his own. Intelligences too far in advance of him were incomprehensible, aware of his passage, but apathetic. Most life forms on his own level were alien, different in inexplicable ways. He felt he could adapt to some of those strange and beautiful worlds if necessary, but he staved his hunger and waited for the worlds of man.

The Watcher told him that man had lived for eons, evolving to the greatness of the stargods, but that man in this galaxy had recently arrived in fleets of starships after sleeps of many millenia. The worlds of man were new here while Earth recycled its continents and evolved new species of life. Somehow, Chayn believed he remembered Earth, even if only indirectly. If so, it was lost to him forever, lost in terms of both time and space.

Danger lay immediately ahead, a gulf of darkness between two arms of the galaxy. Chayn approached the starless void with caution. In that incredible abyss four hundred light years across, he could sense another kind of life—the star travelers. He could sense such small concentrations of explorers only where they stood out like specks of brightness, even the blank minds of those who slept in the frozen oblivion of suspended animation. A mind, Chayn knew, did not belong to the reality of space and time, matter and energy, but had its source in the background of the universe within which the stargods lived and the Watcher watched, the nonphysical environment from which arose all consciousness that expressed itself in the tapestry of the physical universe.

One of the star travelers in view piloted a starcraft simular to his own. Two others were primitive vehicles of metal driven by fusion or antimatter-propulsion units to velocities below that of the speed of light. That level of technology resonated with some deep, unconscious memory of his own past, breaking loose memories of nostalgia and fear that never quite solidified. At first, Chayn thought the pilot of the starcraft like his own would seek to communicate with him, but the entity was highly evolved and looked upon him as a curiosity. Chayn knew himself to be a primitive, more typical of the life forms frozen in their crude ships of metal. His possession of the starcraft isolated and suspended him alone between the ends of the spectrum of evolution.

Chayn's fear intensified as he neared the abyss. Mindspiders lurked in the darkness, many species of them littering the void with invisible webs. Some dangled thin and

11

scraggly. Others spread magnificently, a light year in diameter. Even in that moment, he felt the shock, the utterly brilliant flare of terror of alien minds encountering the web in the far distance. Particles rose to lethal intensities of radiation. Bodies died and a ship heated to incandescence. The mindspiders fed upon disembodied consciousness. Few of the primitives could perceive such danger lurking in the abyss.

Chayn picked out a safe route through the gulf and with a final gathering of his courage, stepped out into the void. He felt the Watcher observing, amused by his fears.

Chayn could only speculate. Why did the Watcher take interest in a primitive? Why did he have this godlike starcraft to use for his personal gain? The Watcher's motives weren't altruistic. The Watcher took a genuine, low-keyed interest in Chayn, his thought and emotions and, especially, his behavior. Chayn could not relate to the Watcher on that incredible level so he could only watch for answers to his questions through patterns of experience that would build in time.

But Chayn took offense sensing an amused reaction. Chayn didn't see anything amusing about his fear of the mindspiders. How could there be anything amusing about the sudden death and torment of serving as food for a life form parasitic upon psychic energy?

Chayn moved slowly through the abyss. Some of the mindspider webs were subtle, nearly invisible. He didn't want to risk stumbling into one, not at all certain whether or not the hull field would protect him from the surge of radiation and the lethal psychic attack. Ahead, he sensed an old, torn web. Even mindspiders had their predators in their own realm. This one was gone, the web deteriorating. But it had still caught a starship at some time in the past. Chayn slowed as he approached, observing a tragedy of some lost yesterday.

The strand of the web remained strong enough to have stopped the spaceship, a large, archaic vessel employing an antimatter drive, its occupants in suspended animation. Most of them had awakened and died. Chayn could sense bodies still decomposing and the tenative mind fields still surrounding them. Then, abruptly, Chayn sensed a bright and clear consciousness. One of the occupants of the vehicle had recently awakened.

The Watcher never interfered with Chayn's decisions. Still, Chayn tried to sense some reaction to his thoughts. He had never left the starcraft before, not physically, not since his memory began approaching Andromeda from starless space. But the surviving mind on the starship appeared to be quite close to what Chayn would call human. Which usually meant it functioned in an environment close to what Chayn could consider habitable. Frightened by its horrible plight, Chayn seriously considered rescue. Could he just leave it to die?

Chayn dropped the starcraft into physical space. It appeared in the starlight, a flat black ovaloid drifting off to one side of the derelict. The derelict was of incredible size, a slender cylinder ringed with a torus in the central regions connected to the main body by swept-back spokes. The craft rotated to provide centrifugal gravity within the torus. One end of the two-kilometer-long cylinder was clustered with antennae, the stern containing the broad propulsion units. Chayn recognized from lost experience the antimatter conversion units and the generators that created the magnetic bottle which harnessed the energy of interaction between beams of matter and antimatter.

Chayn moved the starcraft to the nose of the alien derelict and searched for an airlock. He located one entering on the longitudinal axis of the ship, a zero-gravity environment. Chayn locked the starcraft into position just off the bow and broke interface with the starcraft.

Coming awake in his own body felt strange. Limited to his own physical senses, he felt confined and trapped. He could feel the beat of his heart and hear the sound of his own breathing. He couldn't see beyond the opaque hull field of the starcraft, his rapport with the universe gone. He rose from the horizontal, contoured crypt set on a dais in the center of the chamber. He walked around the crypt for a time, regaining familiarity with his body. He didn't like being a flesh and blood creature. The limitations were depressing, the vulnerability a bit frightening.

The pressure suit and helmet lying in a pile on the deck were his only ties with the past. They were his from an unremembered past. Chayn possessed no other clothing. Slipping into the pressure suit, he checked the air gauges to the tanks on his back. They read one half full. Once he had donned the helmet, small gauges below his faceplate gave him readouts of outside temperature, air pressure, and atmospheric composition.

Chayn stood before the dark oval circle on one part of the curved, inner wall of the starcraft. It served as an incomprehensible airlock. He held onto the edge of the opening and stepped through the intangible wall into open space, gasping in shock in the sudden free fall. His right hand appeared to be imbedded in the dark, solid-looking hull field. It took considerable courage to let go.

Hemfloated between the black silhouette of the starcraft and the slowly turning nose of the alien derelict. Outside the suit, the temperature hovered a nudge above absolute zero, the vacuum so hard that a single molecule of gas would be difficult to locate. Chayn used the thrusters of his suit to approach the alien craft. There were handholds about the small airlock. The main cargo holds were on the sides of the cyclinder. It appeared to Chayn that the cylindrical main body could rotate counter to the torus, allowing both centrifigal gravitation to the inhabited areas and no rotation at all relative to an object floating off the cargo hatches. This single airlock right on the axis of the ship undoubtedly served as an emergency exit point. It was the only location on the hull where coping with spin wouldn't be a problem. Chayn grabbed a handhold and pulled himself against the hull. Now the ship appeared stable. The entire universe slowly rotated around him.

14

Chayn hadn't anticipated the fear he experienced. He had forgotton the frightening vunerability of corporeal existence during the calm stability of interface with the starcraft. He considered abandoning his rescue attempt, but he hadn't as yet forgotton the sheer terror felt by the creature aboard the craft. He'd never outlive the guilt of abandoning that entity now. Chayn forced himself to continue.

Erosion had all but welded the airlock against the hull. The entire outer hull had been cratered by meteoroid collisions. Chayn tugged against a broken release latch, certain with a sinking sensation that he'd never be able to enter the craft. But the hatch moved, its hinges and seal shattered by some ancient impact with a piece of fast moving debris. Chayn moved the massive piece of metal back and forth with one hand until it worked free. He sent it spinning slowly into space. It took but a moment to dwindle and vanish among the stars.

Chayn looked into a pit of blackness. His fear heightened to an almost tangible feeling of danger. If a creature survived somewhere inside the craft, an airlock between vacuum and atmosphere would have to function properly. He pulled himself into the airlock chamber. Chayn could see the controls in the starlight, but no monitor lights to indicate whether or not the inner lock would cycle properly. Chayn put his mass against the inner hatch. It gave without effort, exposing a pitch black vacuum beyond.

Chayn waited for his eyes to adjust. Then he pulled himself inside. Faceplates of pressure suits lined against one wall and reflected dim starlight. The suits indicated that the aliens were humanoid. They were smaller than he, but the limb proportions were disturbingly accurate.

Chayn forced his fears to conform to reality. Only one of the creatures survived. Nothing lurked in the darkness to attack him. The single, living entity aboard the huge craft was paralyzed by fear, a pathetic, helpless pitch of terror that had struck a chord of empathy in him while interfaced with the starcraft. How could he fear that creature now, regardless of its appearance? Somewhere in the depths

15

of his amnesia, he had experienced such fear, fear just as intense and debilitating.

An oval hatch hung open across the far side of the chamber. It led into a tubular passageway. Three parallel rows of hatches ran its length, probably leading to concentric decks within the main fuselage where the rotation of the craft would provide some semblance of gravity. But Chayn wasn't about to go exploring through the huge craft by his sense of touch alone.

Moving into the three-meter-wide tube, his mind had trouble providing him with a sense of perspective. He'd be looking down into a well of darkness one moment and upward toward an impossible climb the next. Weightlessness posed no real hazard, but the shock of a constant shift in perspective began to wear on him.

Chayn opened one hatch after another as he pulled himself along. Life meant heat, light, and power. He searched for monitor lights, anything to narrow down his search. When the open hatches blocked the dim starlight, he backtracked and shut them, then proceeded through increasing darkness. He finally opened and closed hatches by his sense of touch alone.

Chayn opened a hatch. Dim red light flooded down through the opening. Far above—or below—a light glowed. A metal pole ran through the two-meter-wide tube. At regular intervals, hatches lined this tube as well.

Chayn pulled himself inside and along the length of the pole. Within a few meters, his feet had a tendency to swing around ahead of him in the increasing centrifugal gravity. He folded into a ball and allowed himself to swing around, then proceeded downward.

The hatches opened into pitch black corridors, proper corridors with flat decks, walls and a low ceiling. Chayn kept his eyes off those depths of silent blackness and shut the hatches behind him as he approached gradually the red monitor-light below him.

When he confronted the closed hatch with the red light

glowing above it he had just enough weight to make it necessary to hold firmly to the pole. The hatch opened easily for him. Inside, another hatch awaited him—an airlock. Chayn stepped inside the small chamber and closed the outer hatch, but hesitated before moving on. Something alive and alien waited for him on the other side. His courage at that point did not exceed his fear.

There were no controls inside the airlock. Assuming they'd be automatic, he pulled on the latch to the inside door. A sound of rushing air built to a sudden crescendo of noise and stopped. He felt the fabric of his pressure suit relax. Frost formed on the walls around him, melted to beads of moisture, then evaporated. The inner hatch swung open.

Tubes of dim orange light ran along the ceiling. A series of long, rectangular panels lined the wlls, each with a pane of glass set at one end. Black tile covered the deck. Twenty meters away, the chamber ended in another airlock. Two side corridors were also visible from where he stood. Chayn stepped over the rim of the airlock and into the chamber. Gravity pulled so gently, he weaved to and fro as he stood quietly and listened for signs of life.

Chayn sidestepped and glanced through one of the glass panes of the wall panels. Inside the crypt was empty. He moved forward. The second was empty. Below his faceplate, air pressure read in the yellow, temperature in the yellow, air quality in the yellow and just bordering on red. He'd survive here without his pressure suit, but not in comfort. Which implied that the alien would survive aboard the starcraft, but not indefinitely.

The two side corridors at the end of the chamber probably led to locker and prep facilities. Chayn bypassed them, more curious about the second chamber lying beyond, through an opened airlock. Chayn entered the second, identical chamber and inspected one of the crypts. It was occupied.

The aliens had shiny, nonporous skin tinted pale blue.

17

They had curiously slanted skulls, a pointed chin, thin and lipless mouths, and small, human-like noses. Their eyes were closed, but huge and of unknown color and configuration. The ears were in the right place, but delicate and small. The hair was like down and pure white. By the quality of the orange lighting, the low air pressure and cool temperatures, Chayn could guess that they came from a small world of dim sunlight. They were much too human-looking to be really alien.

Chayn could guess as well what had happened to the ship. The computers hadn't sensed an emergency when the ship slowed and stopped against the undetectable strand of the mindspider web. Time passed. Monitor equipment failed. The passengers were safe as long as they were frozen, but some were being revived improperly from time to time. One had survived. Stumbling across a single survivor of a surprisingly human-like species had to be entirely coincidental, but Chayn could hardly accept that.

Movement caught his eyes, something much smaller than him. He looked around and froze, paralyzed by the sight of onrushing, giant gold eyes. The metallic orbs were inhuman, alive with maniacal fury. The slender, naked creature drove an impossible, gleaming, double-edged sword straight toward him. A high-pitched scream tore at Chayn's nerves. He had just enough time to twist away from the point of the primitive weapon. It caught him on the wrist of his left hand. Without penetrating an inner wire mesh, it neatly slid up his arm, slicing his pressure suit open to his shoulder.

Two

The point of the sword jammed in Chayn's suit at his shoulder. The creature's momentum shoved it against the hilt of the sword and threw it off to one side. It struck the panels on the opposite side of the chamber and collapsed panting in a limp heap of slender limbs, its eyes glazed and unfocused.

Chayn cried out against the sudden pain in his head. His ears popped in the abrupt drop in air pressure. He gulped thin, cold air tainted with the stench of death. Frigid air flooded through his suit and he fell back against a crypt in shock and slid to the deck. Without his pressure suit, he was as isolated and doomed as the mad creature lying across from him.

Chayn's thoughts went wild, but slowly spiraled down to the situation at hand. The sword lay on the deck between him and the alien. He ignored it for the time being. The creature had spent itself. It lay jerking in continuous convulsions of terror. It did not appear to be injured, although Chayn unconsciously avoided looking directly at it, satisfied for the moment that it was small, frail, and apparently harmless.

When Chayn stood to inspect the damage to his suit, the creature set up a keening wail, occasionally voicing breathless words in a sibilant language. Its golden eyes focused on him, huge and beautiful, emanating the purest terror Chayn could imagine. Chayn kicked the sword from its reach, unlatched and removed his helmet. He placed it at his feet and stripped the pressure suit down to his waist, gasping as sweaty flesh came in contact with the incredibly icy air. The point of the sword had penetrated several layers of material, but not a metallic mesh. That alone had saved his life. In desperation he thought that perhaps he could find a way to seal the gash. A starship should have resources of that kind somewhere.

Only then did Chayn glance at the alien, prepared now for the shock that coursed through him. Her huge, golden eyes were burned into his memory frever, but for the first time, he perceived the whole of her.

She was nude, far too human to be the product of parallel evolution. She had small breasts, a slender waist and broad
19

hips. She had a navel, nipples and apparently human sexual organs. Her nonporous skin glowed like pale blue plastic, her hair pure white down, thick enough to be opaque upon her head, but elsewhere a fuzz of whiteness that gave her slender body a two-toned effect.

She was quite beautiful. If she could trigger the part of the human brain programmed to respond sexually to a woman, she could not be alien. Somewhere in the past, humanity and her species converged.

Chayn's slightest movement ignited convulsions of terror and her high-pitched wails of anguish. Chayn grew concerned for her. On impulse, he kicked the sword across the deck to her, a stupid move when he thought about it the next moment, but a desperate one to alleviate the nightmarish levels of terror she experienced. She looked at the sword and back to him several times, her reflexes lightning quick. Her metabolism had to be considerably higher than his to account for the quick reflexes and her survival in the cold air. She relaxed, shuddering quietly with her eyes fixed on him. Eyes with gold irises all but unrimmed by white cornea. Eyes with round, human pupils dilated by fear.

"You and I have a few problems," Chayn said.

Her head jerked a fraction of an inch. She blinked her enormous eyes and cocked her head. She let loose with a string of soft sounding syllables.

"You're quite intelligent," Chayn said. "Too bad you overreacted. But I guess I can't blame you."

Again, she responded in an outburst of soft sound.

Chayn put his finger to his eye. "Eye."

She copied the gesture. "Ah!"

Astounded by the speed of her thought processes, Chayn slid back down to the deck and pulled his knees up against his chest. He held up the torn arm of his pressure suit. She blinked and glanced at the sword, then wailed, more of a sob than of renewed hysteria. She spoke with tension in her voice. Chayn could almost sense the meaning of her words. "Yes," he said, "I have a ship."

She broke out in a sudden burst of speech. Chayn shook his head and she fell quiet instantly. Even that gesture had meaning for her. They would be able to communicate in time.

Chayn gestured to indicate himself. "Chayn."

She blinked.

Chayn repeated the gesture. "Chayn."

She put the palm of her hand between her breasts. "Villimy."

"Villimy," Chayn said.

Her thin mouth curved into a wavering smile. "Villimy."

"Chayn Jahil," Chayn said.

She nodded to him. "Chayn Jahil."

"Villimy?"

She nodded and said softly, "Villimy Dy."

"Villimy Dy," Chayn said and sighed with relief. "How do we get out of here?"

She cocked her head in her quick attentive manner. Chayn held out his torn suit. She gazed at it a moment, then quickly stood and trotted out of the chamber through one of the side corridors at the end. Chayn rose to follow, then decided to stay put to avoid the risk of frightening Villimy. She returned with a plastic canister. She knelt on the cold deck a cautious distance from him, seemingly oblivious to both her nudity and the below-freezing temperatures. The canister contained flat, black, flexible patches. Villimy handed him a patch, their fingers only inches apart. Chayn could feel an intense heat emanating from her skin in the sharp, thin air.

The patch had a familiar paper backing. Chayn peeled it off and pressed the adhesive to the fabric of his pressure suit. It didn't stick as well as he would have liked, but still required an effort to pull it loose.

Chayn already had plans made. There were suits near the main airlock. If the patches held, he could retrieve a suit and together the two of them could make it back to the starcraft.

With the arm of the suit draped across his lap, Chayn applied the patches. He knew it wouldn't hold. Villimy stood over him, watching, her large eyes blinking without expression. The same thought must have occured to her. She left and quickly returned with a coil of fine wire. Chayn glanced up at her dumbfounded. Between the two of them, they just might survive after all.

With the job finished, Chayn stood and slipped his arms into the suit. Villimy suddenly bcked away from him and averted her eyes in sudden depression. Her behavior puzzled Chayn before comprehension dawned on him. Villimy thought he was abandoning her.

"No," Chayn said to catch her attention. He pointed to the airlock, gestured to indicate his pressure suit and held up two fingers. He grabbed a fistful of the fabric of the suit, gestured to include the both of them and held up two fingers with clear emphasis.

Villimy brightened. Chayn held out his arm and nodded to the spool of wire she held. Villimy approached cautiously, then began winding the wire around his arm with enthusiasm, splicing the loose ends with a twist. Chayn couldn't bend his elbow, but he still could use his left hand. Testing the seal would be simple. He'd enter the airlock and vent the atmosphere. If the patches blew he'd have a few moments of safety in which to repressurize. If they blew somewhere between the airlock and the pressure suits in the chamber just off the main airlock, the Watcher would have to find himself another primitive with which to play his incomprehensible games.

Villimy fidgeted as he entered the airlock that opened to the access tube. He couldn't convey the subtle assurances he wanted to give her with pantomime. He forced a smile before closing the hatch behind him. He turned and lifted the latch to the outer lock. The sound of rushing air died into silence, the fabric of the suit tensing against the internal pressure. Chayn stood stock still for a moment, his left arm held carefully against his side. He felt something give, but the pressure held.

22

Chayn reached for the shaft in the dark access tube with his right hand. The seal broke with a loud crack that sounded inside his suit. Pain shot down through his left arm. Chayn screamed and sucked ice. His helmet clouded in frost, obscuring his vision. Blinded, air rushing from his lungs, Chayn pulled back and slammed the hatch closed behind him. He turned to fumble with the inside latch with his right hand. His left arm was numb and the side of his neck burned. Unconsciousness overwhelmed him, but not before he heard the rush of entering air.

He awoke, wishing he hadn't regained consciousness quite so soon. The pain in his left arm spoke of severe frostbite. To top off the torture, Villimy had removed his pressure suit. She stood over him, holding a hypodermic needle in one hand. Chayn recognized the device and nodded his acquiescence. Villimy sought to help and he trusted her intelligence despite the risks she took with both their lives.

She gave him the injection in his shoulder, quickly and expertly. In the next instant, a diffuse warmth began to spread through his body. Much of the graying flesh of his left arm remained numb. Chayn tried to ignore that for now. His knees felt weak and his hands shook, but he could think clearly and function now.

Villimy backed away as Chayn sat up. The pressure suit lay beside him. Chayn knelt and inspected the left sleeve. It had blown near the elbow. Chayn had one realization—he'd not survive another blowout.

Chayn applied another patch and rolled the sleeve into a tight bundle. Villimy understood and fetched another coil of wire. Chayn wired the bundle and stood. He shivered and felt odd, wondering what side effects the injection might have. He wanted badly to rest, but didn't dare risk it.

Villimy helped him into the suit. Chayn folded his injured arm against his chest and fought with the self-sealing zipper that ran from his right hip to his left shoulder. Villimy lowered the helmet over his head and locked it into place. Villimy's chances of survival were slim. Chayn's had decreased considerably as well. He didn't know if the air tanks were stored with the suits or elsewhere, whether they'd still be pressurized or not. He'd need to return to the starcraft and the crypt for proper medical attention soon, sensing without knowing that the starcraft had facilities to care for injuries and illness. Chayn had difficulty ignoring the odor in the air. What had Villimy done with the bodies from the empty crypts?

Even before turning to the airlock, he knew something was amiss. He felt ill and the feeling intensified rapidly. But he entered the airlock and cycled it without incident. The rolled-up sleeve held. Chayn reached for the pole with his right hand, forced to shimmy against the slight gravity until he approached the axis of the ship and its weightless environment. His eyes hadn't adjusted to the darkness, but once within the main passageway, he pulled himself toward the main airlock.

Nausea churned within him. Chayn increased his pace, knowing full well what would happen if he vomited inside his helmet. Either from the hypodermic needle or from the air he had breathed, alien bacteria rampaged through his system. It took every last ounce of will power to reject the temptation of the starcraft waiting for him just beyond the outer airlock.

The pressure suits were of an odd design with six small air canisters lined across the back of the suits in pouches. With no way of telling whether or not they were pressurized, Chayn threw two, complete with helmets, across his right shoulder.

He had the shaft casting its red glow into the passageway in sight when his stomach convulsed. He clamped his jaws tight, but the vomit shot forth, blinding and choking him. In free fall, the foul mess inside his helmet threatened to drown him. Driven by desperation, Chayn lunged forward, colliding with the open hatch. He grabbed hold of it and pulled himself inside, pulling himself along the pole until he pivoted around in the increasing gravity. Another bout of nausea threatened, but it no longer mattered. Chayn

24

blinked his eyes against the burning, narrowing in on the red glow filtering through the mess on his faceplate.

He cried out in silent protest against slipping consciousness. He wasn't that ill. But it occurred to him that he had clogged the air circulation pumps that fed the air filters and recyclers in his suit. It wasn't the feverish chill or the ache in his muscles that threatened loss of consciousness. The illness itself he might survive. He felt the satisfying vibration of the outer hatch closing behind him. He turned to the light beyond the inner hatch, half blinded and helpless and wondering if Villimy Dy could help him once again. Not that he had ever intended living forever anyway.

Approaching delerium didn't take him by surprise, but he forgot about the difference between reality and hallucination in the next moment. The Watcher watched and Chayn reached for the security of the stars. They receded and he suffocated in utter blackness. Alone in the void, he heard a crackling noise, ionization, particles of the void sparkling to enigmatic life. The radiation level increased, his limbs tinkling in response.

Mindspider! Mandibles biting into his thoughts, devouring consciousness. Bit by bit the phantom creature pulled them away until nothing remained but a single core of self.

Cold. Intense cold. An eternity of death in the frigid vacuum of space.

And light. Much time passed. Something stung him. He flinched and wondered if the dead could suffer. He blinked in the light and the cold. He lay nude on ice and pain split his head behind his eyes. His lungs burned and his stomach knotted in agony. Gold eyes looked down upon him. When she placed her hand upon his chest, it burned. But the heat spread and he shuddered violently and reached for the precious warmth.

When it passed, he rested. Itsfelt like another kind of dying to breath deep and easy. Thesoftness and warmth he felt oozed through his flesh. He unwound and sank into a deep slumber.

He awoke later and felt the hard places of her body, her

hips and knees and elbows and the contrasting softness of her breasts and stomach pressing against him. He opened his eyes, his body so relaxed, it felt like limp, excess weight. Chayn saw white down billowing before him. He could feel her hot breath on his neck and the rapid beat of her heart. She shuddered occasionally and keened her soft wail so quietly, Chayn almost took it for a sigh. Very quietly, Villimy protested such intimacy with an alien.

It had to be done to ensure her own survival. If he, the alien, died, she would die. Chayn recognized this and formed an undying respect for Villimy Dy. They had both shoved aside their deepest fears of the unknown to save themselves. In abject terror and deep physical suffering, death is never an enemy. Chayn never succumbed to the temptation because of Villimy. Villimy hadn't succumbed because of him.

Chayn waited until Villimy left momentarily before fighting a trace of vertigo to rise and sit on the ledge of the open crypt. Chayn dropped in the light gravity to the deck on his bare feet. The illness had passed, thanks to an alien medical technology that had worked on his physiology and Villimy's ministrations. Now, he needed clothing, some insulation against the incredible cold. Villimy had cleaned his pressure suit and draped it over the end of the crypt.

Villimy rounded the corner at the end of the chamber as he climbed into the suit. Chayn smiled at her, forced to leave the suit half open to leave him the use of his left hand. An oily salve covered the graying, dead flesh of his arm. He experienced no pain, but neither did he have full use of it. With at least some protection against the cold, Chayn turned his attention to the two pressure suits he had retrieved from the main airlock. Chayn examined the six, small air canisters. He held the suit out for Villimy to see.

"Air," he said.

"Air," Villimy said with absolute clarity, but bemused.

Villimy took the suit and pulled a canister from its pouch, disconnecting an air hose. She walked toward the airlock between the two chambers. Chayn glanced ahead and noticed the pressure valves alongside the airlock. Villimy shoved the canister into a valve. Chayn heard the hiss and pop of high air pressure.

"Air," Villimy said.

Villimy pressurized the canisters and climbed into the pressure suit, anxious to leave the graveyeard of her people and the dreams they had shared. Chayn knew that in leaving they abandoned others to the fate Villimy would have experienced. Still, Villimy might have been the first successful revival in centuries. It would take the resources of a starfaring civilization to rescue those still safely frozen in the sleep of suspended animation.

The odor in the air continued to plague Chayn. For the first time, Chayn noticed a third, dark suspension chamber beyond the second one. While Villimy prepared to leave, Chayn walked through the interconnecting chambers to the airlock of the third one. Behind him, Villimy turned away and cringed in anguish at what he would find. Chayn pulled open the outer hatch of the third chamber. The inner hatch hung open. Chayn slammed the hatch shut against the incredible stench that assailed him. The glance he had caught of the pile of rotting corpses told him of the fate of the occupants of the empty crypts. Chayn glanced back at the shuddering, panting woman, frightened by her and by the nightmare she had endured. Even now she teetered on the borderline between sanity and madness, suspended by mere seconds from freedom with her life in the hands of an alien.

They left the chambers together, cycling through the airlock. When they were both in the access tube, the red monitor light went out. The lights in the chambers went out. The ship, sensing the absence of life, had shut the chambers down. The slow death for the survivors continued.

Villimy dived up the shaft with practiced ease. Chayn followed with caution. Relief flooded through him when starlight gleamed like a beacon in the passageway to the outer airlock. Chayn was thinking of the difficulties he might have in coaxing the girl through the hull field of the starcraft. Nearing the outer airlock, a ripple of ice shot through his left shoulder. His ears popped as air pressure dropped. A thin vapor of ice crystals shot from the rolled and wire bound sleeve of his left arm.

Chayn couldn't even manage a feeble cry for help from the silhouette of the alien woman ahead of him. Consciousness faded to oblivion with only a silent, surprised protest to the unmoving Watcher within him.

Three

Chayn's awareness sprang alive in the starfields. The depth and intensity of his own being startled him. Through the interface with the intelligence of the starcraft, Chayn saw the mindspider web strand stretching through the void. The starcraft remained anchored off the bow of the alien spaceship.

Confused by the turn of events, Chayn searched for Villimy, his mind scanning the area like a bolt of lightning. He perceived his own body lying in the contoured dais, a pale corpse, barely alive. He could understand nothing of the complex workings of the starcraft, but sensed the ship in the process of repairing his damaged body.

Chayn located Villimy an instant later. The torus, the main living area of the rotating starship, glared light from a thousand ports. Probing the interior of the ship, he located the girl. She slept on a bunk in the bedroom of a small apartment, curled into a defensive fetal position. A third of the derelict no longer functioned at all, but enough backup systems still worked to provide Villimy with a comfortable environment a safe distance from the death in the suspension chambers. Chayn followed evidence of her passage through the torus, the place where she had eaten, the controls on the bridge she had activated. Emergency beacons broadcast their distress signals to the stars. Villimy had used navigational computers to determine her position in space. Electrical generators hummed and vibrated through the decks.

By now, Chayn could reason out what had happened. When he had lost consciousness just inside the main airlock on the axis of the ship, Villimy had towed him to the airlock. She could only have kicked off in desperation with him in tow when she saw the black ovaloid of his ship hanging just off the derelict. If she had missed the opening in the hull field, they'd both be drifting into interstellar space now, Chayn a quick frozen corpse and Villimy dying of slow asphyxiation. But once aboard the starcraft, the body contour of the crypt spoke for itself. It would not accept a suited form, so she would have removed the pressure suit to place him within the body contour. The interface had been automatic, but not immediate. Villimy must have waited a time for some signs of life from him. When they weren't forthcoming, she had returned to the ship through the axis airlock and made her way outward, through the spokes to the torus.

Villimy Dy dreamed of a green world of cloud-swept blue skies, the orange sun lending an atmosphere of perpetual twilight to her surrealistic dream images. But the surface turmoil of her thoughts sent pangs of fear to churn the dreams to nightmares. Chayn recoiled at an image of himself, a giant, pasty white creature with tiny eyes. Villimy shuddered in her sleep. Her keening wail echoed eerily through empty corridors. Chayn tried to impose thoughts of reassurance into her dreams. Villimy jerked awake, the pupils of her large eyes fully dilated in fear. She screamed.

Chayn backed off, watching the starship rotating slowly, eternally in the void. It would be impossible to lure Villimy aboard his starcraft. Without a pressure suit or the means to dock with an airseal with the alien starship, Chayn had no way to face her in person and try to reestablish the small level of rapport they had shared. Even if he could lure her aboard, what could he offer but isolation in an environment she wouldn't be able to tolerate any easier than he had tolerated hers? She'd be alone in a featureless chamber with an inert, apparently lifeless alien being. She'd have no way of knowing that they moved at faster than light velocities, seeking an uncertain sanctuary.

The time it took for Chayn to make a decision had no meaning for him. He decided to leave the woman to her own world. She had resources to live comfortably now for the rest of her life. Still, he found it difficult to depart. He hovered nearby through several of Villimy's waking and sleeping cycles, watching her explore the ship and establish a rountine of activity. She calmed rapidly, waking during the nights in quiet sobs. But the nightmares passed.

Chayn sensed something wrong, a vibration of the mindspider web strand, a distortion of the space-time fabric itself. He remembered the premonitory hallucination during his delerium, but this time it was for real. From the constant, virtual nuclear interactions of empty space, radiation emissions were rising from nowhere.

Chayn circled the starship and located the nearest airlock to Villimy. Chayn searched with a growing desperation for a way to attract her attention. He nudged the starcraft against the derelict. The entire structure shuddered against the gentle impact. Villimy staggered and fell against a wall, her high-pitched screams echoing through endless corridors. Alarms went off within the starship, first from the control bridge in outrage against Chayn's intrusion, then from radiation-detection devices still operational after countless centuries of disuse.

Villimy ran to the control bridge, her frail form flying through the wide, main corridors of the torus. She switched on screens that gave her a panorama of the stars. She saw the oblong blackness of Chayn's starcraft silhouetted against the starfields, but she'd die if she couldn't differentiate between Chayn's efforts to attract her attention and the real emergency in progress. If the sudden flux'of events over-powered her, his presence would have a reverse effect upon the woman. But even Villimy sensed in that moment the approach of the mindspider.

The sheer emnity of the transdimensional creature ap-palled Chayn, the burning focus of consciousness eating into his thoughts. Villimy clamped all too human hands to her head and screamed, her wailing cries striking a chord of helpless empathy in Chayn.

While she still watched the screens, Chayn rushed to the airlocks and roughly matched the opening in the hull field toward the airlock. She couldn't have misunderstood his strategy.

The cold burn of the mindspider intensified. Chayn braced himself for the onslaught, straining against the utter, driving need to escape the psychic destruction that threat-ened. At the last possible moment, Villimy fled screaming in agony toward the airlock. It would cycle much too slowly and Chayn watched through the interface as she raced for a nearby locker and pulled out a weapon. A beam rivaling the core of a star in intensity lashed out and exploded in cascading, molten metal against the inner airlock. Chayn had no way to warn her that he had no airseal to provide for her protection. Villimy blasted through both airlock hatches. In an instant, the atmosphere of the torus burst out through the airlock in an icy vapor engulfing Chayn's star-craft.

Thrown forward by the hurricane, Villimy fell, then slid across the deck and rolled through the still glowing edges of the burned out airlock. The hull field of the starcraft deflected the blast of frozen air and debris. For a brief moment of horror, Chayn thought it would deflect Villimy's tumbling body as well. For a fraction of a second, she fell through the airless, heatless void, naked against the uni-verse—and through the hull field airlock of the starcraft.

She struck the dais upon which Chayn's body lay and slumped to unconsciousness. With a mute scream, Chayn let go and the starcraft vanished from space-time and shot through the abyss, streaking across the light years toward the distant wall of stars.

Chayn had no way to help Villimy. Grimly focusing on the space ahead, he reached for the warmth and the mind fields of the cliff of starlight, only then slowing to speeds that put space-time back into its normal perspective. Gradually the burning touch of the mindspider faded. Some inexplicable damage, a scorching of the edges of his psyche, healed, tendrils of his thoughts spreading to reclaim the areas of consciousness consumed by the mindspider. Chayn trusted his intuition, the silent voice of the Watcher. It told him that the mindspider had been young, recently born, that the hazard had passed and no permanent damage inflicted upon Villimy or himself.

Once back within the starfields, Chayn searched for human civilization with renewed vigor. Chayn didn't know the whole story as yet, but an eon ago, humans had penetrated this spiral galaxy in fleets and caravans of starships, sleeping their death-like sleeps of suspension, awakening here and there to explore and colonize new worlds. They adapted to those worlds, either evolving genetically to fit into the biosphere and environments of their new homes or practicing genetic engineering to force fit themselves into alien enviroments. The Watcher told him that many of those worlds had regressed and spent millenia in slow, social evolution before reaching the stage of explosive, technological growth. Many were still planet-bound. Others had formed empires of many worlds and star systems. A few had already achieved the status of stargods, moving beyond the environment of space-time, rejoining their ancestors in the galaxy of man's origin.

Chayn searched for worlds on a technological level within his comprehension, knowing the gold star to be his destination, but unable to accept that he'd stumble upon it coincidentally despite the Watcher's quiet provisions of information. He searched his way through the mind fields of the stars, anxious to find sanctuary before Villimy recovered. He failed.

Villimy awoke and panicked, and Chayn stopped the starcraft and broke interface. His psyche fell through a funnel that condensed the essence of him into human flesh. Chayn moaned and struggled to rise against the pain in his left arm and shoulder.

Villimy backed against the resilient hull field, her wide, gold eyes bright with subdued terror. Chayn climbed from the crypt and walked around the dais once, studying the damage to his left arm. If it hadn't been for Villimy, he would have lost his life. The starcraft had salvaged his arm. Pink tissue covered the wound without scarring.

He turned to Villimy, unable to communicate. They experienced apparently normal gravity. There were no inertial effects while maneuvering, no screens or ports through which to view the stars in motion. Villimy had no direct, perceptual way of knowing the silent chamber moved. To top it off, here were no stores of food or water for a passenger. The starcraft provided for a crew of one.

The Watcher watched dispassionately, a bright window of inhuman consciousness.

"Villimy," Chayn said. "How do I communicate with you?"

"Chayn! *Vla dys mon!*"

Villimy suffered. She panted, her mouth open. The heat, Chayn recalled. The environment wasn't suited for her any more than her ice-cold, thin air suited him. Chayn could only move on in search of refuge for the both of them.

Chayn walked over to stand in front of the airlock. Either one of them could step through the oval outline in the hull field without impediment and fall unprotected through the stars forever. But Villimy had passed through it twice. She'd remember the first experience vividly. Chayn indicated the outline of the airlock. He mocked stepping through

33

the center of the outline, clutching his throat and giving his best performance of death by asphyxiation, decompression, and quick freezing. Villimy shuddered and backed away, obviously aware of the hazard involved.

Gesturing for her to approach, he showed her the metallic disks in the body contour of the crypt. He formed a claw with one hand, clamped it to his head and pantomimed the catalepsy of interface. He pointed to the bow of the craft and ran in place to communicate the notion of speed and movement.

Villimy stared at him.

Chayn stared back. "Do you understand?"

"*Ki son,*" Villimy said, still panting heavily to ventilate excess heat. She pointed to her mouth, clutched her stomach and bent at the waist, using pantomime of her own to indicate either hunger or thirst, probably both by now.

Chayn nodded his understanding. To indicate her own, Villimy sat against the wall on the far side of the chamber from the airlock and rested, her eyes fixed on him. Chayn climbed back onto the dais, frightened and saddened by her plight. He lay his head back down into the body contour and the stars sprang to life around him.

Chayn took the starcraft past the speed of light. The stars ahead brightened into the ultraviolet, the stars behind dimming into infrared. A starbow formed around the circumference of the starcraft at light speed. Then the stars sprang back to their normal perspective, the nearer stars moving visibly at an increasing pace. Beyond the speed of light, the starcraft moved outside of space and time, providing him with an interpretation or translation of his progress. The starcraft itself piloted. Chayn provided only the will and intent. An enormous intelligence operated the craft, something other than the Watcher. Chayn thought of it as a computer that seemed not to have a consciousness of its own.

Chayn stopped twice in his journey, once to orbit a world of quasi-human creatures locked in a perpetual, planetary

34

war. Chayn had no way to investigate a planetary civilization. The starcraft would touch down on an airless, planetary surface, but would not enter atmosphere. Chayn had already tried once to coax it down to the surface of an Earthlike world. Later, he slowed through a planetary system of a large, K5, spectral-type sun, remembering the gold star the color of Villimy's eyes. The mind field about the large, orange star shown bright and calm from a considerable distance, but the species that inhabited it were far too alien. Fast moving ships intersected with his trajectory and escorted him through the system without a show of hostility. Once on the far edge of the system, Chayn reluctantly accelerated to hyperlight velocities, leaving the alien ships far behind.

Chayn broke interface twice to check personally on Villimy. The second time, she had fallen unconscious. He could not awaken her. For the first time, he felt her smooth hot skin. He lifted her arm and felt the fragile skeletal structure beneath her shiny, bluish skin. Her light build helped explain her incredibly quick reflexes. But she felt like a woman, like a human being, and for the first time, he felt the stirrings of sexual desire which was more alien to him than Villimy could ever be. Chayn pegged her preference for nudity as a cultural norm. Chayn would have felt more comfortable dressed in her presence, but the only possessions he had consisted of a torn, useless pressure suit and its helmet.

Chayn returned to interface and sent the starcraft speeding into denser regions of the galaxy. Despite the incredible velocities he reached, the size of this galaxy awed him. It would take a thousand lifetimes to pass simply within sensory range of each of the billions of stars washing past the starcraft like a vapor of light. And among it all, the Watcher told him that he searched for one, specific destination, the worlds of the gold star, coincidentally or not, the color of Villimy's eyes.

Chayn found it and felt less in control of his destiny than

he would have preferred. He touched the mind field of the system and altered course slightly, directly toward what later turned out to be the gold star, sensing but ignoring just as intense of a mind field in the regions of a nearby black hole. Not a single planet of the system of the gold star could support a naked human upon its surface, but it was a system rich in metallic content. Civilization proliferated in colonies orbiting every world and satellite in the system with a population numbering in the tens of billions.

They were human, too close to humanity as Chayn knew it to detect any differences from a distance. He approached the system with trepidation. This was it, his first contact. He could travel no further and expect Villimy to survive.

Chayn's psyche brightened with fear. He hadn't the slightest idea of how to establish contact. The starcraft had capabilities he hadn't explored or even suspected as yet. From here on in, he'd be stumbling through the limitations of his own ignorance and forced to explore those new potentials.

Dropping into normal space, Chayn passed the outer worlds, sensing the enormous industry of the civilization. They were mining the atmospheres of the gas giants, sending insulated icebergs of frozen, purified gases sprialing down into the inner system. Closer to the star, an incredible heavy industry formed a band orbiting the sun. solar collectors soaked up energy, heat radiators glowing white hot to dissipate the excess heat of factories processing ore mined from the inner worlds and a double band of asteroids. They were a primitive civilization by Watcher standards. They might have been slightly less advanced than the civilization of his origin, but he doubted if his own people had colonized any one system this heavily.

Chayn scanned for spaceships, the nearest concentration forty light minutes away, not close enough even to have detected his presence as yet. Chayn moved across the system at hyperlight velocities and in seconds appeared in the midst of a large, stationary fleet positioned a few light minutes away from the largest gas giant of the system. When they perceived him and accelerated to surround him, Chayn focused on the mind fields of the men aboard the craft. He felt their cold, calculating intent. And fear. An alien craft had invaded their space. They reacted with hostility.

Even their maneuvering to surround him took an excruciating amount of time. Villimy would die soon if he didn't find help. One of the largest of the approaching ships emitted modulated electromagnetic radiation, a form of communication. The intelligence of the starcraft translated for him without effort.

"Unidentified spacecraft, this is the Defense League of the Rashanyn Empire. Identify yourself."

"I am Chayn Jahil." His voice translated back in the form of radio waves. "I am in need of medical facilities. I have an alien aboard who requires medical assistance."

"Who are you?" the voice returned. "Where are you from?"

"I am human," Chayn responded. "I do not know my origin."

"Prepare for docking."

Chayn grew increasingly agitated. "Do you have medical facilities that can handle an alien physiology?"

They did not respond, but their weapons turned on him. Chayn zeroed in on a single individual aboard one of the craft and tried to make sense of the man's nonverbal thoughts. Chayn could not speak their language on his own, but he caught a visual image of the large base circling the gas giant. Chayn looked in that direction, sensing the concentration of a mind field. The fusion powered military craft surrounding him would take too much time to reach that base.

"I haven't time to waste," Chayn said. "I need help now."

Chayn moved the starcraft. The spaceships about him opened fire with a combination of coherent light beams, focused particle beam-accelerators and thermonuclear missiles. Space flared to incandescence while Chayn shot across the void in a blue wake of radiation. The military base opened fire as he pulled within range. Chayn waited out the wavefronts of radiation until the barrage ceased.

"I am Chayn Jahil," he radioed. "I am human, but this craft is of stargod origin. I have an alien aboard in need of immediate medical attention."

Silence accumulated.

"This is Commander Cornoben speaking. You are requesting medical aid?"

"Desperately. I need help. You can'tharm this ship, but neither do I have offensive capabilities. I request aid on a peaceful basis."

"We have no medical facilities to handle an alien physiology. We have just received word that nearby forces encountered a craft and voice communications matching your pattern."

"That was me," Chayn said. "They had no medical facilities."

"Your craft travels at speeds faster than light?" The voice sounded taut. Chayn could imagine the impact he would have on these people.

"It does."

"One moment please."

Chayn had a rough idea of what would be happening. Despite the invulnerability of his highly advanced starcraft, he spoke and behaved like an individual in trouble. Therefore, they would comply with his requests, but would attempt to separate him from the starcraft. And Chayn would have to comply to ensure their cooperation. Chayn didn't consider himself to be risking his or Villimy's welfare despite the loss of his ship. These people were basically peaceful. He could detect no evidence of internal warfare anywhere in the system and it had taken long term and peaceful cooperation to build a civiliation of this magnitude. They would comply with his needs. They would have the starcraft in trade.

"Chayn Jahil."

"I am here."

"The largest city orbiting the fourth world of this system possesses exobiological facilities. When you arrive, you must disembark peacefully and turn your craft over to Reylaton military authorities. Will you comply with these terms?"

"I will."

"Please do not disembark until we communicate with Reylaton authorities."

Villimy's life force declined rapidly. She barely breathed, her flesh cooling with the approach of death. Maybe these people could save her, but they had no interstellar commerce. What would they know of alien physiology other than the primitive life forms of the worlds of this system? And in giving up his starcraft, he'd probably be stranded here forever. Chayn knew his own kind well enough to know they'd take jealous possession of the starcraft and never let him approach it again. He did not know what kind of society and culture these people possessed, but they would be his from here on out.

Chayn traded his freedom among the stars for Villimy Dy's life.

Four

Chayn marveled at the size of Reylaton. These people had spent millenia building their space-faring civilization. They no longer built colonies so much as small, self-contained worlds. Reylaton turned slowly, perpetually facing the golden sun, a torus many kilometers in diameter centered with a huge, flat, cylindrical hub connected to the torus by three spokes. The bottom half of the hub contained a mirror-complex feeding sunlight through the inside, glass skylight of the city. The top half of the flat cylinder contained three monstrous docking bays. A circle of strobe lights guided Chayn to a smaller docking bay off to one side of the metal landscape.

Again, Chayn could only align the hull field airlock with a personnel airlock inside the smaller docking bay. Chayn didn't bother locking the starcraft in place when he broke interface. Even if it drifted free of Reylaton, it would be safe in its half-million kilometer orbit about the large, volcanic planet. No harm would befall it in the hands of Rashanyn authorities. They'd not be able to pilot, disassemble, or otherwise damage the craft. One way or another, probably with a large net, they'd undoubtedly move it to a location of their choice.

They promised Chayn a response time of a fraction of a second. Leaping through the airlock into vacuum in his damaged pressure suit felt like a suicide attempt. He tumbled through a zero G-enviroment which at least gave him the reassurance of seeing the outer hatch slide shut behind him. Inside a squat, circular chamber, air pressure slammed with an even force about his leaking pressure suit. With his healed left arm tucked against his chest, Chayn grabbed for a handhold with his right hand.

The inner hatch slid open to reveal a brightly lit corridor large enough to run the starcraft through. Black-helmeted guards in blast armor lined the corridor in groves with knees hooked through rungs in the walls, freeing both hands to brace and aim wicked-looking weapons. At the end of the corridor, a portable beam accelerator anchored to a wall swung its business end around to focus on him. A number of officers with gold emblems on their black helmets pulled themselves behind transparent blast shields.

"*Doeic*!" a voice rang out. "*Temeo selpedon kisa*!"

"Oh, great!" Chayn muttered. "That's all I need."

Chayn let go of his handhold for a moment, floating free

to hold out the palm of his right hand in what he hoped to be a universal gesture of peace. The corridor turned and twisted slowly with the rotation of Reylaton, disorienting Chayn and threatening nausea. Chayn grabbed for another handhold and closed his eyes for a moment. Then he pulled himself into the corridor, using the plentiful rungs welded across the circular walls. Behind him, the inner hatch of the airlock slammed shut with an ominous finality, a sudden barrier between him, Villimy, and the starcraft. But they knew about Villimy. They'd cope with one alien creature at a time. The quicker he cooperated, the quicker they'd attend to Villimy Dy.

A section of bulkhead at the end of the corridor opened. An open vehicle anchored on tracks running the length of the corridor rolled forward. The vehicle approached and stopped a few meters away from Chayn, just off to his right.

"*Ilopines! Beleio koi, ohilbim!*"

Chayn assumed the amplified voice to be coming from a nearby officer who pointed to the personnel carrier from behind a blast shield. Chayn pulled himself along the rungs with his one arm and grabbed for a cage-like structure covering the open cockpit of the vehicle. Four of the nearest guards joined him. The vehicle jerked into motion, retracing its path along the rails. Once back inside the chamber from which it had emerged, the bulkhead doors slid shut. Chayn heard the sound of machinery. After a short while, his weight began to reappear. They were descending through one of spokes into the city. Chayn silently wished Villimy Dy the best of luck in the care of her new hosts.

The doors opened again on another corridor, one with a flat floor, walls littered with plumbing and conduit and a ceiling lined with bright yellow flourescent strips. The guards jumped off the vehicle and moved back, their weapons still trained on him. Other guards waited in the otherwise empty corridor stretching ahead. One gestured for Chayn to move forward, then to stop after a few meters. The elevator closed behind him.

41

From one of many side entrances, a tall, slender, black-haired male with lavender eyes led a procession of people into the corridor. The lavender-eyed, olive-skinned man and half of the group were dressed in neat fitting, white coveralls, the other half in blue and gold military uniforms. There were racial differences among the group, but in general, the Rashanyns were dark-haired with an olive tint to their skins. They all had blue eyes, most a dark lavender. Chayn stood taller than the tallest of them and outweighed them by at least fifty percent.

The tall, dark man approached Chayn fearlessly. He smiled and nodded his greeting, already aware that they spoke separate languages. He gestured for Chayn to follow. He turned and reentered the room beyond the doorway. Chayn followed.

They entered a laboratory of considerable size. Isles criss-crossed geometrically arranged tables filled with equipment that threw Chayn for a loss. A handful of the original procession followed the two of them across the lab and into a back room. There were two examination tables positioned next to a wide array of equipment. Two teams of white-smocked, solemn looking men stood behind each table. A small and glum looking individual dressed in irridescent green tunic and trousers stood alongside one of the examination tables. Two military officers entered the room. The doors were shut on the others. There were no armed guards.

Upon command, the small man in the green clothing undressed and stretched nude upon one of the examination tables. The man with the dark lavender eyes gestured mildly for Chayn to do the same. Reluctantly, Chayn complied, but glad to be rid of the pressure suit. He could do with a more extensive wardrobe.

It didn't take long for Chayn to understand the procedure. He appreciated the consideration. Each step of the examination procedure was performed on the civilian volunteer first, giving Chayn a chance to observe what they would be doing with him. A needle withdrew a blood sample from his arm. X-ray machines scanned him from head to foot. Physicians bent over him, their faces contorted with concentration, examining the exterior structure of his body. There were vague differences in proportion between Chayn and the Rashanyn, but no differences as pronounced as the ones Villimy displayed. The examination lasted hours. When the two military men left, Chayn could imagine the problems they'd be having with the starcraft. After the examination, Chayn's counterpart sighed in relief, dressed and leaned over to shake Chayn's hand, a familiar gesture from an unremembered past.

Chayn was handed a pair of white coveralls. Chayn sat up and inspected the clothing before dressing, surprised to discover the coveralls would serve as an emergency pressure suit. The wide, flexible collar was designed to accomodate the helmets he had seen. Concealed vents rendered the thin, but well insulated fabric tolerable for everyday use. To top it off, the coveralls fit perfectly.

The lavender eyed individual stepped before him. "*Vos sa*, Trenton," He pointed to himself. "Trenton."

"Trenton," Chayn said. "Okay, I'm Chayn. Chayn Jahil."

"Chayn," Trenton said with satisfaction.

When they left the examination room, a single guard fell into step behind them. Chayn looked around for some evidence of Villimy's presence in the lab, but the large room had emptied of personnel. Trenton led him through a maze of corridors, then entered another, dark, and somber looking lab. Several technicians greeted Trenton and escorted them to a glass partition dividing the small room. Beyond, enclosed in a tent of clear plastic, Villimy Dy lay on a bed with a white sheet pulled to her neck. She lay with her head turned toward him, her eyes closed, her bluish skin contrasting morbidly with the white sheets. Her breasts rose and fell rapidly but evenly.

Chayn put his hands to the glass with rising elation. He turned and grinned. "Damn, you have no idea how much

I appreciate this.'' On the inside of the tent, Chayn could see frost. That alone indicated that these people knew what they were doing. Villimy Dy would be in good hands.

Trenton turned to leave, gesturing for him to follow. They left the lab. An elevator nearby took them to another floor and through a corridor sparsely populated with civilian pedestrians in a variety of dress styles. They were, on the whole, dark-skinned and somewhat frail to Chayn's eye, but attractive. He stood in sharp contrast to them and received a series of expressions of surprise. Trenton escorted him through a large office filled with desks and small computers. In the corridor behind the offices, Trenton led him through a door into an apartment.

There were four rooms. Trenton showed him the food preparation area and demonstrated the drink and food dispensers. Sanitation facilities were partitioned off in a corner of the bedroom. A screen that dominated the living room filled the entire surface of one wall. A couch, two chairs and end tables facing the screen were the only furnishings. A fourth, small room contained a machine. A chair faced a keyboard. A small screen curved above the keyboard. Trenton gestured for Chayn to be seated. Chayn sat. Trenton placed a thick metal band around his wrist. A cable connected the band to the console. Chayn heard a hiss from the band and something stung his skin. In the next instant, he felt a shock like that of awakening from a daydream.

A round, black circle formed on the screen against a white background.

"*Dos*," the machine said.

Trenton urged him on. Chayn shrugged. "*Dos*."

Two circles. "*Das*."

"*Das*."

Three circles. "*Tim*."

"*Tim*."

Chayn laughed. The process took five minutes at the end of which he could count in Rashanyn to one hundred. He did not forget what he had learned, an anomoly which explained the medication he had received. The wrist band probably contained a monitor to keep the medication at a certain level. The simple lesson demonstrated to Chayn that he'd be quick in learning to speak the language.

Chayn followed Trenton back to the apartment entrance. Trenton shook his head when Chayn moved to follow him outside. *"Tioke eos kolx*, Chayn," the man said.

Chayn understood and backed away, more than content to stay put. The apartment would provide him with sustenance, comfort, and a chance to assimilate this fascinating new world. Trenton left. The door remained unlocked. Chayn went back to the teaching machine and began lesson number two.

There were twenty-five hours in the day, marked by the rotation of Gilderif, the planet that Reylaton orbited. Once a day, a massive continent passed below on the surface of the world. Smoldering volcanoes on the eastern coastal region belched ash and smoke across the planet-sea. Constant rains and heavy clouds masked most of the face of the world, but a towering range of mountains on the western coast of the continent blocked the clouds. A vast desert, both uninhabited and uninhabitable, shone in the sunlight of Star Rashanyn. The length of the day seemed about right to Chayn and he adapted to it.

Chayn lost track of time, but wasn't given the chance to feel imprisoned. Once a day, Trenton arrived and escorted him on a tour of the city, a walk Chayn felt to be more for the sake of exercise than education. Trenton spoke with him in a slow, simple, condescending manner, underestimating either Chayn's intelligence or his progress with the teaching machine. Chayn listened and made no attempt to correct Trenton's misconception.

On alternate days, Trenton took him to a lab where he could watch Villimy's progress on a wall screen. It amused Chayn to note that she seldom bothered dressing except in the personal company of the scientists who interviewed her in the same condescending manner they showed him. Chayn didn't like the idea of a hidden camera in her apartment until he saw her glance at it on occasion, evidence that she knew of its presence. Chayn felt certain that there were no hidden cameras in his apartment, but Villimy had attracted most of the attention of the scientific community. Her huge, gold eyes were captivating, her quick, animal-like movements unsettling but graceful. Chayn was treated as a stranger, but as a man. Villimy was a true alien who churned man's unconscious and brought to the surface feelings of strangeness and wonder.

Chayn became restless as time passed and noticed stress in Trenton's manner as well, evidence of an undercurrent of events that Chayn didn't have access to. But he could guess that Trenton was having problems with the military. They'd have a team of specialists working with the starcraft. By this time they'd be thoroughly stumped without even a background in theoretical physics to explain the nature and functioning of the alien artifact. Soon, they'd be wanting to interrogate him.

From the beginning, Chayn had known of the simple, numerical counter in a rear compartment of the teaching machine that recorded his progress through the continuing educational programming. Wingnuts held the cover in place. Each time Chayn returned to the apartment after one of their walks, the wingnuts were in different positions. If dishonesty had been a larger part of the Roshanyn culture, the counter would have been monitored outside his apartment. Chayn continually reset the counter, keeping it a third of the way behind his actual progress with the machine.

At the end of the first month, Trenton brought a visitor with him one evening. The white-haired, aging officer in an elegant blue and gold uniform stood just short of Chayn's height and threw him a look of sheer enmity as he entered the apartment.

"There are many races among us," the officer said to Trenton. "He looks like a laborer from the inner factory satellites."

46

Chayn feigned a confused interest in the conversation, following Trenton and the officer on their inspection tour of the apartment.

"The important differences are genetic," Trenton said. "He's not Rashanyn despite the controversy that will cause. Neither is he anything less than human."

"The stargods are a myth," the officer said.

"Of course, General Pak, but stargod is a term that applies to any life form or civilization beyond comprehension. The craft is of stargod origin in that respect. Obviously, he isn't an agent of the black hole aliens. He shouldn't be treated with suspicion."

"He remains a potential threat to our security," General Pak said with a tight note of hostility. "I've managed to place the alien under tighter security, but I don't like the freedom you give this man."

"The Supreme Rashanyn Council gave us these two people to study. You have their ship. The military has no business interfering with the affairs of the Institute."

The general moved into the room containing the teaching machine. He openly removed the back panel and inspected the counter. "This is impossible. He's skimming through the material. Your estimate of his level of intelligence is obviously exaggerated."

Trenton glanced nervously at Chayn. Chayn had a good grasp of Trenton's problems with the general. He recognized the type from somewhere, the kind of arbitrary authority that would give any society problems.

"General, I firmly believe we seriously underestimate his capacity to learn."

The general ignored him and returned to the living room. "I want to question this man as soon as he can speak the language with a basic fluency. How much longer will it take? Another month?"

"Try two weeks ago," Chayn said from behind the man.

General Pak spun around, an expression of incredulity on his face.

Chayn grinned. "I couldn't resist. Pay a little closer attention to Trenton in the future. He suspected me all along."

The general kept his narrowed eyes fixed on Chayn. "Trenton, I want to speak with you shortly!"

When he left, Chayn walked over and sat on the couch, giving Trenton a chance to regain his equilibrium.

"I really had no idea you've progressed this rapidly," Trenton said. "You altered the counter?"

"It's just as important for me to learn about you as it is for you to learn about me. I couldn't afford to bypass the opportunity."

"General Pak will not appreciate the deception."

"He'll be delighted. He wants answers to questions. Not that I have the answers he wants, but I can tell him that with a certain degree of fluency now."

"Where did you get that spacecraft?"

"I don't know," Chayn said. "If the military wants to put it to good use, I'll cooperate. I can pilot it. I don't understand how it works. How's Villimy doing?"

"She progresses rapidly," Trenton said. "She's still under pretty tight security. She's obviously alien. You're human. All humans are supposedly Rashanyn. The law doesn't contain provisions for non-Rashanyn humans."

"Am I in a good enough bargaining position to give her a hand?"

"If you mean more freedom, it's likely. She falls under military jurisdiction. They're likely to grant reasonable requests from you in order to ensure your cooperation during formal interrogations. I wouldn't push it too far though."

"I'd like to be able to communicate with her. Eventually, I'd like for the two of us to be able to function in this society of yours. I knew and accepted that I'd loose the starcraft when I arrived. I don't have any illusions about that. Villimy and I need a place to live and Rashanyn is as good a place as any."

Trenton still stood by the door. He walked over and sat

in a chair, relaxing for the first time during the course of the conversation. "Sounds good, Chayn. I can arrange for a screen channel between your two apartments. It'll be monitored by General Pak, though. As for arranging a meeting between the two of you, even adjacent living quarters, it wouldn't be at all difficult to arrange. With Villimy close by, the general is in a position to keep track of you as well. As long as you don't object."

"Can you discuss it with Villimy? Does she speak your language well?"

Trenton gave him a broad grin. "She's frighteningly intelligent. She communicates just fine. May I ask what your relationship has been? I've refrained from asking personal questions until we've had a chance to know each other better, but I am curious."

"Friends," Chayn said. "We've saved each other's life. I think we trust each other now. It would take awhile to tell the whole story."

"I'll be honest with you, Chayn. I work for the Reylaton Institute of Exobiological Studies. I'm a specialist in the field of intercultural relations, a cross between a psychologist and an anthropologist. I work for three different employers, myself, and my own insatiable curiosity, Reylaton civilian government and, indirectly, with the Rashanyn military on security matters. I mentioned the loophole in Rashanyn law that gives you the equivalent of citizenship. As long as you cooperate with the Institute on matters of scientific interest, the military won't have much ammunition to put you under its jurisdiction. They have some over Villimy Dy, but she'll remain connected with the Institute as well. If you can tolerate the situation, neither of you will have problems fitting yourselves into Rashanyn society. You'll always be curiosities and it might take years before we understand you much, but your future here looks good to me."

"I like the arrangement," Chayn said. "I'll admit I have a mild antipathy for the military. I have no memory of my origin, but I have attitudes and feelings that must arise from it.''

Trenton stood and prepared to leave. ''We have more in common in that respect than you might imagine. I'll see what I can do about reducing Villimy's isolation. In the meanwhile, congratulations on your lack of tact with General Pak. The more often you can throw him off balance like that, the easier life will be for the both of us.''

After Trenton left. Chayn spent the evening watching entertainment programs on the wallscreen, but lost himself in thought for much of the time, oblivious to the movement and color on the screen. He went to bed long after the artificial nightfall.

Before dawn, a beeping sound awoke him from a light sleep. It came from the wallscreen. Chayn knew the screen served for personal communications, but it took a moment to locate the channel to answer the call.

A face appeared on the giant screen, an alien equivalent of a hesitant smile quivering about thin lips. Large, gold eyes blinked at him.

''It might scare the daylights out of me to hear you talk,'' Chayn said in the Rashanyn language.

''It is odd, is it not?'' Villimy said, her voice a whisper, her words still sibilant and graceful. ''We were like animals to one another.''

Chayn grinned. ''I understand it was easier for me to accept you than for you to accept me. You're beautiful by my standards. I am something of a monster by yours. So must be the Rashanyn.''

''My values change,'' she whispered.

''Mine don't have to. I've wanted very badly to be able to communicate with you.''

''Friend Chayn. I am not among my own people. I am not among comrades. But you look upon me with favor and I am honored. It is with pleasure that I speak with you.''

''It will not be easy for us, Villimy.''

''You are like the Rashanyn, but in some ways you are more like me. For the two of us, it will not be impossible.''

Five

Four pairs of boots echoed through the corridor. Civilians formed a clear path ahead, pressing against the walls with blank expressions as the formation passed. Chayn resisted the hypnotic tendency to walk in time with the stone faced guards and with a grin, skipped a step to put himself out of synchronization with his escort.

They led him through broad, double doors into an amphitheater. Empty and darkened for the most part, a half dozen military and civilian authorities sat overlooking a large, upholstered chair on the lighted stage. Cameras and recording equipment squatted off to one side, prepared to record the interrogation.

Trenton rose from among the group, a worried expression on his face. He met Chayn on the stage and gestured for him to be seated. A second man rose from the group, dressed in a white uniform with a gold emblem on the left side of his chest. By his expression, Chayn assumed he took himself quite seriously.

"Chayn Jahil. I am Administrator Georing, representative of the Supreme Council. I understand that you have agreed of your own will to this interview. In addition to myself, you will be speaking with General Pak, Military Commander of the City of Reylaton and Lieja Corsa, vice-chancellor of the Reylaton Council. Our other guests will funnel their questions through the three of us. You may consult Trenton before answering at any time you wish. Are you in agreement?"

Chayn made himself comfortable. "Yes."

Administrator Goering seated himself. "You name yourself as Chayn Jahil. Genetically, you are human. You arrived recently in a highly advanced, alien spacecraft seeking medical attention for an alien female of possibly distant, human ancestry. Her name, Villimy Dy. She is not, in the legal sense, human, and cannot be extended the same rights as a citizen of Rashanyn. She can be offered a permanent

51

visitor's visa subject to minor restrictions.

"You claim to have no memory of your origin, your point of departure, your personal past or the history of your people. Can you amplify this?"

"Not really," Chayn said. "My first conscious memory is of entering this galaxy. I have no conscious memory of anything previous to that, but obviously I have a background, a foundation of past experience upon which to draw. I suspect I'm something of an orphan set loose in human space to seek a life for myself. The stargods must have other motives for providing me with the starcraft, but it's a waste of time to carry speculation too far."

Heads paired off and quick whispering echoed through the empty confines of the amphitheater.

"You use the term stargod," General Pak said, his voice harsh and loud in the stillness. "The word has religious connotations in our society. I've been informed that you do not use it to denote entities of supernatural origin. What can you tell us about these stargods?"

"Nothing. I've seen nothing of them. I remember nothing of the events connecting me with the starcraft. I have a store of knowledge to draw from, facts I take for granted, but I don't have access to their sources. I admit, it is unnerving sometimes. The beings I've encountered that use craft of that degree of sophistication are physical entities far in advance of humanity. But the stargods are nonphysical entities. They don't inhabit time and space as we know it."

Again, the background of harsh murmuring arose. Lieja Corso spoke in apparent anger. "How can you know of such things?

"The starcraft enables me to perceive mind fields. I can't describe what that means in words any more than I could communicate the color blue to a blind man. I can only state that life in the universe we perceive is expressed in physical terms, but past a certain point it's nonphysical. Physical reality is like a prop. Past a certain stage of evolution, consciousness interacts directly with reality and the props are no longer necessary."

52

"Let's get down to more practical considerations," General Pak said. "There are those who suspect you of being a spy and would deny you your freedom on the grounds of being a security risk. How would you answer such accusations?"

"That's easy," Chayn said. "Who would I be spying for? For the entities with a technology that can build a starcraft? A race that far advanced wouldn't need me to spy for them. They could do it themselves without being noticed. They could enter minds, manipulate at will, handle a bunch of primitives such as ourselves without effort. Perhaps I am a puppet in some respect, but again, that's a matter of the motives of entities far too advanced for useful speculation. If such entities have designs on Rashanyn, I'm totally irrelevant to the situation. It would make more sense to place a spy within the government, a native Rashanyn, trusted, with access to inside information. I am an outsider and I'll always be an outsider. Another consideration to keep in mind—interfaced with the starcraft, I could see into the mind and the thoughts of Rashanyn, and the starcraft could accurately translate our spoken languages without any of the usual means of data acquisition. Why did I turn the craft over to you? Why was Villimy Dy's life more important to me than the freedom and powers I had interfaced with it?"

"Can we question you about the starcraft?" General Pak said aggressively.

"Do so."

"How is it operated?"

"By an interface between the mind of the pilot and the mind of the craft, the intelligence that actually operates it, perhaps some kind of computer. I provide the will, the direction. The starcraft does the rest."

"What is it made of?"

"Force fields generated in other dimensions. It's a multidimensional artifact. What you perceive of it is only its three-dimensional expression."

"Why haven't our technicians achieved this interface of

which you speak?"

Chayn smiled. "I don't know. I suspected that it would respond only to me."

"Why would stargods provide this service to you?"

"I don't know."

"Where did Villimy Dy come from? Where did you find her?"

"On a derelict, interstellar spaceship. The ship was deteriorating, the occupants frozen in suspended animation and being improperly revived spontaneously."

Administrator Goering spoke. "Our history tells us that humanity evolved in a nearby galaxy over a million years ago. You speak of human civilizations throughout this galaxy. That does not coincide with our knowledge."

"Then your knowledge is in error," Chayn said. "Humanity is seeded throughout this galaxy. Villimy Dy is proof of that. Maybe she's an example of human adaption to an alien enviroment."

"She is not genetically compatible with homo sapiens," Lieja Corsa said.

"She's a close miss, though," Chayn said. "Isn't it a bit too coincidental to believe an entirely alien life form could evolve that closly to human parameters? It doesn't take much for genetics to drift. Separate two identical species long enough and they'll diverge. They still have a common origin. That's the basis for evolution, isn't it?"

"Where did you obtain your education?" Corsa said.

"I haven't the slightest idea. It exists. I'm not stupid, nor uneducated. At least not by Rashanyn standards."

"Surely, you're curious about your personal past. Haven't you ever bothered to speculate?"

"Yes. I'm a survivor, an orphan. I come from a civilization slightly in advance of your own. Villimy Dy and I have a lot in common. We're both lost in space and time. My people lived eons in the past in another part of the universe. Villimy Dy's people as she knew them lived perhaps several millenia in the past a few tens of thousands of light years from here, on the other side of the Rift."

"You spanned the Rift?" Goering exploded.

"It took a few days," Chayn said, matching the man's angered volumn. "It was only four hundred light years across and it wasn't a pleasant voyage."

"Chayn Jahil, your claims violate everything we know of the universe, every fact and truth we've ever established in the fields of physics, exobiology, and human history."

Chayn laughed. "My claims or my presence? It isn't necessary to be so conservative! I assumed that you'd be delighted to receive the knowledge I have to offer of the universe around you. I wanted that to be a value we could trade for the imposition we've made on Rashanyn."

Trenton stepped forward and gestured for silence. "I speak for the scientific community. Chayn is entirely correct on this issue. We are not interested in the claims he might have to put forth, but by his presence and the presence of the starcraft and Villimy Dy. Rashanyn has, in our opinion, failed to advance in several fields of the sciences, relying too heavily on historic and religious dogma for centuries. If Chayn Jahil, Villimy Dy, and the craft they arrived in undermine our beliefs about the universe and Rashanyn history, then it's time to be more careful, to differentiate between beliefs and facts. In the days and weeks ahead, I'll be interviewing Chayn Jahil in depth. If you have questions and interests in some specific area of Chayn's experiences, present them to me. I'll provide you with more detailed information as I obtain it. You requested this interview in order to meet Chayn Jahil and to gain some idea of what he is like. He is like us. His psychological profile is like ours. Even his cultural background is not entirely foreign to ours. Villimy Dy poses impersonal, scientific challenges to be met. Chayn Jahil poses more direct, personal challenges simply because he is human. We can live with that."

"I can substantiate what I say," Chayn said when silence fell in the amphitheater.

"How?" Goering said.

"I'll take you for a ride. I'll take you for a short spin around this part of the galaxy. I'll show you the worlds and the life forms I speak of. You'll need a pressure suit. The starcraft doesn't have provisions for a passenger. We'll have to go outside the ship to view those scenes."

Administrator Goering declined.

When the meeting broke up, Trenton put his hand on Chayn's shoulder. "I'm almost tempted to apologize for them. They're political and military leaders. Not scientists."

"Are they serious about this spy business?"

"Not really. We have a few problems that you'll run into soon. You'll understand the paranoia without holding it against them."

"What effect does that have on me for the immediate future?" Chayn asked.

"None, really. They can balance the necessity for rationality with their fears without much trouble. But you'll be closely watched."

Chayn laughed. "I'm used to being watched. I might be a bit paranoid myself on that score. Do I get to see Villimy Dy?"

"That's been arranged. You have new, interconnecting apartments. I take it you're familiar with Villimy's environmental requirements?"

"Cold," Chayn said, awed by memories. "She's a hot-blooded one, isn't she?"

"Body temperature, one hundred twenty degrees. She likes her environment just above freezing, pressure on the thin side, oxygen on the high side. Her metabolism is considerably higher than ours. She's incredibly active and intelligent."

"Can the Institute afford to provide for her indefinitely?"

"We're having a field day with her. It sounds inhuman, but it's to her advantage. She'll be cared for."

"And myself?"

"The same applies. More than half of Rashanyn is not employed full time, but you can see the standard of living we enjoy. You can spend your life pursuing your own interests, but to get to know our society better, I'd suggest you develop a marketable skill and take a part in Reylaton society. That is only a suggestion."

"I'm not going to have problems with those people?"

Trenton looked uncomfortable. "Rashanyn has problems and people tend to get defensive and intolerant. I won't be more specific than that right now. You'll learn for yourself." Trenton looked around the deserted amphitheater. "We'd better be going. I'm supposed to remain objective. After some time has passed, I'll be stopping around for personal visits if that's all right with you."

"I'd like that."

"You have new living quarters. Your personal effects have been transferred. It's situated near our research labs and will give you some privacy from public harassment."

For the first time, they used public transportation, a monorail bus filled with quiet passengers intimidated by Trenton's white uniform and Chayn's massive build. A four-passenger ground vehicle guided by a single track took them along an open pavilion running the length of a canyon of stepped buildings rising on either side. The city curved upward. In the hazy distance, Chayn had a three-quarter view of the terrain before the arch of the skylight overhead cut it off. The mirrors guiding sunlight into the city from the Hub blocked Chayn's view of the rest of the torus of Reylaton. The city was ancient and huge. There were thousands of such colonies scattered through this planetary system.

Reylaton glowed in golden daylight, the sky of glass bright with reflections of sunlight. An open corridor took them on foot into the depths of the city and an elevator took them downward a level or two. The doors opened upon a bustling corridor of white-uniformed, competent-looking people of the Institute.

Trenton stopped at a door in a deserted side corridor. "It's a smaller place than you had, but better furnished. Villimy's apartment is larger, but she understands that she's not as free to roam the city as you will be."

"Has Villimy had any objections?" Chayn said.

"On the contrary. She finds our environment a bit oppressive and except for you, she doesn't seem to be interested in social relationship with anyone. The records show that I put her near for her own psychological welfare."

"Is her confinement permanent?"

"Did I give you the impression that she's being confined? Once you're familiar with the layout of the city and we find a way to cope with her enviromental needs, she's free to leave her apartment with an escort. Technically, you qualify."

"Will we still have those teaching machines to work with?"

Trenton found that amusing. "They're a permanent part of any residence. What's more important, you have full use of the wallscreen. You'd be surprised how versatile it can be."

"I have a lot to learn," Chayn said. "A whole foundation of the mundane to pick up."

"If the situation were reversed," Trenton said, "I'd be utterly fascinated."

Chayn explored the new apartment. The automatic vendors in the kitchen offered a wider variety of food and appliances to prepare his own meals from basic ingredients. The bedroom contained a closet supplied with clothing specially tailored for him as well as a bed with a liquid-filled mattress large enough for a small crowd. The living room spread before him in rugs of light blue and a ceiling of glowing yellow. The screen occupied the largest wall and a painting on the opposite wall showed an incredible view of the gold sun filtering through the fragile superstructure of a space colony under construction.

Trenton left without Chayn noticing immediately. Chayn entered the small, featureless chamber that contained the teaching machine and located the only other door in the apartment, the one that apparently led into Villimy's apartment. He stood before the door and searched his own motives for wanting Villimy close by. Did he plan on approaching the alien woman sexually?

Chayn knocked on the door, knocked again and waited.

The door opened to a blast of cold air and dim, orange light. The brighter light from Chayn's apartment cast his shadow across the floor inside. Villimy stood off to one side, inhuman and exotic in the dim light.

"Enter, Chayn."

Chayn stepped into the apartment. Villimy closed the door behind him and moved around to face him with a quick, odd grace that Chayn found both graceful and disconcerting.

"Welcome."

The cold bit through Chayn's ventilated coveralls. Villimy had dressed for the occasion. She wore a shiny, bright-yellow-orange blouse that draped loosely from her shoulders to mid-thigh, an obvious concession to Roshanyn sensitivities. But the orange light distorted color for Chayn. Her eyes were darker now, throwing jewel-like bits of dark gold light.

"We don't know of each other's way," Chayn said. "If I offend you in any way, tell me so that I can modify my behavior with you."

"Be yourself," Villimy said. "It is enough that we know of our differences."

Villimy escorted him to the living room. The Rashanyn had offered her the courtesy of specifying the furniture design she preferred. Dense white furs lined the dark tiled floor around a low table. A tray of drinks sparkled in the colored light.

"We share the same tastes in food and drink," she said. "Come and sit with me."

Villimy eased down into a crosslegged position and touched a remote control, the screen blossoming to life, showing a scene of the starfields of space. A banded, yellow and slate-red planet slowly transversed the stars.

"Can you adapt to all of this, Villimy? Are there any discomforts?" Chayn spoke quietly in her presence, aware of acuity of both her hearing and eyesight, especially her hearing in the slightly denser air she had adapted to. It made a pressure seal between her apartment and the outside world unnecessary.

Villimy gave him her version of a smile, a distortion of her lipless mouth. But her eyes burned their way to the core of his being. "These are a fearful but good people."

"I'm sorry you suffered aboard the starcraft."

Her eyes widened. "I suffered! I did not understand! I trusted you, but feared I would die without you even knowing!"

Chayn looked around at the apartment. "Well, this is what we have to work with for the rest of our lives. It's not all that bad. Not bad at all."

Villimy shifted closer to him. "But Chayn, there are things that are wrong!"

"Wrong?"

"I can show you. I've studied hard. These people are at war and there is great danger!"

Chayn felt a sinking sensation and rising anger. He didn't doubt Villimy's perception for a moment. He had suspected all along that things were going too smoothly.

"I haven't seen any indications of any trouble," Chayn said. "Their military is a little active for a peaceful society."

Villimy pointed to the starfields. "The danger comes from without. I think they are being invaded."

Six

The first probe incident in over a century swept in on the planetary ecliptic from interstellar space. An armada of meter-long, sensory devices moved in on a vast, sweeping arc toward the orbits of the outer worlds. Warning of their approach sped through the system at the velocity of light, but only twenty-five percent faster than the progress of the invading probes themselves.

From defensive positions scattered on the outer perimeter of the Rashanyn system, tens of thousands of missiles flew from the launch tubes of military spacecraft, weapons platforms, and from the giant military spacecraft, weapons platforms, and from the giant military bases orbiting the gas giants of the golden Star Rashanyn. Sirens wailed their mournful cries through the atmospheres of thousands of colonies basking in the warmth of the inner system. Defense lasers whined their power buildups. The streets of the great toruses and cylinders emtied, populations huddling close to pressure chambers. Silence fell and the populace waited.

The probes sped inward in impossible quantities. Missiles intersected their trajectories in billowing spheres of thermonuclear fury. From the densely populated regions within the double band of asteroids, lasers began flickering their multimillion kilometer tongues of starcore fury. The starfields flickered with new life, tiny stars born and dying in microseconds.

Then, from the population centers of the inner system, the heavy construction factories and open shipyards, darting threads of light began the tenacious and tedious process of defending themselves against the blind, ballistic probes. Less than ten probes shattered through the glass skies of the space colonies throughout the system. For the first time in the memories of their inhabitants, populations screamed in the winds tearing through their cities, but within minutes, sheets of reinforced plastic rose skyward, held against the holes leaking atmosphere to vacuum by internal air pressure.

The probes passed the gold star, hundreds falling blindly into the thermonuclear fires. Their thinning numbers slowed perceptibly as they began the long, outward journey, continually running the barrage of laser and missile fire, defenseless and uncaring. Ten percent of the original numbers of billions moved into interstellar space, pursued by the armadas of Roshanyn's military. The ten percent became four percent before the ships turned end for end for the long voyage home. Again, the sirens wailed, the sound unchanged, but to the ears of the people, sounding a note more cheerful. Anxieties faded quickly to dull undercurrents of fear. The black hole aliens would not risk mutual destruction. There'd be no interstellar war.

The first haunting wail of the sirens took Chayn Jahil by surprise. They tore through his idle thoughts and sent shock coursing through his body. He walked alone on a boulevard running alongside a canal alive with fish and bordered with flower gardens. He squatted along the protective railing lining the walk at the superhuman howl of warning, watching crowds in the distance run for cover.

Why hadn't he been warned of this? Villimy had suspected, but Trenton had dismissed his concern, speaking in vague tones of a centuries-old fear of a nearby alien civilization.

The explosion overhead rumbled through the cavernous spaces of the torus of Reylation. A white hot light flickered across the city, casting black shadows and drowning out the soft, golden sunlight. Chayn glanced skyward to see shards of glowing, sparkling glass tumbling slowly in the air. A rain of sparkling reflections of sunlight fell a kilometer away, a high pitched hissing and ringing sound echoing from the billowing cloud of dust.

The wind jerked into existence from behind him, throwing him to his knees on the pavement. His jaw agape and his mind paralyzed by the scale of the catastrophe, Chayn looked upward at the gaping hole in the sky and at the snowstorm of frozen air billowing into vacuum beyond. The smooth surface of the canal lashed into whitecaps. The flower beds tossed colored petals and green leaves spiraling skyward.

Even before it occurred to Chayn to take shelter against the ear-popping drop in air pressure, a dull booming sounded nearby. A white bundle flew skyward, unfolding as it rose, an umbrella of steel webbed plastic caught and guided into place by the invisible whirlpool of escaping air.

The umbrella snapped into place, grew taunt and, despite the distance, Chayn heard the crackling of tension. Within minutes, spidery maintenance machines moved up along the glass sky and its intricate webwork of metal framework. Chayn sat down on the pavement and gave a shuddering sigh of relief. Whatever the nature of the colliding object, it had struck a glancing blow and hadn't entered the city.

Chayn waited before returning to the apartment to see how Reylaton would react. Within minutes, the city returned to normal, the pavilion filling with pedestrians, their pace no more hurried than before, the monorail traffic no heavier. Overhead, the broken panes in the skylight were replaced with incredible rapidity, a hovercraft rising to retrieve the umbrella before it dropped back down into the city. A half hour passed and several pedestrians passed, more upset by Chayn's appearance than by events of a short few minutes ago.

The reaction, or the lack of it, unsettled Chayn. By his standards it indicated something seriously amiss with the people of Reylaton. The excitement should have taken time to wear off. Once the adrenalin had drained from his system, the new mystery plagued him worse than the trama of the near catastrophe.

Chayn decided to make his job interview on time. He'd learn more on the streets of the city than he would back in the isolation of his apartment. He located Reylaton Electronics and entered an office environment of nostalgic familiarity. A willowy, rather beautiful receptionist looked up, startled by Chayn's intrusion, but smiled vaguely and pointed out an office partitioned off from the rest of the room. Inside, another woman with dark brown hair and blue eyes looked up at him with studied impartiality from behind a desk. She gestured for him to take a chair.

"You're Chayn Jahil? I had a call from the Institute about you."

Chayn sat down. "I'm Jahil."

The woman leaned forward. "Did you see what happened outside?"

"Something knocked a hole in the skylights," Chayn said. "It didn't seem to bother anyone too badly."

The woman gave him an ambiguous shrug. "It's scary, but it happens occasionally. But I've never seen a probe incident before. I'll have to be sure to watch the news tonight."

Chayn wanted to question the woman, but decided he'd have enough information waiting for him back at the apartment. The newscasts were impressively complete. The woman shifted gears, quickened her pace, and picked up a file lying on her desk. "From what I've heard, I don't need to ask your history of previous employment. Is it true that you're not native to Rashanyn?"

Chayn gave her a firm nod, watching her reaction.

"The church claims it can't be so, but I've read articles about evidence of human civilizations elsewhere, especially on Tycon's star, that third world they explored a few hundred years back."

"How far out has Rashanyn explored?" Chayn asked.

She glanced into space for a moment, her eyes snapping back to his. "I think about two hundred light years. I don't know much about that sort of thing."

"How many other inhabited worlds do you know about?"

She smiled. "A few, I guess. Tell me, citizen Jahil, are you familiar with the field of molecular electronics?"

"I know about it."

"Field interfacing?"

"The terminology might throw me, but I know what you're talking about."

She gave him a puzzled look. "I don't suppose I have to ask about educational qualifications."

"I must have some," Chayn said with a grin. "I have no memory of anything specific."

"Well, about all we can do for you is to offer you an

aptitude test in high-level computer logic. It's an intuitional ability to discriminate between subharmonics, the ability to sense a discordant rhythm in a function analogue. The job of a computer technician sounds like a hands-on kind of job, but it's really an art, perceiving a visual and audio representation of field harmonics and picking out the discordant harmonics that indicate a malfunction.''

The woman stood. "If you'll follow me, please?"

Chayn fell in step behind her. The woman had an incredibly attractive build, but Chayn had already noticed the lack of defects in the Rashanyn. They were advanced enough to weed out unsuitable genetics before birth, but aesthetic enough to allow considerable genetic variation. The woman led him along a wall through the outer offices and into a small room equipped with a console faced with a curved screen before it. Chayn sat before the console at her urging. She reached in front of him to press a key on the console, then placed a set of headphones on his ears. The screen danced with light.

"The green button is for 'go.' Push it when you're ready to start and when you've finished with a problem and are ready for the next one. The blue and red buttons on the right are for accept or reject. If you sense a disharmony, reject that analogue. If you do not, accept it. The disharmony will be both visual and audio. There are three practice analyses and two hundred problems in harmonic discrimination that should take you an hour to complete. Do you have any questions?''

Chayn shook his head and pushed the green button. The woman watched Chayn ease his way through the three practice exercises, then slipped quietly from the room and closed the door behind her.

Emerging from the room a few minutes later, Chayn made his way back to the woman's office and stood in front of her desk. She sensed his presence and glanced up at him, startled. "Do you have a problem?"

"I'm finished."

She opened her mouth to protest, then decided not to bother. She forced a smile. "We'll call you when the test results are analyzed."

Dusk had set in outside, deep golden light flooding through the skylights overhead from a sun that never really moved from its central position in the skies of Reylaton. Chayn could see the structure of the mirror clusters and hints of the curve of the rest of Reylaton. In bits and patches of black sky, the stars shone. Looking out over the upward curve of the hazy, distant landscape, birds darted in the sunset, snapping up the insects spiraling and dodging in the warm, evening air.

Chayn walked along a ledge overlooking the lower levels of the city. A few pedestrians glanced at him as they passed, glancing back over their shoulders to puzzle over the gray-eyed, muscular individual. Trenton had assured him that most people would assume him to be a foreigner from some distant, isolated colony, even those who had heard of the man from the stars.

A hand reached out from an alley passageway and clamped onto Chayn's arm. Chayn pulled away, throwing a tall, gaunt man off balance.

"My apologies, citizen," the man said with a slight nod. "You are Chayn Jahil."

"I am."

"Why do you claim to have come from the stars? The Word of Rashanyn says that men are unique to the worlds of Rashanyn. Why do you deny the Word?"

Chayn turned away and continued on. He glanced back to see if the man followed. The sidewalk was empty.

Returning to his apartment, Chayn slipped into a chair and picked up the remote control for the wallscreen. He punched out Trenton's personal number. A woman answered and put him on hold.

Trenton's image appeared. "Good evening, Chayn."

"What the hell happened this afternoon?"

"On the remote control you're holding is a button marked memory. Press it and punch in this code number." Chayn

66

did as he was told. "That's a catalog number for a briefing course on the black hole aliens. Push the release button and it'll be presented automatically for you."

"Was it some kind of invasion?"

Trenton shook his head. "A probe incident. The last one occured one hundred and fifty years ago. It's their way to keep track of our technological progress. We have our ways of accomplishing the same thing. There have never been hostilities."

Chayn refrained from asking further questions on the subject. "What's the Word of Rashanyn?"

Trenton sighed. "It's a book of the Church of Rashanyn,. a powerful, ancient religion. It's that ultraconservative dogma you've encountered, the kind of simple structure of belief some people need in order to cope."

"I seem to conflict with their beliefs."

"Keep your distance from them," Trenton warned. "Keep Villimy away from them. You can't reason with them and the lower your profile the less harassment you'll have to tolerate."

"Okay. Thanks, Trenton."

Trenton nodded. The screen went blank.

A pair of hands like fire and long, slender, pale blue fingers brushed his cheeks and slid down his chest from behind. Chayn put his hands over the slick, soft skin. "Want to watch a documentary on your invaders?"

"I was frightened this afternooon," Villimy said.

"Wait until I tell you my story. Are you psychic or something? Did you have some way of knowing what would happen?"

"No. The incident was coincidental. But despite what happened, I still believe the situation is more serious than Trenton makes it out to be."

"Let's watch the show and discuss the matter."

"Your place or mine?" Villimy said in her soft, sibilant voice.

Chayn could picture the teasing smile on her lips. "Mine," he said. "I froze my ass off in yours last night."

Seven

Rashanyn history extended only two thousand years into the past. The original colonists took up orbit about Jasper, the largest of the gas giants, the fifty-world just beyond the twin asteroid belts. Of the thirty thousand passengers in suspended animation under twenty thousand survived resuscitation and radiation injuries incurred when they awoke admist the intense, fluctuating radiation belts surrounding the world. Less than five percent of the gene bank survived and practically nothing of the memory banks that would have provided a continuation of the old levels of culture and technology.

Sometime during the early years of the budding Rashanyn Empire, a quasi-religious organization wrote the Word of Rashanyn based on the surviving records and personal memories of their origin. Science clung tenaciously to the sparse facts known of their origin and purpose in making the unbelievably long journey from another galaxy, preferring to build a future on little more than human ingenuity and the resources of the extensive planentary system they had stumbled across. A minority had always clung just as tenaciously to the ambiguous Word of Rashanyn as a literal history of the race and a handbook for the structure of Rashanyn society.

The Rashanyn Empire grew from that first complement of colonists to a civilization of twenty billion human beings thriving in the extensive, metal rich system of Star Rashanyn. Chayn frowned at the use of the word "thriving." Birth rates had soared early in Rashanyn history, then tapered off with the advent of population control. But those programs had been dropped almost three hundred years ago. Present birth rates indicated a slight population loss and had for over a century.

The nearest world orbiting Star Rashanyn consisted of a solid nickel-iron core two thousand kilometers in diameter missing its mantle of rock from some early cataclysm. The second and third worlds were contrasting twins, one molten beneath a dense atmosphere locked in a greenhouse effect, the other locked in a perpetual ice age. Gilderif, the fourth world, and Reylaton's primary, could not be colonized, but its orbiting cities served as a way station between the deep inner system and the furthest regions of the outer world colonies.

Jasper's gravitational perturbations had never permitted the next two planets to form. The dense, twin asteroid belts supported an industry employing billions. Beyond, four gas giants orbited Star Rashanyn, Jasper, the world that had never quite made the grade of sunhood and just beyond, a familiar-looking, banded world with a ring system sprawling in a flat plane to incredible distances around the light-weight planet. The inner worlds possessed no satellites, but the four giants shared over forty moons between them and had been extensively colonized. Still further out, a series of smaller, rocky worlds circled at distances of up to a tenth of a light year, some in renegade orbits leaning almost ninety degrees to the ecliptic.

Trenton hadn't told him the entire truth. Early in Rashanyn history, alien spacecraft had indiscriminately destroyed a number of small colonies. Over a span of five centuries, several other sporadic attacks followed, ending when Rashanyn technology regained its capacity for interstellar travel and followed three of the alien craft back to their source. Thus was discovered the civilization of the black hole aliens inhabiting the orbiting debris of the first black hole ever discovered, lying only three light years away. Since that time, exploratory probes had discovered Black star industrial colonies in the lifeless planetary systems of three nearby, red and white dwarf suns. No recurence of Black star hostility had followed a missile attack upon one of the dwarf settlements. The military believed the unknown creatures to be intelligent enough to know for certain that there'd be no defense against interstellar war, not for the Rashanyn, but neither for themselves.

Once every two or three centuries thereafter, a probe

incident occurred, the massive barrage of meter-long devices passing through the Rashanyn system. Likewise, the Rashanyn military sent its own observational probes into the black hole system, keeping tabs on the slow expansion of the alien civilization. The Church of Rashanyn believed the Blackstar aliens to be the creation of the Dark Stargod, the balancing force to good in the universe. Despite the protest of the scientific community, the Church influenced public opinion heavily enough to prevent large-scale attempts at peaceful contact.

Chayn watched Villimy's eyes dart about the screen during the documentary, convinced that she'd prove to be the more intelligent of the two. "What do you think?" he asked of her.

"I think there will be war," she said. "I think the two civilizations cannot stagnate and survive. The Blackstar aliens have little mineral wealth. Perhaps they considered the Rashanyn system to be their property, planning on eventual colonization."

"That explains the paranoia of the Rashanyn military. Why don't they suspect us of being Blackstar agents? They were never too enthusiastic about the possibility."

"You know the answer to that," Villimy said with a smile. "You are testing me. The Blackstar aliens do not have a technology to create a device like the starcraft. Also, the black hole aliens are physically small creatures, very alien with no direct contact with humanity."

"I am not testing you," Chayn said. "I trust your observations. Why do you believe the two civilizations to be stagnating?"

Villimy rose from her place on the couch alongside Chayn and selected several light pencils from their container near the screen controls. She selected a channel on the screen that would allow her to draw diagrams. In the center of the screen, she drew a series of colored circles and white arrows. "The gold star is Rashanyn. The blue star is the black hole, the home of the aliens. The red and white circles are

70

the dwarf colonies of the aliens. The arrows show their relative trajectories. All share a common, renegade trajectory that moves at a sharp angle past Star Rashanyn. Rashanyn is passing through their midst even now. Rashanyn authorities know that the black hole strongholds are very mineral poor. The Blackstar aliens are very ancient. Therefore they stagnate, but do not have a technology capable of moving their entire civilization to another stellar system, although, as I mentioned, it seems likely that they intended colonizing Rashanyn as it passed through their suns over a period of thousands of years. In a few thousand years more, Rashanyn will depart from the presence of the black hole and its attendent dwarfs. If the black hole aliens want this system for their own, if Star Rashanyn means survival for them, they will attack soon in overwhelming numbers. The increasing frequency of the probe incidents lends support to the hypothesis.''

Villimy sat back down beside him.

Chayn studied the diagram. Villimy's observations were inescapably obvious. "Do Rashanyn authorities know of this?"

"They must. I have read of this Church of Rashanyn. It is oppressive and fanatical. Fear breeds support for the Church. In turn, the Church breeds more fear. Rashanyn stagnates as well. They have lived with fear for too long. If the authorities publicize the seriousness of the crisis, social upheaval might result, perhaps the destruction of Rashanyn democracy and a takeover by the Church of Rashanyn.''

Chayn leaned back against the couch. "What's the chance of our leading a peaceful life and dying of old age before this whole thing blows up in our face?" A thought occurred to him. "How long do your people live?"

"Forty or fifty Rashanyn years."

"How old are you?"

"Sixteen years."

Chayn sat up straight, genuinely shocked. "Sixteen

years? You're still a child!''

Villimy crossed her arms in her characteristic gesture of displeasure. "And you are an old man!"

Chayn recovered just as quickly. Sixteen years at her metabolic rate would make her the human equivalent of twenty to thirty years of age. He slipped his arm about her waist and gave her a reassuring squeeze. "A dirty old man."

"I think," Villimy said, "that we arrive at the turning point in Rashanyn history. I think we are to take part in events to occur. You said you knew of the gold star before you arrived. Your arrival, ctherefore, is not coincidental."

And the Watcher watched, silently from the background.

"Coincidence or not, I take things at face value. Villimy, you can't live a day-to-day life on an incomprehensible level."

But other thoughts emerged and fell into place, foremost among them, memories of the sheer power of the starcraft. But even if he had access to the starcraft, what effect could one man have on the inexorable events involving entire civilizations and tens of centuries?

Villimy leaned close. Her huge eyes were like windows to her soul, but, in turn, his lay naked to her unearthly gaze. Chayn held an alien body in his arms, his hands exploring her slender contours.

"I saw the break in the skylight this afternoon," Chayn said. "Can you imagine a catastrophe on that scale? Fifty million people asphyxiated on the streets of their own city?"

Villimy shuddered. "My people do not live like this."

She had told him of her people. He could vividly imagine the green worlds she described to him. Her people had colonized eighty planetary systems within a sphere of two hundred light years of their original worlds. Chayn thought of the challenge of locating and visiting those worlds someday. He had tried not thinking of the loss of his starcraft, but in just such indirect ways he failed. He had accepted the inevitable at first, but already found himself speculating on their eventual departure. He could return Villimy to her lost home. They could return to the derelict and retrieve the navigational data they'd need and together retrace the path of the doomed colonists.

Villimy brushed her hot cheek against his. "Life is full for us. Live from moment to moment to the fullest, Chayn. Tomorrow grows from the roots of now."

"I still think you're psychic."

Villimy stood and held out her hand, leading him to the bedroom. Chayn turned the thermostat to its lowest setting, turning back to her to see her pull the shift over her head. The way she held her clenched fists at her side and slightly back with her torso arched signified anticipatory delight. Slowly, he began to know her, but continued to experience guilt toward their sexual relationship. But when he undressed, he swept her into his arms and laid her across the bed, her heated flesh igniting an all too human lust in him. Quickly aroused, Villimy emitted her eerie, husky wail of desire, her body convulsing as Chayn entered her. She raked his shoulders in an instant, continuous orgasm, her body churning beneath him with a life of its own. Chayn joined her in an explosion of esctasy a moment later. It had to be quick for her. Her nervous system couldn't sustain such intensity for long.

Interspersed with sudden and violent bouts of lovemaking, they lay quietly together during the night, Villimy warming him against the chill in the air and from her perspective, Chayn cooling her against the sweltering heat. They couldn't rest well together.

Only once had Chayn gathered the courage to ask how he compared to the men of her own species. "You are big and slow and powerful and I am very perverse." He'd need even more courage to ask what she meant by "perverse."

The wallscreen beeped at daylight. Chayn rose to answer it, keeping the visual off.

"Chayn Jahil," he said.

"Citizen Jahil, this is Reylaton Electronics." The voice

was male. "Can you report to our offices at nine for an employment interview?"

"At nine. I'll be there."

"Thank you, citizen."

Chayn showered and dressed. Villimy slipped into her own apartment, preferring her ice water. Some things, he decided, they'd never fully share without concessions.

"I go with you today?" Villimy called from the other side of the closed door.

"I know the heat bothers you," Chayn said, "but you'll have to dress."

"Trenton gave something to me." She emerged wearing a white coverall. A square bulge on her right shoulder emitted a whispering rush of intense heat through a metal vent.

"A refrigerator suit? I'll be damned."

Villimy slipped on a pair of large, smoked sunglasses similar to those the public wore on occasion, although much darker. With the glasses covering her large, golden eyes, she looked surprisingly human. Even her white hair would pass. The Rashanyn tended to loose hair coloring with age.

"You'll pass—for an anemic."

"Insult! Let me see you disguise all that muscle and pass as Rashanyn!"

Chayn shook his head in mock disapproval. "What a weird pair of Reylaton citizens we're going to make."

Villimy ate a breakfast three times the size of his, her caloric intact incredibly high by Chayn's standards. Together, they left the apartment, nodding in the corridors outside to a few of Trenton's technicians who interviewed them and poked at their anatomies from time to time. Among the pedestrians on the streets, they would never have passed without reactions of shock and surprise, but Villimy reacted with open delight at her surroundings. She behaved like a tourist. Trenton had suggested that they'd experience little trouble with the populace if Reylaton took

74

them to be tourists from some exotic, far reaches of Rashanyn. It worked. Villimy pointed out the upward curve of the landscape, the bow of the skylight curving overhead and commented on themcolor qualities of the sunlight. She bent to inspect flowers, ran her fingers over the grass and dug into soil with her fingernails. She speculated on the technology behind the transportation system, the monorails running the length of the pavilion and the hovercraft passing overhead. Like Chayn, she considered the Rashanyn somewhat backward technologically.

Nothing escaped Villimy's attention. "We're being followed."

Chayn glanced around casually. Three men followed. One turned off into a side alley and another joined the remaining two.

"They're trying not to be obvious," Chayn said.

"Who are they?"

"Church of Rashanyn."

"Trouble," Villimy decided.

Three men and two women stepped from an alley. Chayn and Villimy stopped. Chayn recognized the gaunt man who had accosted him the day before.

"I am Hadak, Elder of the Reylaton Congregation."

Chayn said nothing. Villimy moved up against him, quivering.

"You are not Rashanyn," Hadak said. "The creature at your side is not human. You are agents of the Dark Stargod. It is not coincidental that your arrival coincides with the probe incident. The Blackstar aliens move against us."

Chayn glanced at the three men to their rear. None appeared to be armed. Chayn would have preferred simply to walk around them, but to their right towered the concrete face of a building and to their left, a railing overlooking a thirty-meter drop to a sidewalk below.

The pair of close set eyes glared at Chayn in raging frustration, Hadak would not even look at Villimy. If Trenton, even General Pak, represented the voice of reason in the city, these people represented the opposing extreme, the prejudiced, the self-righteous, the voices of a defensive culture fearful of its security.

"The Elders of the Church of Rashanyn wish to question you. You will come with us now. Without resistance."

The three men moved in from behind. The two women stepped forward to take Villimy. Chayn yanked two of the men who grabbed at his arms, then clamped one hand around the back of each of their necks and shoved them into the two advancing women. All four fell together and, for a moment, struggled against one another to regain their footing before falling to a heap on the pavement. Chayn pivoted to confront the remaining man coming up from behind. He pushed him backwards with a strength born of rising anger. The man fell against the railing and almost tumbled over it, his eyes bulging as he got a good look at the empty space beyond.

"Take them!" Hadak bellowed.

The two remaining men standing alongside Hadak moved forward, dressed in loose, shiny black coveralls. By their cautious approach and slight crouch, Chayn figured they'd be more effective street fighters. Chayn stepped forward to put Villimy behind him. One of the men slid gracefully up to him, feigned with an open palm, theen struck Chayn in his solar plexus with the other fist when he reflexively blocked the feign. Chayn doubled in pain and surprise and suddenly found his right arm being twisted behind his back.

Another of the men reached for Villimy, expecting no trouble from her. Chayn expected nothing of her. Villimy looked too frail to defend herself.

Villimy's sudden, high-pitched scream of rage sent hackles rising on Chayn's back. A slender arm shot out, blocking the man's reach. Her other fist lashed out, jabbing the man hard in the throat. He staggered back, two others moving in on both sides of him. In a single graceful movement, Villimy kicked off the shoe of her right foot, leapt into the air and cracked the man closest to her across the bridge of his nose, sending him careening back against Hadak. The second man retreated.

Recovering from the unexpected violence, Chayn stepped forward, tearing himself free from the grip that jammed his arm up against his back and planting his massive fist against the side of the jaw of the retreating man. Chayn felt bone shatter. Blood poured from the man's mouth and with an expression of astonishment, he fell forward, face first onto the sidewalk.

Chayn stepped over him. His next adversary moved in, one of the men dressed in shiny black, open palms inscribing delicate circles in the air. An open palm lashed out and Chayn stepped inside and turned to take the blow harmlessly across the muscles of his upper back. Chayn grabbed the man by the throat, lifting him bodily into the air. Pretending to throw him over the railing, Chayn pivoted at the last moment and threw the screaming fanatic across the legs of his advancing comrade.

They still considered Villimy the weak link in the two-link chain. The two women recovered from their fall and moved in on her. Villimy lashed out at them, raking their faces with clawed hands. She leapt forward with inhuman reflexes, the heel of her right foot smearing a nose across a face, mangling another face before her shocked opponent fell unconscious to the pavement. She tore through the remainder of Hadak's men, the air reverberating with screams of terror and Villimy's wailing shrieks of rage.

Chayn moved back in shock, frightened himself of Villimy's murderous attack. Then silence fell with the moans of the injured increasing in volume as they realized the extent of their injuries. There were three men and two women scattered across the bloody sidewalk with Hadak and his remaining two survivors disappearing into the distance in a mad dash for safety. Villimy crouched panting in the midst of the carnage, her hands still clawed and rigid. She glanced rapidly from side to side, her movements light-ning-quick. Slowly, by gradual degrees, she relaxed, her panting slowing to the normal, quick rise and fall of her breasts.

"I'm sorry, Chayn," she said. "I lost my temper."

"Villimy, if you loose your temper over domestic quarrels, you're going to have to wear mittens to get within ten feet of me."

"I'm sorry." Her body shuddered in a final reaction of fear. She gave him a quivering smile.

On the pavilion far below, the police arrived in a flurry of flashing red lights. Tiny figures poured from the vehicle and disappeared into the building below.

"Relax now," Chayn said. "There'll be trouble, but we have Trenton to help us. Don't fight the police."

Villimy moved up against him. Chayn slipped an arm around her shoulders. The police poured onto the walk ahead and from behind, their weapons drawn. An officer stepped forward from their ranks, pulling a transceiver from his belt.

"Patch me into the Exobiology Institute, the department housing the two aliens. Their pets just single-handedly massacred the Church of Rashanyn."

While he waited for an answer, the officer knelt beside one of the injured men, ignoring Chayn and Villimy. "Jesir. I might have known. The next time you consider incorporating a little violence into your sick games, think of your poor nose. It'll break even easier the next time."

Eight

A black robed figure gesticulated wildly on the wallscreen, his head thrown back in passionate frenzy, his mouth contorting with each unheard word. Silence dominated the room. Trenton paced in front of the screen. "I can't reason with emotion," he said, his calm voice betrayed by his restlessness. "I can't stop fear with logic and there's no way to keep an entire population from acting on emotion rather than reason."

Chayn sat beside Villimy on the couch facing the wall-screen. Villimy shuddered at the vehemence of the Church spokesman delivering his heated message.

"What do they want?" Chayn said.

"Control of the government. A change of policy. A society cannot live in fear forever. It's debilitating and demoralizing."

"What did they want us for?" Villimy asked in her soft tone, forcing Trenton to consider words spoken in contrast to his anger and the display of anger on the wallscreen.

"Propaganda," Trenton siad. "Some of them really believe you're agents of the Dark Stargod. Regardless, they intended to interrogate you, film the episode and broadcast it on the Church channel. If they had asked you the purpose of your mission for the Dark Stargod, even a denial would have sounded suspicious to a citizen who believes in that crap. The form of their questions would have thrown you into a defensive position. They wouldn't have caused you any physical harm."

"There is real danger," Villimy said.

"No kidding!" Trenton said. "We face a war we don't want, one that is bound to destroy civilization as we know it. Billions will die whether or not we initiate hostilities." I should have known better than to assume we could keep the truth from you two."

"Let me have my starcraft back," Chayn said. "I'll visit the black hole and find out what you're up against."

Trenton relaxed, depressed by the reasonableness of the suggestion. He reached to the side of the screen and turned it off, then sat in a chair off to one side of the couch. "I've already put the suggestion to General Pak."

"How did he react?"

"Even if he's game, he doesn't have the authority to release the starcraft to you. The military is biding its time, hoping to find a way to coerce you into revealing its method of operation. They've given up trying to figure out how it functions."

Trenton leaned back and crossed his legs. "I trust the both of you. I trust your objectivity. The fact that Villimy could spend two days here and clearly see if what the military spends billions hiding from the public is evidence enough that you could be useful to us. But the more immediate problem is the Church. If the elected Council looses a vote of confidence, you two have real problems."

"Any suggestions?" Chayn said.

Trenton seemed not to hear. "You didn't get to Reylaton Electronics."

"At least your jails are comfortable."

Villimy shuddered. She hadn't enjoyed the experience at all.

"I'll call in the morning, explain the situation and underplay the extent of the problem. Get yourself employed, Chayn. That'll validate your citizenship to where even the Church will have trouble contesting it. You have an unusual talent with computers. In a society regulated by computers, it might come in handy."

"Where's the starcraft?"

Trenton gave him a cold look. "Transferred to Cornoben's command, the military base orbiting Jasper."

"That's the big gas giant. I talked with the man when we first arrived."

"Jasper is a long, long way from here, Chayn. That ship of yours is lost forever to you. I'm sorry."

"You would have helped me hijack it," Chayn said with a grin.

Trenton suppressed a smile. "Damn right. You two don't deserve this crap."

"What do we do if the Church gains power?" Chayn asked.

"Try to make it to the maintenance levels below the city. Play it by ear from there. Survive. I won't be in a position to help. The Church would take sadistic delight in replacing the staff of my research department with their own people. We work with heretical knowledge."

"Things fell apart in a big hurry," Chayn said in a depressed tone of his own.

"I'm sorry. It was the probe incident. It happened at a bad time. The Church has never been this active during a probe incident before. Otherwise, we would have taken it in stride."

"We'll help," Villimy said.

Both Chayn and Trenton looked at her. "How in hell can we help?" Chayn said.

"You and I," Villimy said. "We'll help. And then we'll leave. Even in your own mind, it's what you want."

"You're telepathic," Chayn said. "Right?"

"No, Chayn," Villimy said with a laugh. "You are slow and so very predictable."

Trenton stood, preparing to leave, not taking Villimy seriously. "Lay off the newscasts," he said. "They're depressing as hell."

Chayn and Villimy sat quietly in front of the blank screen, Villimy with a slight smile on her face, waiting for Chayn's thought processes to lead to inevitable conclusions. Chayn picked up the remote control for the wallscreen and punched for a catalog of data requests. Chayn searched the alphabetical listings for what he wanted. Finally, he punched in his coded request.

A torus filled the entire screen, a white line drawing on pitch black filled with an incredible amount of detail. Chayn exploded the drawing. It rushed forward, the detail expanding to expose even more detail. They were looking at the technical readouts for the city of Reylaton.

Chayn rotated the schematics, viewing them from various angles to gain an idea of the capability of the computer-generated images. Finally, he managed a cross-sectional view and expanded that until he could discern a recognizable view of the city's construction. He could switch between electrical, plumbing, and basic construction schematics, or outline different systems in various colors. Chayn focused down to the maintenance levels below the surface that lay open beneath the skylight.

"Damn, look at the size of it." The maintenance levels were more extensive than he could have imagined.

"Mn work down there," Villimy observed. She could see the living quarters and transportation facilities.

"Yes, but there must be kilometers of tunnels and very few people to go around. I see what Trenton's getting at. A person could hide down there indefinitely."

Later, after Villimy had returned to her own apartment, Chayn watched the public news broadcasts. Chayn considered it odd that the arrival of two aliens from the stars could attract so little attention. Nothing was mentioned of the Church attack on them, but neither had the Church used them in their propaganda. Panels were openly debating the merits of Church dogma versus science, democracy versus the necessities of self-defense and the chances for peace versus the possibility of destruction. Even the Church warned the public against panic, but Chayn did notice that they had a good grasp of the threat and were advocating more action to counter it than the military considered publically advisable. Despite the beliefs and tactics of the Church, Chayn could almost sympathize with their stance. The military functioned with too much secrecy.

Before turning in for the night, Chayn checked on Villimy. He found her sitting comfortably nude in her comfortable environment considerably below freezing. She sat before her own wallscreen, going through the catalog at breakneck speeds, stopping or hesitating as something caught her attention. She had a photographic memory. Later she'd backtrack and study the material she wanted in detail.

They made a good pair, complementary allies, Villimy with her intelligence and quick reflexes, Chayn with his methodical planning and brute strength. Villimy did not rely upon him for support more than Chayn found himself relying upon her. Despite his amnesia, it seemed to him that in the world to which he had belonged women were more subordinate to men than necessary. Even Rashanyn women were the equals of their male counterparts.

Suspecting that Villimy would join him during the night, Chayn set the thermostate to its lowest setting and turned on his new, electric blanket. Thanks to Trenton, that one, potential domestic conflict had been eliminated. Chayn grinned, reminiscing the street fight. Not that Chayn appreciated General Pak's filming of the incident from a distance, delaying intervention out of curiosity. Villimy had fought like an animal, yet displaying the most helpless, sophisticated level of indignation at the police station. Secretly, Chayn had enjoyed himself.

Basking in the security of their ability to cope with the worst Reylaton had to offer, Chayn's eyes shot open to the hair-raising, trilling scream tearing through the apartment. He rolled off the bed and onto his feet in an instant, dashing through the subdued lighting and bursting through the door that separated him from Villimy Dy with enough force to slam the door back and crack the plastic wall. Villimy stood in the center of the room in the cold, orange light. Something alive bulged the ventilator grill inward, a rectangular grid located in one corner of the room. The grill sprang loose with the sound of snapping bolts and bounced across the floor.

The creature fell to the floor, a flexible body uncoiling, two rolls of legs struggling for equilibrium. Green eyes on black flesh focused on the sound of the screaming. A red tongue flickered, tasting the cold air.

"Villimy!!"

Villimy glanced at him with an expression of horror. In the same instant, the creature raced across the floor, its mouth gaping, two fangs gleaming white in the dim light. Villimy jumped straight into the air, the fangs missing her right ankle by inches.

The creature stopped, sensing for a disturbance in the

83

environment, darted forward, stopped. Chayn froze in disbelief, not daring to move. Quicker than Chayn could follow, the creature attacked again and Villimy jumped to one side faster than Chayn could ever hope to move. Even so, the creature grazed her flesh.

Chayn backed into his own room, his heart pounding. In his mind's eye, he searched the apartment for a weapon, but turned back to the door instead and held it half-closed, waiting for Villimy to notice him, not daring to distract her again. Villimy stood panting, backed against the far wall. The creature squatted before her, shifting from side to side to gain perspective. Villimy glanced at Chayn, but the instant she took her eyes from the creature, it shot forward in a blur of pounding legs.

Villimy dodged, leaped and raced for the door. She breezed past him into his apartment and Chayn slammed the door behind her—but not before the creature shot past his legs. Villimy leapt, pivoting in the air. She landed on the couch and froze, her eyes fixed on the creature.

The thermostat poked Chayn in the back. The two apartments had been used in the past by the Institute to house specimens of primitive life from the ice-locked third planet of the system and were capable of heating or cooling the apartments to impractical extremes. Chayn reached around and turned the thermostat to its highest setting. The temperature began climbing on the thermometer even as he watched.

A minute passed, then two. Reacting to the heat herself, Villimy began backing off the couch. The creature scurried around the couch, its movements visibly slowed in the increasing heat. Villimy continued to put the couch between herself and the creature. When the animal finally squatted on the floor and did not move, the two of them backed into her apartment. Chayn pulled the door closed behind them.

Villimy sank to the floor in convulsions of delayed reaction to her terror. Chayn called Trenton on the wallscreen. "Something with a bunch of legs and two long, white teeth just came in through the ventilator in Villimy's apartment. It's in mine now. Don't let anyone barge in. I think it's deadly."

Trenton's face paled. "Quite lethal. Stay put. Help is on the way."

Chayn helped Villimy to the couch. She recovered rapidly. "I know who did that."

"Hadak," Chayn said, voicing their common suspicion.

A commotion sounded from Chayn's apartment, a crash followed by a shout of fear. A man cried out in horror and a crackling sound followed. A moment later, the interconnecting door opened. A helmeted soldier followed the snout of a laser rifle inside.

Two more followed, taking up positions on either side of the door. General Pak entered the room, looked around suspiciously and nodded his sober greetings.

"It's clear in here," Chayn said. He pointed to the ventilator shaft. "It came from there."

The general signaled for them to join him in the adjacent apartment. A man lay on the floor, his face swollen and discolored. Smoke rose in tendrils from a scorched arc across the tiled floor, ending in the charred remains of the creature. The acrid fumes burned Chayn's eyes. Villimy turned and darted back into her own apartment.

General Pak stared at the dead creature and his dying trooper, apalled. "How could you have survived?"

"Villimy did all the moving. It didn't even notice me. The heat slowed it down." Chayn had forgotten about the thermostat. The air rippled with heat. He reset it. "What was that thing?"

"It's from the equatorial regions of Chatlo, the third planet. It lives in a cold environment. Its reflexes are incredible."

"A fitting adversary for Villimy," Chayn said.

The general tensed. "We'll increase security. This won't happen again."

"Why do they want to kill us?"

"If the Church can't use you and the woman in their propaganda efforts they fear we will use you against them."

"How can you use us?"

"A documentary can be made of your presence in our society. An interview can be conducted, an honest one. Your very presence contradicts Church doctrine. If their reputation is damaged now, during the height of a crisis, they may never recover."

"If you get around to it, we accept. It might take the heat off us if we're too well known to assassinate."

"My thoughts as well." The general nodded curtly to the body on the floor. "Do you wish a change of quarters while we're cleaning this mess up?"

"I'll stay with Villimy," Chayn said.

General Pak glanced at him, but said nothing. Chayn had noticed that even Trenton avoided mentioning Chayn's closeness to the alien woman. They were curious in a morbid way, but Chayn had yet to learn what subtle taboo he violated in his relationship with Villimy.

"You won't have further trouble tonight," General Pak stated. "Trenton's crew is ensuring that you'll be safely isolated until at least morning."

"Thank you, General."

General Pak turned away and left the apartment, followed by his men. Medical personnel entered the apartment, unrolling a stretcher without reacting to the sight of the carnage.

Chayn rejoined Villimy. She stood gazing up at the open ventilator shaft. "Hadak is frightened of you, Villimy. This was quite an exteme to seek revenge. Fear is our weapon as well as his. For the moment, it's in our hands."

Villimy glanced down at the scratch on her leg. "It was not intelligent, but I felt akin to it almost. I would personally have enjoyed returning it to this Hadak person."

"I wonder what they have in store for us as an encore?"

Villimy nudged up against him. "When this is over, I want to go home."

Chayn payed little attention to her statement. Villimy required little sleep, but catnapped often, four or five hourly periods whenever the need came over her. She napped for an hour while Chayn studied the readouts of the city. Between the two of them, they would grow to learn a great deal about the layout of the city. Villimy awoke during the night and continued studying the schematics. Chayn retrieved the heated blanket from his own apartment, wrapped himself in it and crawled into Villimy's bed.

Trenton called after daybreak. With a new appointment at Reylaton Electronics in an hour, Chayn and Villimy set out across the city on foot with the golden rays of Star Rashanyn glowing against the arced landscape of Reylaton in a perpetrual, deep summer haze. Villimy wore her white coveralls with its small, air-conditioning unit and Chayn, a two-toned tunic and trousers of white and blue. Two police hovercraft followed their progress, moving parallel to him over the canyon formed by the stepped buildings rising on either side of the central, open strip of pavilion. To the casual eye, the slender woman in white and the unusually stocky male walked alone. More than a few eyes followed then in envy of the flowing grace of the woman's walk or the impressive physique of the foreigner.

Entering the outer offices of Reylaton Electronics, the receptionist took notice of the woman escorting citizen Jahil with subdued disappointment and showed them into the office of Administrator Jarl as she had been instructed. With employment a bonus rather than a necessity in a society supported by automation, it wasn't unusual for a mated couple to share one job opening. Jarl stood and gestured for them both to take seats.

Jarl studied the unusual woman for a moment, bothered by the color of her skin and the large eyes behind the dark sunglasses. He already knew Villimy not to be native to Rashanyn, but mistakenly considered Chayn Jahil to be native to some distant colony in the system, remembering only that he was said to be fully human.

"You scored unusually high in our tests," Jarl said to Chayn. "I've personally not encountered an individual with your sensitivity to subtle disharmonies. We can be of service to one another."

"I'm not fully familiar with your electronic terminology," Chayn said to the graying, deeply tanned official. "I don't know my way around the city. I might mention that we've had a few problems with the Church and may not be free to travel as openly as we'd like."

"That will be no problem. We provide company transportation. As for your unfamiliarity with our technology, we'll provide technicians to show you the aspects of the job that you'll need to know. Our employment practices are standard. One week's probationary period, retroactive pay deposited to your account, pay grade ten."

That did not concern Chayn. "Why do I get the impression that the rate of computer malfunction is a bit on the high side?"

Jarl leaned back in his chair and interlaced his fingers. "Inadequate shielding. Molecular electronics are quite sensitive to damage by high energy, subnuclear particles, cosmic rays. Reylaton itself is electrically shielded against background radiation, but if a high energy particle passes through a computer core, it distorts the circuitry. We can compensate for mathematical error, but in high level computer functioning, the damage causes distortion, the equivalent of neurosis. The core at fault must be located to be replaced."

"You don't have computer interface with the human neural system, some potential for feedback?" Chayn asked, suspecting that he overstepped himself. "I know your electronics works with interaction between magnetic fields, but there are ways to correct distortions through feedback."

"That's still experimental," Jarl said. At first, he had thought Chayn to be overemployed because of a special skill, but now questioned his own judgment. "I'll talk with some departmental heads and see if we an arrange further testing with what we have on hand. It's an interesting idea if you think you can handle it."

Jarl looked again at Villimy Dy. "The two of you will be working together?"

"I understand it's not an uncommon arrangement."

Jarl spoke direct to Villimy. "You're not a citizen, are you?"

"Technically speaking, neither am I," Chayn said in challenge. "You've spoken with Trenton of the Institute about us?"

Jarl had lost himself in Villimy's large eyes. He looked at Chayn, startled. "Yes, of course. There's no problem. You mentioned some trouble with the Church."

"I understand that's not unusual either."

"No, it isn't," Jarl said, "but we have few dealings with the general public. We'll take good care of you."

On the way back to the apartments, Villimy asked, "Why is employment here important to you?"

"Reylaton Electronics is international in scope. If the trouble with the Church blows over, that gives us access to interplanetary commerce."

"Yes," Villimy said. "I see what you're getting at. Your starcraft."

In the early afternoon hours of the day, the screen awoke Villimy from a nap in her apartment. She donned her sunglasses and answered the screen.

A frail, aging man spent a moment recovering from mild shock. "I'm Ken Davi. I've been instructed to deliver Villimy Dy and Chayn Jahil to a job site for Reylaton Electronics. Are you prepared to leave?"

"Immediately, citizen Davi."

"I'm parked in front of the Institute's receiving dock on the pavilion."

"We'll be right with you."

Villimy skipped into Chayn's apartment, a bright smile on her thin lips, her gold eyes bright with exitement. "I make a good secretary!"

She jumped at Chayn. He caught her by the waist and spun her around once. "A beautiful, live-in secretary. Boy, do I have it made so early in my career. Now, what's going on?"

"A chauffeur waiting outside."

Ken Davi turned out to be a small and slender, aging man who gave them both a confused but friendly smile as they slid into the rear seats of the enclosed hovercraft. Chayn slid the doors closed and Davi pulled away from the dock, rising high into the air above the pavilion. The stepped buildings converging on the ground level fell below with their many levels of railing protected walks. They rose above the glass faced buildings and for the first time, saw the vegetation that stretched to meet in the distance with the skylights. Chayn made a note to plan a visit to the parks and forests, to see what kind of artificial ecology Rashanyn had put together with their genetic engineering. From ancient pictorial texts and the surviving gene banks of the original colonists, the Rashanyn had literally created a world of living things to share their many colonies with.

They flew close enough to the skylights to study in detail the metallic framework supporting the transparent, silicate panels. They flew slowly through filaments of water vapor, a thin stream of clouds that circled the torus of Reylaton near the skylights where water vapor condensed against the twin panes of insulated glass. It rained in Reylaton occasionally, with a little help from the city engineers.

"Are you a technician?" Chayn asked Davi.

"No, just a driver. I don't work for Reylaton Electronics directly. They lease my services, Davi Security. I've heard about you two. Glad to have you aboard."

They dropped back down into the canyon of concrete to the pavilion, set down on rubber tires, and rolled into the receiving dock of a bustling commercial center. A crane tipped with a specialized claw reached over, grasped their hovercraft and placed it on a parking rack above several levels of similar vehicles. The three of them stepped out onto a catwalk and walked along the metal cliff to a door.

Inside, a corridor led into the depths of the complex.

Davi led the way, turning into a suite of offices where a technician in white coveralls with a Reylaton Electronics insignia on his back spied them and called out to Davi. They filed through a side door into a dimly lit chamber filled with banks of computer terminals.

Davi stepped off to one side. For the first time, Chayn noticed the man was armed. Villimy caught Chayn's eyes and smiled. The technicians had their equipment set up and ready to go, Chayn recognizing nothing except the portable console with its screen and earphones.

"This equipment services the navigational computers of the traffic control division of Reylaton Transport," one of the technicians explained. "They've had some problems with traffic crowding. You wouldn't believe the amount of data these computers handle. These are just access terminals here. We haven't located the malfunction, but someone's liable to get hurt if we don't get the problem solved."

"How does this equipment work?" Chayn asked.

The technician handed Chayn a remote control device connected by a thin cable to the small console set on top of one of the computer terminals. "The large button is a circuit advance. Push it to move from one circuit to another. I've already programmed in the circuits we have to scan. Just stop if you sense a disharmony. Administrator Jarl thinks you're sensitive enough to help, but we haven't had much luck so far."

Chayn pulled up a stool and donned the earphones. The patterns of color on the screen and the stereo tones of sound were hypnotic, isolating Chayn from outside interference. His psyche submerged in a universe of resonance and bit by bit, he focused on the myriads of frequencies, following harmonics down the spectrum and searching for the discordant rhythym that indicated trouble. He moved from circuit to circuit, each a new symphony of beauty until he found the grating, disruptive flow.

Before he disengaged, he flowed deeper, abandoning

himself to the depths of the indecipherable intelligence. He tried to interface in the same way he interfaced with the starcraft, handing over the challenge of interpretation of the harmony fields to his unconscious, aware that he lacked the artificial intelligence that aboard the starcraft served to synthesize the calculation he perceived.

Suddenly, the Watcher intervened. He hadn't given any thought to the entity that observed from the depths of his psyche for days. The Watcher hadn't abandoned him. For the first time, it took an active role in his psyche. It absorbed the harmony fields, processed the data and fed back to him a sensory image of its significance.

Chayn saw thousands of spacecraft, images of unseen things moving in a three-dimensional void. He wasn't dealing with the kind of data that would allow him to see images of the ships in usual terms, but he could sense them in terms of size and mass in relation to one another and to the great mass of Reylaton. He could feel the forces at play moving them about and feel the calculations of the computers in moving them about in safe, efficient patterns.

Chayn couldn't feed himself into the pattern or take willful control of the computers and their programming, but given some kind of feedback into the system, he'd indeed be able to do just that.

Chayn withdrew and reoriented himself. "Block five, circuit level nine, board five and processing core eighty-four. It's shorted through and feeding garbage into the system."

"How could you possibly have that kind of information?" the technician demanded.

"Just check it out."

The technician jotted the directions down on a clipboard. "Davi, take these people home. Our field representative will get ahold of you later this afternoon, citizen Jahil."

Villimy expressed no concern for Chayn's success or lack of it. They followed Davi back to the hovercraft, Villimy soaking in the environment with cheerful alertness. Once in the air and gaining altitude, she pointed out something below and Chayn leaned forward to follow the direction of her wavering finger. A black, seething mass filled a plaza.

"What's that?" Chayn asked of Davi.

Davi banked the craft for a better look, then began losing altitude. "I'll be. Looks like a riot."

"Does that happen often?"

"Never heard of anything like this happening. Might be dangerous. It has to be a Church demonstration."

"What do they want?" Villimy said.

Davi took the hovercraft to a nerve-racking, low level over the scene of violence and hovered. "They want the Council to take a public vote of confidence. The Council has refused so far."

Police on the perimeter of the mob were having a difficult time containing the churning throngs. The rioters turned over a ground vehicle and set it on fire. Dense smoke billowed alongside the hovercraft.

"I think we'd better be moving on," Davi said, tipping the nose down and climbing skyward at a sharp angle.

A collection of hovercrafts were arriving from a distance, red lights flashing. More police poured from a monorail bus.

A pencil beam of light flashed through the sky alongside Davi's window.

"Oh, damn, someone's shooting at us."

The laser beam appeared to dissipate before reaching the skylights, was Chayn's first thought in the confusion. Suddenly, the cherry red light flickered past his window.

Something was burning. Villimy grabbed for him in sudden fear. The engines failed, a generator winding down to low-pitched uselessness. The hovercraft dipped its nose and picked up speed, the sound of rushing wind filtering into the cockpit.

"This is a first for me as well," Davi said in an even, calm tone. "We've just been shot down."

They rushed down the vast tube of Reylaton, gaining

speed second by second. The pavilion below blurred to a gray strip at the bottom of slanted walls of glass and concrete. Davi banked from side to side in the final seconds before impact. With Villimy clutching at him painfully with clawed hands, Chayn understood Davi's strategy during their last moment of flight.

Davi dived for the canal, the winding river that circled the city of Reylaton.

Nine

The hovercraft skimmed the surface of the canal, sheering the undercarriage away. The blades of the two fans exploded in a horizontal spray of shrapnel. The hovercraft rebounded, tilting its nose into the air in a moment of silence, then struck water again in a lurch of deceleration. On the final rebound, Davi tilted the hovercraft to the right, using the small airfoils on the side of the fuselage that bit into the spray of water instead of air. The flat nose of the craft dug into the loose soil of the flower gardens, churning dirt up over the windshield. The hovercraft spun around once and came to a halt.

Chayn couldn't breath for a moment, having taken one of Villimy's elbows in his chest. Villimy disentangled herself and looked outside with quick, nervous movements of her head. Chayn leaned over the front seats and pulled Davi back from the steering pillars. Davi struggled to consciousness, blinking away blood that poured into his eyes from a gashed forehead.

Villimy tried unsuccessfully to tear a piece of cloth from Chayn's tunic to stem the flow of blood.

"Hey!"

Villimy smiled, her lips quivering. "Blue is a distasteful color anyway."

"Considering that weird stuff you call sunlight," Chayn said, struggling with the jammed door, "it's no wonder." Chayn leaned back in his seat and kicked. The door bent outward, then sprang open.

Chayn climbed outside, tripping over the loose, moist earth. A crowd of people converged on them from the near distance. The red beam of light could still be seen battling the police vehicles. Even as Chayn watched, a brighter beam of white darted into the crowd. A moan of fearful protest arose from the rioters.

"We've got sightseers coming our way," Chayn said. "Let's get Davi out of there and get lost."

Between the two of them, they dragged the half-conscious chauffeur from the wreckage of the hovercraft. In tacit agreement, they dragged him toward the store fronts lined beneath an overhang.

"Do you know where we are?" Chayn said. Villimy just nodded, but even Chayn had an idea of how to return to the Institute without exposing themselves along the open pavilion.

They entered a small apparel shop, startled patrons and horrified clerks backing away from the blood splattered threesome. Villimy darted off to one side and snatched a small piece of white cloth from a clothing display, handing it to Davi and pressing his hand against the head wound. Chayn backed through a rear door dragging Davi behind him. Villimy threw one of his arms over her shoulders, supporting as much of his weight as she could.

Clerks in the stock room backed away, but one ran forward and held a swinging door open in the rear of the shop, exposing a loading dock beyond and the huge transportation tunnel with its six sets of monorails overhead. Monorail trucks were parked along the docks, electric lifts loading and unloading merchandise. Chayn headed for the nearest truck as a driver pulled the side doors closed and walked toward the cab. When the man glanced up at the approaching trio, he dropped a clipboard and moved forward to block their path.

"Wait a moment, citizen . . . ."

Chayn dropped Davi. Villimy struggled under the full burden, easing Davi to the ground. Chayn reached out for the truck driver and bunched the front of the man's coveralls in his fist, raising him off the ground. "We're hijacking your truck. It's not a nice thing to do, but under the circumstances, it's expedient."

Davi recovered and struggled to his feet. Blinded by blood congealing over his eyes, he needed Villimy to guide him to the cab of the truck. Chayn pulled the truck driver in after him.

"Drive," Chayn said. "Villimy, how far?"

"Six kilometers."

"Six kilometers," Chayn said with a grin.

The driver, a small man with sad eyes took one look at the blood on Davi and decided not to protest. He slammed his door shut. A turbine hummed to life. He moved the truck forward, operating foot-controls to shift the truck onto the second monorail as it came up behind another truck parked along the dock.

The truck gained speed with each shift to an outer monorail. On the last one against the far wall of the tunnel, it rushed soundlessly down the endless tunnel.

"This tunnel goes clear around the torus, doesn't it?" Chayn asked of Villimy.

"Yes. There are other tunnels beneath this one, conveyors for heavy cargo."

Minutes later, the truck slowed and began shifting back along the monorails. The docks stretched endlessly, teaming with the business of a somewhat unusual city. The truck driver glanced at Chayn questioningly.

"Anywhere along here," Chayn said.

The driver pulled into an empty dock area and climbed out of the cab. Chayn, Villimy, and Davi followed. Villimy and Davi headed directly for a pair of swinging doors. Chayn turned to the driver. "Sorry to inconvenience you. It was rather pathetic of me to treat you like that." Bewildered and shaken, the trucker watched the freakish trio vanish into a stock room.

Chayn led the way through the isles of a food store where patrons shopped for items not included in the automated dispensers. Exiting onto the pavilion, they were only a few doors down from the Exobiological Institute. When they entered the building, technicians rushed forward to help. Davi was taken from them. Uniformed guards escorted Chayn and Villimy to the Institute's security office. Minutes later, Trenton entered the room.

"What happened?"

"Rioting. Davi's vehicle was hit. He works for Reylaton Electronics." Chayn grimaced, rubbing his bloodied hands on his tunic. "I don't think he was hurt too bad."

"Pak's tied up in a security session. I heard about the rioting. Better stay put in your apartments until we have an all-clear on the situation."

In their apartments, Villimy vanished into her own and didn't emerge for an hour. Chayn showered, changed clothes and rested. An hour later, Villimy appeared in clean clothes and together, they watched the rioting from the safety of the couch facing the wallscreen, Chayn with a hot drink in his hand, Villimy with ice in hers.

"Have you ever experienced anything like that?" Chayn asked.

Villimy glanced at him with bright gold eyes. "My people are more reasonable."

"Looks like fun in an irresponsible sort of way."

"Your species experiences emotion in a more intense manner. Violence is the way of animals. Even they put it to better use."

"Your people are perfect?"

Villimy turned back to the screen. "Yours are more interesting."

After the newscast, a documentary on the background of the civil strife in Reylaton caught Chayn's full attention. Reylaton with its population of fifty million was an important city orbiting Gilderif, but not the largest, nor the capital of the Rashanyn Empire. Chayn had wondered if the Church of Rashanyn was a universal religion. It was not, just a purely local phenomenon, but the issues in question were universal. The Church of Rashanyn had aligned with other religions and political or social organizations on the issue of the Blackstar alien threat. In the Gilderif region, the Church led the way for social change. They called for a war economy, construction of the largest, most advanced warfleet imaginable and an attack on the Blackstar aliens and their settlements—regardless of cost. Eventually, they argued, there'd be war and great loss of life. Living with that fear perpetuated an atmosphere of anxiety. The military advocated holding off on an attack as long as possible in order to await development of new weaponry, perhaps a breakthrough weapon that would destroy the Blackstar aliens without risking human lives.

"How would your people handle a situation like this?" Chayn asked Villimy.

"In my opinion, they would launch a military fleet against the enemy and a survival fleet in the opposite direction to salvage the knowledge of civilization. What about your people, Chayn?"

"I suspect they'd conduct themselves pretty much like the Rashanyn."

"The Rashanyn disable themselves by having no common voice of decision and action."

"The majority will rule in the end," Chayn said, "but it will be weakened."

The riots were organized and had spread through hundreds of major cities. Governments were calling for votes of confidence and were toppling here and there to the cries for war. As each city fell, the pressure increased on others to join in. The military had always operated subservient to civilian law, but for the first time in recorded Rashanyn history, there was talk of a military take over of civilian governments. Chayn listened to the voice of Commander Cornoben demanding that military decisions be left to the military, that survival depended upon the expertise of specialists guaranteeing the most efficient use of resources and time.

Chayn considered the rioting mild, but Councils listened to the demands of the populace and requested votes of confidence. If they were not forthcoming, new elections were held. Most of the news dealt with new elections and their outcomes. Chayn continually referred to a map of the Rashanyn system to keep the geography and politics straight in his mind.

The screen flashed, indicating an incoming call. Chayn put the call on the screen.

"Can you report to our labs immediately?" said Administrator Jarl of Reylaton Electronics.

"How's Davi?"

"Davi has received first aid. He is unharmed. In fact, we're sending him to pick up you and citizen Villimy Dy of you are free at the moment. We'll explain when you arrive."

"What do you say, citizen Dy?"

"I like being called a citizen," Villimy said.

"It's those big bright eyes of yours." Chayn turned back to the screen. "We're available."

Chayn turned the screen off and leaned back against the couch, feeling the effects of fatigue. "No rest for the wicked." He glanced at Villimy. "Did your people believe in evil?"

"No, just stupidity and ignorance. And please do not refer to my people in the past tense."

Ten

It had been a long hard day. The mirrors were tilting on the Hub, turning down the golden light of Star Rashanyn. As evening fell the city quieted. Chayn could still smell the odor of the fires burning in the distance. Guards stood outside the Institute, watching as Chayn and Vilimy waited near the landing pad where Davi would set down with the hovercraft.

"I'm tired," Villimy said. "I've had enough for one day."

"Nap on the way. There shouldn't be any more trouble."

"Will your skills with their computers be advantageous to us? Or will they cause further trouble?"

"Both," Chayn said. "But if we play dumb, we're of no use to anyone and they're liable just to lock us up and forget we exist."

The hovercraft set down fast and neat. Davi offered them a weak grin as they climbed into the back seat. "You two probably saved my life," he said. "I'm inclined to appreciate that."

"Are you okay?" Chayn asked. "I'm not inclined to ride with drivers with nasty bumps on their head."

Davi touched the bandage on his forehead. "I volunteered for this. Don't make me feel unappreciated during after hours."

"Just fly high and fast."

They arrived at Reylaton Electronics without incident. Davi escorted them through deserted corridors to a laboratory. Two men waited inside, Administrator Jarl and the technician who had supervised Chayn at the job site earlier in the day. Villimy napped during the short trip and now took a seat off to one side, crossed her legs, laid her head back and closed her eyes. Chayn joined the two men.

"Do you recognize this piece of equipment?" Jarl asked.

Chayn looked at the squat, metal device centered on a table. He could hear a motor running, suspecting some superconducting, cryogenics to be involved. "It might be a big, empty box with a fan in it. I'm not familiar with the details of your technology. I've never been an electronic or electrical engineer as far as I know."

Jarl held out a shieve of papers. "How do you explain this? Your test reports and the results of your repairs for that computer unit you looked at today. You located the malfunction in some other unit rather than the one you were working with. There were over fifteen hundred molecular core units in that piece of equipment. Using our analysis equipment, we might have found the problem in a week or two. You located it in less than five minutes."

"Am I expected to defend myself?"

Jarl sighed and dropped the papers on the table. "No, of course not. I've been speaking with General Pak. He's told me something about a neural computer interface, direct, conscious control over the functioning of a spacecraft. He said that you are non-Rashanyn and that your technology offers interesting possibilities for us. General Pak contacted me for a specific reason. We're the largest military contractor on Reylaton. You must be aware by now of the push for technological innovation.

"Citizen Jahil, our latest computers are infinitely more efficient than early generation models, but they are not as reliable as we would like. Our technology is flawed and repairs to sophisticated equipment is expensive in terms of time, our most valuable resource. Regardless of your relationship with the military and the mystery of your arrival and the problems the general is having with your spacecraft, things he will not discuss with me, you have an unusual aptitude for harmonic discrimination and you have applied for employment. You'd be a handy person to have in our maintenance department, but we're after more than that. Much more."

Chayn leaned against the table. "General Pak thinks I'm

holding back on him. I'm not and I am interested in helping Rashanyn as much as I can. I take it you've accepted my suggestions about a feedback capability for your equipment. I can't promise that your own people can handle it as well as I can, but I'd like to be able to show you that it can be done, that your technology is on the right track. There's more potential for molecular electronics than you've dreamt of yet."

"Then you're a step ahead of me," Jarl said. "This is relatively crude equipment." He picked up a mesh helmet connected by cable to the equipment scattered both on and beneath the table. "We can detect and amplify bioelectrical brain activity associated with consciousness and feed it back into computers to interact with the electromagnetic fields of the cores. The visual and audio representation of those field interactions can show us the effect we have on them. But as far as we know, the human mind cannot interface with the intelligence of computer operation. In other words, the human mind cannot interface with computer operation and control effects in the same way the brain interfaces with reality, understanding and affecting aspects of its environment."

"It would be impossible if computers did not function in the same reality that the brain functions in," Chayn said. "But they do. The trick is to feed the brain a translation of what's happening inside the computer in human terms. The only technology you have left to develop and perfect is a mediation or buffer device to perform that function. I can do without it, but I'm not going to even try to explain how. Obviously, you've set this equipment up to try something out."

Jarl smiled. "Maybe we are being tricky. Do you mind?"

"No," Chayn said. "Maybe the general will believe what I've told him about the starcraft if I show him what can be done with your own equipment."

"Then what we have," Jarl said, "is a navigational computer for a drone in nearby space outside Reylaton. Several

102

cores have been deliberately damaged, but my engineers tell me that there's a potential of directly repairing those distorted cores if we did have a mind capable of handling this interface equipment. That means you.

"The general and his people are controlling two other drones with their own equipment. This is to be a practical exercise. The general will try to destroy our drone. You are to escape the destruction. My engineers are recording and observing the outcome. Do you think you can handle it?"

"Perhaps," Chayn said.

"You have about two minutes to effect repairs. If you succeed, you will have demonstrated the feasibility of in-service repairs, something that has never been possible before."

"Let me take a crack at it and see what I can do."

Chayn seated himself, letting the technicians unfold their suitcases before him, a high resolution viewscreen and a pair of earphones. When they had connected the equipment, Chayn donned the mesh helmet and earphones. When the screen came alive and his head filled with the symphony of harmonics, Chayn relaxed to let the hypnotic quality take him into a deep level of concentration. But his own thought processes both conscious and unconscious were interfering with the perfect harmonics. One of the technicians pointed out a control that allowed Chayn to adjust the feedback to where it required an effort of will to interfere with the patterns. Still, Chayn agreed with Jarl. Under normal circumstances, it would be impossible for human thought process to make sense of the patterns of light and sound and to effect an intelligible modification.

Chayn lost himself in the harmonics, having little difficulty on his own in locating the distorting cores. When Chayn concentrated on shifting them into synchronization, the Watcher came alive, interceding in the process of translating the patterns into familiar, sensory terms.

Something moved in a void. Chayn sensed reactive and centrifugal and inertial forces at play. Two other objects moved in the void, shifting and swinging about to intersect with Chayn's drone. Chayn had already achieved his objective. The distorting cores were functioning again. The drone responded properly to its programming and was well on its way toward escaping the attacking objects.

Chayn wanted more. He wanted to make an impact on the military, a demonstration of his abilities. Ultimately, he wanted Rashanyn to know that he could be of service, that he could be trusted. Chayn wanted his starcraft back.

He overpowered the drone's programming. Swinging the drone around, he searched for weapon circuitry. The attacking drones were firing lasers, aiming for the likeliest trajectory probabilities of his drone. Chayn used the drone's own programming to keep the drone moving unpredictably while moving in for the kill.

Chayn found the laser firing circuit, but held off until he maneuvered the drone, forcing the attacking drones to approach on direct collision courses with his drone directly between them. Unable to fire on him without risking hitting each other during the last milliseconds of the maneuver, Chayn opened fire. Both attacking drones blossomed and faded, the radar representation of their destruction.

Chayn disengaged with a new respect for Rashanyn technology, but also with an awareness that he hadn't put his own abilities to their best use as yet. "Was that adequate?" he asked of Jarl.

"We'll know as soon as we hear from General Pak." Jarl nodded to a blank, nearby communications screen.

Villimy opened one eye from across the room. "Did you get us into trouble, Chayn?"

"Brace yourself for some excitement."

Jarl ignored the two of them. When the screen beeped, Jarl walked over and switched it on. General Pak's face appeared, his dark eyes sweeping across the room. "Jarl, pack up your equipment. Report to launch bay twelve and wait for Trenton and his team. We disembark at 0200 hours. Hold Jahil and the woman until the security team arrives. I've just dispatched them."

Chayn rushed to the screen, shoving Jarl aside. "Pak, what the hell kind of stunt are you trying to pull?"

"Reylaton's civilian government has just fallen," General Pak said. "Regent Kraken, or so he calls himself, of the Church of Rashanyn has just announced temporary appointments to the Council, Chayn, there are directives out for the detention of you and Villimy Dy."

"Are we under some kind of protective arrest?"

"Chayn, it's us or the Church of Rashanyn. Take your choice. You're important to us, but I can still afford to give you a free choice. Your options are rather limited."

Villimy pressed up against Chayn, bewildered and frightened. General Pak glanced at her, startled and captivated by his sudden view of her surrealistically huge, golden eyes. The screen went blank.

Chayn turned to Jarl. "Is he on the level?"

Before Jarl could answer, sirens sounded in the distance. Color drained from the man's face. Jarl gestured tentatively to the technician. The man began quietly and efficiently to disconnect and pack the equipment.

"What does it mean?" Chayn said.

"Military alert."

"Then this is for real?"

"The Church probably moved in without waiting for the Council to loose a vote of confidence," Jarl said. "They've got the city worked up to a feverish pitch. I've suspected they might take advantage of the situation."

Villimy took a seat and watched Chayn walk slow circles around her. Jarl sat at the blank communication screen, tense and unsettled. The technician tinkered with the equipment, reducing it all to four suitcases set in the center of the room.

The door burst open. A helmeted officer entered with a laser rifle held at hip level. "Administrator Jarl!"

Jarl turned and slipped from his stool. "Here."

The officer gestured with the barrel of the rifle. "Let's move."

There were six soldiers in the corridor outside. Two of

them shouldered their weapon to help the technician with his equipment. The officer hustled Chayn and Villimy from the room, assigning two of his men to guard them with a curt gesture. The formation moved out along the corridor toward the rear of the complex. A military vehicle on the monorail of the transport tunnel pulled up to a small receiving and loading dock. The group filed aboard.

"Launch bays," Chayn said to Villimy as they took a seat together near the rear of the bus.

Villimy nodded her understanding. The launch bay meant an ascent up one of the three spokes to the hub of the city. There'd be no escaping their benefactors once they entered that weightless realm.

The bus began moving, accelerating as it shifted to the outer rail. Chayn estimated that the nearest spoke lay no more than twenty kilometers ahead. The windows in the bus were narrow slits, just large enough to provide a view of the less than scenic tunnel.

"How well organized would a Church take over be?" Chayn said to Villimy.

"Well organized," Villimy decided. "They risk a great deal to engage in theatrics. They would have gained power legally without risking civil disobedience."

"What are they trying to accomplish?"

"They ride a crest of a wave of fear," Villimy said. "They must keep it in motion or it sinks back into apathy."

"Then brace yourself for trouble," Chayn said. "They can't hope to cope with the military unless they can disrupt troop movements within the city."

Villimy glanced at him in alarm. Chayn relied upon Villimy for her powers of observation and projection, but Villimy relied upon him for their practical application.

A brilliant flash flickered through the window slits.

"Monorail's down ahead!" someone called from up front.

The bus jerked and rolled from side to side. A sudden deceleration threw Chayn forward. Villimy reacted quicker, her thoughts racing ahead to the impending crisis. The bus dipped and nosed into the concrete floor of the tunnel.

The impact sent Chayn sprawling into the aisle. The bus skewed to one side and fell silent. An explosive concussion rolled past, echoing through the huge tunnel. Shrapnel rattled against the bus. The lights flickered and went out.

An emergency door halfway down the aisle burst outward, half the troops deploying to the right and left outside. Villimy helped Chayn to his feet. While the officer directed two of his men to help Jarl's technician with the equipment, Villimy and Chayn moved to stand alongside the emergency exit. A laser beam scored its way across the floor of the tunnel toward one of the troopers. The man dived from its wavering path and returned the fire, an eye-searing beam of split-second duration darting from the tip of his rifle.

"Let's move out!" the officer called out. "Move out!"

Jarl scrambled out of the bus, hesitating to search out the source of the laser fire. A soldier grabbed him by the arm and dragged him across the empty expanse toward the protective cover of an overhanging loading dock. Chayn and Villimy filed out last. Villimy grabbed his arm, pulling with a weak but emphatic insistence toward the rear of the bus. When Chayn hesitated, the laser fire suddenly intensified, giving him little choice but to give in to whatever Villimy had in mind. Nearby, one of the soldiers fell soundlessly, the air filled with the stench of burnt flesh.

Safe behind the bulk of the bus, Villimy panted in excitement, fitting her sunglasses back into place. Jarl and the officer were yelling at them, urging them to sprint across the open expanse of concrete, their voices echoing in the cavernous tunnel.

"Manhole covers," Villimy said, pointing out a distance behind the bus. "Electrical conduit."

"An escape route?"

She nodded.

More of the laser beams were sliding across the metal hull of the bus, the air acrid with the vapor rising from molten metal. Chayn took Villimy's hand. They moved away from the bus, keeping its bulk between them and the laser fire. Before he risked exposing himself, Chayn looked for the nearest of the manhole covers. They were spaced at thirty-meter intervals, the nearest to them a few meters beyond the cover of the bus. Chayn waited a moment for the firepower to drop off, then dashed for the manhole cover. He yanked it free and sent it clanking across the concrete. A shiny tube led downward into darkness. A ladder provided access. As laser beams rapidly scored across the concrete toward him, Chayn sat on the edge of the hole and lowered himself to safety.

Halfway down, he waited for Villimy, his nerves on edge. She waited until the firepower returned to the others beneath the overhanging dock. When she darkened the circle of light above Chayn, he hurried to the bottom, a nearby light coming on when he touched the bottom rung. He stood off to one side, lifting Villimy from the ladder and setting her down beside him. Only then did he take note of their environment.

They stood in a metal tube about five meters in diameter, one side crammed with masses of small-diameter tubing and banded cable. The air crackled around them like a living entity. Chayn's hair crawled. The air smelled fresh. "Ozone," he said. "Keep away from the cables."

Villimy turned and began walking. Chayn followed, knowing better than to question her memory. He tried to recall where the conduit tubes led. He had a vague notion of relay stations and an exit point to maintenance levels. Villimy's pace hurried. Finally, she broke into a run.

"Hey, what's the hurry!"

"Current surge!" she called back. "This tunnel is part of the field coil!"

Chayn remembered. Reylaton was surrounded by an electric field that deflected charged solar and cosmic radiation. He tried to keep pace, but within minutes his lungs burned and a crippling ache developed in his side. As they ran into darkness, another light would come on ahead, the light behind them giving way to darkness. Villimy hadn't even bothered removing her sunglasses, but Chayn silently thanked the engineers that had planned Reylaton down to such detail.

Villimy easily outdistanced him. "Please! We must hurry!"

Chayn opened his mouth in protest when he noticed Villimy's wooley, white hair expanding around her head. The crackling in the air became more pronounced. Chayn tensed. A bluish corona surrounded the masses of cable in the darkness ahead.

"Oh, damn!" Impending danger gave Chayn his second wind. He caught up with Villimy. "How far!"

"Close!"

Blue sparks began jumping between Chayn's feet and the metal tube as he ran. "Villimy, run on ahead! Find the relay station!"

"I'll stay with you!"

But she took the lead. Blue fire danced about her clothing.

Chayn's skin began to itch. The intense ozone burned his lungs, then numbed them. He began staggering, his eyes unfocusing. His footsteps jarred through him, each step becoming a conscious effort.

Villimy screamed. Chayn caught himself veering toward the cables.

The lights went out.

Blue fire danced in the air. A human outline ran just ahead of him, louder snapping noises sounding against the rushing, wind-like sound of static electricity. White sparks jumped from the cables to the sidewalls of the tunnel, intense enough to kill a man.

Villimy cried out in the keening wail Chayn recognized as her expression of abject fear. She stopped abruptly. Chayn ran into her, knocking the both of them to the heated metal floor of the tube.

"Villimy, run!"

Villimy thrashed on the floor ahead of him. Chayn reached for her in desperation. A white spark snapped within inches of his face.

Chayn's hands went numb. Blinded by the afterimages swimming in his vision, he groped in the emptiness for the girl.

Villimy had vanished.

Eleven

Chayn fell through a hole in the floor and into a void. Something partially broke his fall, his head and shoulders impacting against concrete. A clang of metal rang through an enclosed space.

"Chayn? Are you okay?"

The afterimages faded to darkness. When his fingertips could feel the texture of the floor, Chayn rolled over and sat up.

"That was close. Where are we?"

"We're in a relay station," Villimy said.

"Am I blind?"

"There are no lights. There's some equipment in here, circuit breakers and gauges. There's a door, but I haven't opened it yet."

Chayn looked around and saw a sliver of light from beneath the door. "You can see in this?"

"The light is adequate for me."

Chayn pulled himself to his feet, using the metal ladder alongside him. He had fallen through the trap door at the top. Chayn reached out and grasped Villimy's arm. She shook uncontrollably, but he could hear the humming of the small air-conditioner in her coveralls. "I think we'll be okay," Chayn said, rubbing at his itching flesh. "Do you want to rest or move on?"

"I cannot rest."

Chayn felt his way through the darkness and cracked the door open. Dim, yellow light flooded into the small room. The corridor beyond stretched twenty meters across and into endless distances to either side. A monorail passed down through the center of the isle near the ceiling, evidence that some large machinery or vehicles passed through occasionally. Entrances to side corridors lined the far wall at regular intervals.

"What do we find down here?" Chayn said.

"Water purification, sanitation, food processing and air-conditioning plants, repair and manufacturing shops, warehouses and storage tanks, pumping stations, and data processing substations."

"We'll need a base of operations, food and water and a place to rest. Something secure."

"The living quarters down here are only fifty percent occupied."

"Why?"

"I'm not sure. I think Reylaton's been more heavily populated in the past."

Investigating the living quarters for the maintenance personnel would be first on the agenda, but it sounded too good to rely on. Perhaps they'd be sealed off and inaccessible. Villimy would be growing hungry and thirsty a lot sooner than he would.

Chayn heard voices and the sound of a motor in the far distance. They stepped into the huge maintenance tunnel and Villimy nodded out the proper direction. Chayn took the lead. The darkened side corridors spaced every few meters would provide cover if anyone passed.

"How far?" Chayn asked.

"A kilometer."

They walked side by side down the center of the passageway.

"Why didn't you want to go with General Pak?" Chayn said.

"It wasn't a good idea as long as there were alternatives available, was it? What did you do with that computer?"

Chayn wondered if it would accomplish anything to explain about the Watcher. Even now he could feel the entity observing through a clear and bright hole in his psyche to elsewhere and elsewhen. "I managed an interface with the computer. They would have discovered the potential sooner or later with the right people. What do you think? Are we better off here than on Jasper?"

"It depends on what you hope to accomplish," Villimy said.

"I'm not out to accomplish anything. I just want a place to live."

"These are your people. You can help them."

Chayn looked at the woman. She had tucked her sunglasses into a chest pocket. Her large eyes shown a deep gold in the dim, overhead lights. Those eyes and her inhumanly graceful, quick reflexes disturbed him at some deep level. Not that he could forget the human ancestry she belonged to nor the kind of relationship they had drifted into.

"They aren't my people," Chayn said. "My origins aren't here. Neither are yours."

"They are human, like us. More like you, Chayn. Why do you think the stargods send you into these spaces?"

"I don't know."

"You will spend your life searching for the reason."

"You said you wanted to go home when we finished here? Do you really think that's possible?"

Villimy smiled at him. "Wait and see."

The noise in the distance intensified. A light appeared, distorted in the distance but steadying as it approached. Chayn took Villimy's hand. They moved across the wide aisle, ducking into one of the side corridors and backing into darkness. At the end of the corridor, they could see light, probably another main aisle.

112

A large truck passed on the monorail in a roar of subdued turbines. Behind it, two young boys followed in whining, electric carts. They dodged and weaved down the aisle, calling and laughing to one another. Chayn hadn't seen many children in Reylaton, but knew the schools and the university to be almost halfway around the torus from the Institute.

"It looks like a pretty informal environment down here," Chayn said. "We should have one of those carts."

"There should be recharging stations along this tunnel."

They continued on and saw increasing evidence of the maintenance population. A man walked down the aisle in the distance with a clipboard, reading pressure gauges on some plumbing, but finally climbing back into a cart and passing by in a soft hum of noise.

The side corridors were illuminated here, taking away their cover of darkness. The main aisle widened and brightened. Chayn decided it to be time to investigate one of the long, interconnecting corridors. They might have been a kilometer long, three meters wide and lined on both sides with doors spaced at irregular intervals. Chayn investigated a few at random. One led into a darkened laboratory of some kind, another into a pitch black stairwell.

"Where do you think it goes?" Chayn asked. A winding staircase led both upwards and downwards into darkness.

"There are other levels. This must be for emergencies."

They finally discovered an apartment. It contained three interconnecting rooms. Chayn found a light switch and Villimy checked out the food dispensers in the kitchen. "No food. No water," she called to him.

Everything looked clean, but disused. The wallscreen had no power. "If we can find an apartment that isn't shut down," Chayn said, "we have it made."

They stepped back into the corridor directly into the path of a moving machine. Chayn and Villimy froze. The machine stopped, binocular cameras on its squat, insect-like body rising to focus on them. After a slight hesitation, the machine swung around them and continued on its way.

113

Chayn leaned against the wall, waiting for the effects of shock to pass. "Damn, that thing scared the daylights out of me."

Villimy gave him a quivering smile. "What was it?"

"Makes sense, I guess. They must have robots or remote controlled drones to do rountine monitoring. This is a pretty big place to keep an eye on. Might as well be a camera."

The machine reached the end of the corridor and turned. "It didn't seem to pay us much mind," Villimy said.

"Let's hope it didn't. It might be computer-controlled and not programmed to respond to people."

It took five minutes to reach the end of the corridor. They stopped in silence, startled by the spectacle beyond. The corridor entered onto a wide ledge lined with metal railings. Stretching ahead of them were a series of huge pipes ten meters in diameter beneath a sky of concrete far above them. In either direction, the monstrous tunnel curved upward and out of sight.

"These people are excellent engineers," Chayn said, his voice hushed in the utter stillness of the scene.

Villimy walked to the railing and stood gazing out over the landscape of metal. She pointed out vertical stands of piping in the distance. "Water," she said. "These pipes must come from the surface and return to the water plants."

There were groups of people standing on the plain of concrete far below. They were tiny black objects in relation to the huge pipes. It didn't seem necessary to behave too discreetly in this vastness. Villimy put her sunglasses back on. The lights overhead were as intense as sunlight, duplicating the golden light of Star Rashanyn.

Villimy turned away after a time. "I'm hungry, Chayn. Let's find something to eat."

They turned back into the corridor to check on a few more doors. These too were apartments. Villimy went directly to the kitchen. "Chayn! Food and water!"

Chayn tried the wallscreen. It sprang to life in bright color. "Home sweet home, Villimy. Suppose anyone lives here?"

Together, they searched the apartment and found no evidence of personal effects. "What do you think?" Chayn asked. "Shall we give it a try?"

Villimy nodded enthusiastically. "There are no eating utensils, though."

They ate with their fingers and drank directly from the water spigots in the sink, sitting together on the counter without speaking. Chayn became aware again of the hum of the air-conditioning unit in Villimy's white coveralls.

"How is that powered?"

Villimy glanced at the device on her shoulder. "Batteries, I suppose."

"What if it runs down?"

Villimy shrugged. "It's a little cooler down here, but still very warm. I will have troubles if it stops."

The beds had no blankets, but the living room contained the standard issue furniture. Chayn turned the wallscreen over to a channel that presented a running update of general news items.

"Oh, oh."

Villimy turned back from the door, checking on the corridor outside. A familiar figure filled the ceiling high screen. "That's Kraken," she said.

Chayn turned up the sound.

"In the name of Rashanyn!" Kraken thundered. "We haven't the time left for tradition or sentiment! The life of humanity itself is at stake! Democracy is a tradition, a sentimentality in a universe where only power rules! Democracy is the painless means for the majority to voice its choices for the structure of society, but democracy rules even in a tyrannical monarchy where the victims of fear haven't the interest or courage to demonstrate the power of the masses! But they remain responsible for the liabilities and suffering of their conscious, deliberate acquiescence!"

Chayn and Villimy sat together on the couch. Villimy leaned her head on his shoulder.

"The Church of Rashanyn has taken power by force! We have violated tradition and insulted sentimentalities! If we are accused of being advocates of violence, tyrannical dictators ruling by fear and threats of death, so be it! The threat of death is very real!

"But I say to you, citizens! Do we threaten your welfare? Have you risen in force to depose us as you rose in force to depose the Council and the military forces on Reylaton? No! Because we represent the majority! The military and other civilian governments of Rashanyn look in disfavor upon what has occured on Reylaton! They move against us, but we offer the only salvation possible from the threat of wholesale slaughter by the hand of the Dark Stargod and his inhuman legions of the Blackstar! Never have we witnessed such events transpire with such frightening rapidity! The arrival of aliens who claim themselves human when the Word of Rashanyn denies such a possibility! The second probe incident in less than two centuries and the knowledge the military thought to withhold from us of the movement of Star Rashanyn into the midst of the Blackstar strongholds!"

Chayn turned down the sound. "That was us he mentioned. With the military out of the way, he can use us against them."

Villimy gave a momentary shudder. "Kraken is a patriot. He is a fanatic and firm in his own ignorance, but he voices the fears of his people and absolves fear by inciting violence."

"Shall we try to steer clear of him?"

"Yes," Villimy said. "Please."

Chayn turned up the sound again. " . . . united Rashanyn and an armada the universe has never seen and feed the legions of the Dark Stargod to their whirlpool of annihilation!"

The door behind them burst open. Chayn jumped to his feet and pivoted as two men in blue coveralls sidestepped to clear the doorway. A third man entered, as tall and nearly as heavily built as Chayn. Beneath a shock of disheveled, black hair, slits of dark blue eyes took in the room and focused on the couple standing between the couch and the wallscreen. The man glanced over them into the piercing eyes of Kraken and sneered.

"Shut it off!"

Chayn stepped to one side and shut off the screen.

"Who are you two?"

"Chayn Jahil and Villimy Dy," Chayn said.

The man grinned. "You refugees from topside?"

Chayn nodded to the screen behind him. "From him."

Villimy still had her sunglasses on. The man fixed his gaze on her with a sudden expression of fearful disdain. "What in the name of Rashanyn is that? Lady, take those glasses off."

Villimy removed her glasses and shoved them into her shoulder pocket. Orbs of golden eyes blinked at the man and her thin-lipped mouth quivered a smile. The man backed off a step. "Mother of Rashanyn, it's the aliens!"

Two laser rifles leveled on Villimy. Chayn stepped forward, his hand outstretched. "We're not your enemies."

The leader of the trio regained his composure. A crowd pressed close in the corridor outside. He closed the door and backed against it. "That military bus that nosed itself into the deck in the conveyance tunnel. You were with them, weren't you?"

"Are they okay?" Chayn asked.

"We found one body. How the hell did you get down here?"

"The conduit tunnel," Villimy said to demonstrate that she could speak and display a reasonable intelligence. "We went down through a manhole and into this level from a relay station."

"Without getting fried?" The man studied her with a cold detachment. "That was quite an accomplishment. So you figured you'd make yourself home down here, huh? Like the apartment?"

Chayn didn't like the sarcastic tone. "It was either this or Kraken."

"You the agents of the Dark Stargod he mentions?"

"Do you believe that nonsense?"

"Some people do. Who the hell are you, then?"

"We're not of Rashanyn. We arrived in this system a few days ago requesting medical aid and sanctuary. They took our ship away from us."

"It doesn't matter," the man said. It didn't seem to Chayn that he could quite believe in human extraterrestrials. "Kraken's got one hell of a price on your head. You might be of use to us. Jo, Edkar, tie them up and put them in the bedroom."

They shouldered their rifles and moved around both ends of the couch. One of the men grabbed for Villimy. She shrieked, but Chayn didn't have the opportunity to watch the action. As his adversary grabbed for his arm, Chayn spun the man around, grabbed him by the scruff of the neck and threw him to the foot of the couch. The one who had made the error of tackling Villimy went down with a heel mark across his forehead. Chayn pulled him to his feet to use as cover.

The laser bolt shattered the wall screen in a spray of glass. "That's enough, damn it! Freeze! The both of you!"

Villimy crouched to attack. Chayn dived for her, protecting her from her own temper and the laser rifle the third man held level toward them. She threw him off with unbelievable strength. Chayn struck the back of his head against something quite solid. He fought the descending cloak of unconsciousness with a hurt protest.

And awakened to darkness. He moved and found his hands bound behind his back. Villimy lay beneath him, face down on the bed and moaning softly. He felt intense heat emanating from her and tried to discern the source of his growing panic.

He listened to the silence.

Villimy's air conditioner had failed.

Twelve

Chayn rolled off the bed and onto his feet. He shuffled his way through the dark room to where he figured the light switch should be. A touch of his elbow flooded the room with light. Villimy moaned in protest and buried her face in the mattress.

His wrists were bound tightly but not so as to cut off circulation. He strained just short of injuring himself to break the cords. They held firm, but stretched somewhat.

Chayn paced the floor, working his wrists around until he felt increasing freedom of movement, then renewed his struggles until the cords began pulling loose. Ignoring sharp pains of broken skin, he pulled one hand loose, then the other. He held his wrists out to the light. His injuries were superficial.

He untied Villimy, rolled her onto her back and unzipped her coveralls. He lifted her shoulders and pulled her arms free, then stood at the foot of the bed and pulled the coveralls off her body. Villimy tossed her head from side to side in half-conscious delirium, panting to ventilate excess heat. Chayn shook his head in exasperation, wondering what kind of metabolism could generate such heat. Her flesh glowed in the overhead light. Her nonporous skin couldn't sweat. Chayn spread her limbs to help her radiate as much heat as possible, then turned to the closed bedroom door.

He cracked it open with infinite care. Despite the technology of the Rashanyn Empire, the doors were simple, hinged affairs seldom equipped with locks. Chayn peered through the crack into the living room. One of the drones squatted in the middle of the room, the binocular-cameras on a meter-tall stalk rotating slowly to scan the room.

It wouldn't take much to destroy the drone, but Chayn minimized their chances of escape. Once alerted, the lower-level citizens of Reylaton would converge on the apartment. They knew their world far better than he. Still, from what he had seen, these weren't the most compassionate citizens of Reylaton and he preferred not to throw himself on their mercy.

Chayn timed the rotation of the cameras on the robot. He estimated the weight of the machine. When the cameras swept past the bedroom door, Chayn stepped into the living room. He bent, grabbed onto the most convenient hand-holds, pulled the machine back against his legs and hoisted it into the air. Wheels spun and motors whined. With a cry of agonizing strain, Chayn lifted the drone high enough to dash it against the floor. The cameras shattered. The machine bounced and spun around, its wheels spinning air. Blinded and helpless, at least it couldn't be used to follow them. Of course, if there were guards in the corridor outside. they wouldn't be going very far.

Chayn went back into the bedroom. He rolled Villimy's coveralls into a bundle and placed it on her stomach, then scooped her feverish body into his arms. The corridor outside the apartment appeared to be deserted. Chayn turned toward the ledge overlooking the landscape of oversized plumbing, then moved away from the populated areas, glancing down each dark side corridor as he passed. Minutes later he stopped when he felt a breeze of cold air. He turned down the corridor and walked into darkness.

Regaining consciousness, Villimy twisted in his arms. Chayn ignored her struggles, searching out the source of the cool breeze. He couldn't see in the darkness, but stopped when he sensed himself entering a large, open area. The cold was more pronounced. He turned slowly and walked in the direction of the breeze. He began sliding one foot forward at a time, taking care not to walk into walls, machinery or an imagined abyss lying ahead.

His foot touched something solid. He laid Villimy down

on the cold, moist pavement, fighting an instinctive drive to keep her feverish body warm. She thrived on just this sort of environment. Chayn reached out and felt meter-diameter pipes. The one closest to the floor felt cold to the touch. Above the pipe, he felt a flat-surfaced catwalk or mesh guard. He climbed onto the rough surface. A meter or so back, he felt cold stone. He climbed back down, spreading Villimy's coveralls across the catwalk. Scooping Villimy from the floor, he hoisted her onto the catwalk, laying her carefully on the coveralls.

He climbed up alongside her and sat, wondering what else he might accomplish before she recovered. He couldn't see. If a lighted cart came down the corridor, they'd be spotted in an instant.

Villimy's breathing slowed to near normal, her panting sounding like some large animal resting beside him in the darkness. She recovered quickly. When she put her hand on his arm, Chayn helped her to sit up.

"You okay?"

"Where are we?"

"I don't know."

"We escaped?" she said.

"Can you see?"

"I can see. It looks like a pumping station of some kind, but the machinery is all shut down."

"Is it cool enough?"

"I have a headache. My batteries went dead. I'm sorry I hurt you. Maybe you saved my life again."

It amazed Chayn to discover he had a headache himself. He hadn't paid it much attention.

"Are you okay, Chayn?"

"I think we'll both survive if we try hard enough."

Chayn heard a rustle of fabric. He heard a click and a snap. Villimy shoved something into his hand, a heavy, square piece of smooth metal or plastic.

"Is this the battery?"

"Yes."

121

Chayn shoved it into his trouser pocket. "Where to now?"

"There are doors to your left, just around the corner from the corridor. Shall we take a look and see what they are?"

Chayn dropped to the floor, slid his hands up the curve of her wide hips to her narrowing waist. He lifted her and set her down beside him. Her knees gave slightly and she leaned against him for support.

Villimy slipped her hand into his and led him forward at a nerve-racking pace through the pitch blackness despite her incomplete recovery. She stopped and he stumbled into her. He heard the latch of a door give and the creak of hinges.

"Gauges and stuff," she said.

She pulled him sideways and opened another door. "Storage, I guess." Her voice echoed through a large, empty space.

She led him to a third door. "Oh, this is interesting!"

"What's interesting?" Chayn said with growing irritation. "I can't see a damned thing!"

"That's because you're eyes are so beady." She pulled him into the room. The door closed behind them. "Were my glasses in the coveralls?"

Villimy located the glasses in her shoulder pocket and tossed the coveralls against the wall. "Cover your eyes," she said. "I'm going to see if the lights work."

They worked. When Chayn's eyes adjusted to the sudden light, he turned slowly to scan the room with bewildered elation. "How damned coincidental," he said.

They were in a garage. Drones lined one entire wall of the room. There were different species of them, robots little more than half a meter high to monstrosities on tracks three meters long and two wide. Most had cameras mounted on stalks like the one Chayn had grappled with, but some had claw-tipped arms in addition. "Wouldn't it be neat," Chayn said, "if we could get one of these to work?"

A number of control consoles lined the opposite wall of the garage. Chayn walked down the ranks of the drones and back up the row of consoles. "They're remotely-controlled, monitoring robots," Chayn said. "When times are busy, it must cut down on the footwork."

"What would you do if you could get one to work?" Villimy said. She stood before one of the consoles with her tiny fists resting on the broad curve of her hips, both an exotic and erotic figure, unsettlingly alien.

Chayn took note of the speaker grilles on the drones. "It would be a convenient way to contact our hosts and try reasoning with them."

"If there are lights here, there should be power to the consoles." She reached out and touched a button. The console lit up, the screen coming to life in a blur of static. "See?"

Chayn stood over her and studied the controls. There were no labels, but most appeared to be self-explanatory.

"That selects the drone," Villimy said, pointing to a small keyboard and readout. She walked over to the robots and selected a medium-sized one with mechanical arms. She located an identification plate. Returning to the console, she punched it into the keyboard. Behind them, the robot hummed.

Villimy looked up at him. "Shall I?"

Chayn shook his head. "Looks like too much fun. Me first."

Chayn slipped into the contoured couch. He felt foot controls beneath his boots and slipped his hands into glove-like controls to either side of the couch, trusting Villimy's acute powers of observation in reasoning out the rest of the controls. She turned on the video, giving Chayn a rear view of a slender, blue-skinned woman standing nude behind a man seated in one of the console seats.

"Gee, will you look at that?"

Villimy poked him with her fist. "Pay attention."

Chayn flexed his hands in the gloves. The mechanical

arms on the drone followed suit. Depressing both pedals moved the drone forward at varying speeds. Releasing both pedals stopped it. Depressing only one pedal turned the drone. Within minutes, the drone drove up and down the length of the garage, waving its arms and snapping its claws.

The screen gave a split view of directly ahead, to the rear and both sides. The drone moved on treads and appeared to have considerable power. "I'd say the arms are for removing access panels," Chayn said. He discovered that a heel button would raise or lower a stalked camera for gaining a view from different heights.

Villimy slipped into a couch beside him and chose a drone smaller than his. Soon, the two machines were chasing each other about the garage. As Chayn developed a growing rapport with his drone, he reached out, grabbed Villimy's smaller machine by the chassis and lifted it into the air.

"What is that supposed to be?" Villimy said with disgust. "Rape by proxy?"

Chayn eyed the large doors at the rear of the garage. Villimy beat him to it. The doors rolled upward, exposing a darkened corridor beyond. Villimy turned headlights on her drone. It took Chayn a moment to locate his. They took the drones into the aisle. Villimy lowered the doors behind them.

Chayn sighted the headphones hanging off to one side of the consoles. He took a moment to put them on and turned on the audio circuit. Later it would come in handy.

Chayn led the way, driving down the dark corridor, his headlights gleaming off metal and concrete. Entering the main aisle, he clipped a corner, caught a clawed hand on the wall and spun himself in a circle. Villimy circled him, inspecting for damage.

"Clumsy."

Chayn straightened out and continued down the center of the main aisle, picking up a comfortable speed. "How do we find them?" Chayn said.

"There should be someone near the apartment where they imprisoned us by now," Villimy said.

Chayn lost his bearings. Everything looked the same on the screen. Villimy pulled out ahead of him and Chayn followed the smaller machine weaving down the aisle. Villimy turned abruptly into a side corridor. Chayn braked hard and swerved to follow. His drone stopped dead.

"Whoops. I don't fit."

Villimy's machine stopped ahead of him. "There's nobody down there anyhow."

"Then let's move further down the main aisle. We're bound to run across someone."

Chayn backed into the middle of the aisle. Villimy swung around and they continued on. In the distance, a man in blue coveralls climbed into a cart. The cart sped off, moving away from them.

Ten to twenty passenger elevators lined the side of the aisle ahead of them. As they approached, several doors opened. A small crowd of armed, black-robed figures emerged. Villimy slowed and parked against the opposite side of the aisle, ready to duck into the side corridors in case of trouble. The group milled about for a moment, obviously members of the Church of Rashanyn.

"What do you suppose is happening?" Chayn said, his voice hushed despite the fact that they were safe in the garage, more than two kilometers from the scene on the screens.

"Let's wait and see."

Four armed guards remained at attention by the elevators, rifles held diagonally across their chests. The rest of the group began moving down the aisle away from them. Villimy moved to follow. Chayn tensed and started to voice a protest, then moved out to follow her. If the guards fired on the drones, they could always send out others.

They passed the guards stationed by the elevators. The guards watched without interfering. At one time or another, the entire group turned to observe the drones following them, but promptly ignored them, probably taking them to be piloted by curious maintenance personnel. They entered a widening in the aisle, a brightly lit group of offices centered in a large, open area. Villimy pulled up behind the group as close as she dared. Chayn stayed behind her, raising his cameras to look over her.

There were ten of them, five armed guards and five church officials. Chayn took an interest in the tallest of them. "Who does that look like?"

"Kraken," Villimy said. "It's Kraken himself."

A group of six men in blue maintenance coveralls emerged from one of the offices. Several children dashed past, vanishing from view. Chayn got the impression that the sublevel world of Reylaton was more familial than life on the surface.

They couldn't quite hear the conversation through the microphones the drones carried. Villimy crept forward until she received a look of mild vehemence from one of the guards. Chayn followed suit, leaving it up to Villimy's superior reflexes and judgment to keep them out of trouble. Less than ten meters from the group, they still couldn't overhear the conversation. Chayn looked for the three men who had overpowered him and Villimy, but they weren't there.

The conversation didn't appear to be going too well. The maintenance personnel became agitated. Kraken gestured wildly in anger. Three of the men in blue coveralls stepped forward to voice their angered response. Chayn didn't quite catch the first sign of trouble. Two guards moved in, lowering their rifles. Two of the maintenance men leapt into action, overpowering the two. The other guards moved in to protect Kraken. A laser rifle fired. One of the blue-uniformed men fell over, trailing smoke from a fatal head wound.

The maintenance personnel weren't armed. Kraken gestured and the group backed away, then turned and began walking at a brisk pace down the aisle toward the elevators.

One of Kraken's guards had been injured somehow. Another helped him to one of the carts and together, they sped on ahead.

They headed almost directly toward Chayn's cameras. Chayn clenched his mechanical claws. Villimy heard the sound through her drone's microphone. "What are you thinking?" she asked.

"I have something to say to Kraken."

"Do so," Villimy said. "What do we have to lose?"

Chayn let the procession pass, then spun around, reaching out with the mechanical arms and opening the pinchers. He rushed forward, one of the guards turning at the sound of the drone's whining motor. He fired wildly, the beam passing over Chayn's cameras. Chayn grabbed the man by the arm, feeling the feedback through the glove. The guard screamed and Chayn pivoted, throwing him around in a wide circle to scatter the group.

The maintenance men ran for cover. Villimy sped forward, unarmed but not helpless. She chased a second guard for several meters. The man dodged and would have evaded Chayn, but not Villimy's inhuman reflexes. Her small drone turned and tipped onto its wheels. She hit the man from behind, flooring him. Churning tires climbed onto the downed guard, tearing into his clothing and flesh. Screaming, the man lunged upward, overturning Villimy's drone. Chayn let go of the guard he spun in circles. The man sailed off across the concrete floor, his arm broken and bloodied, his laser rifle flying off at a tangent. That left the third guard. Chayn turned his cameras and saw him running toward the elevators, Kraken close on his heels.

Chayn gave chase. He caught Kraken easily, reaching out with the mechanical arm to grab him by the back of the neck. Kraken cried out in rage and flailed his arms about in an effort to break the grip of the drone. Chayn pulled the man off to one side, out of the direct line of fire from the guards still at the elevator.

Chayn turned on the speaker. "Kraken, if you don't

recognize the voice, this is Chayn Jahil. Villimy Dy is the one with her wheels in the air.''

"Let go of me, you demon!"

Chayn squeezed the claws a bit tighter and Kraken screamed. Chayn didn't want to kill the man, but his anger needed venting. "There's only one thing wrong with the use of violence to accomplish something," Chayn said. "It's a two-edged sword. Like you said yourself, the most powerful rule. I could pinch your head off, but it would accomplish nothing. Therefore, I give you a warning. Rashanyn cannot defend itself while conducting a civil war. If your acts of terrorism are typical of the way Rashanyn conducts its internal affairs, then Rashanyn will be in no position to pool its resources for defense against the Blackstar aliens. Listen to the voice of reason, Kraken, before it is too late.''

At that moment, Chayn took a laser blast across the side of the drone. His screen went blank. Villimy looked shocked, an expression that seemed inappropriate to the situation—until he felt something hard and cold press against the back of his neck.

"Quite a show, citizen Jahil," a familiar, male voice said.

Thirteen

Chayn stood slowly, stepped from behind the chair and turned to confront the nozzle of a laser rifle wavering off the tip of his nose.

"My name is Jaklin Tellord. Jak, for short." The laser fell away. Jak slung it over his shoulder. "You should have killed Kraken while you had the chance."

Chayn shook his head. "There's someone standing in line behind Kraken. Their strategy against us won't be as desperate if we don't kill wantonly."

"Kraken wanted you pretty badly," Jak said. "It's always been our policy to cooperate with the ruling party topside, but I should have known better than to try to deal with the Church. I killed one of my own men."

Villimy stood and slipped into Chayn's arms, looking up and into Jak's eyes. Jak stepped back in surprise, his eyes darting the length of Villimy's slender body.

"Why in the name of Rashanyn haven't you got any clothes on?"

Chayn held out Villimy's left arm. "Touch her. I want to show you something."

Jak hesitated for a moment, then decided to comply. He reached out to touch Villimy on the wrist, more fascinated than repelled by her smooth, shiny skin. He jerked his hand back when he felt the heat.

"Her metabolism is much higher than ours. The suit she wore was air-conditioned." Chayn retrieved the battery from his pocket and tossed it to Jak. "The battery died. She would have suffocated within an hour or two."

Jak took a moment to assimilate it all, trying without much success to keep his eyes off Villimy. Villimy smiled openly at him, amused by his behavior.

"I heard something about that," Jak said. It occurred to him that he was speaking around Villimy. He looked at her. "I didn't mean to hurt you."

"Yes, you can speak to me," Villimy said in her hushed tone. "I am human also in ways that count. I have feelings just like your cold-blooded variety. I accept your apology, Jak Tellord."

Jak studied the two of them in turn, understanding that no permanent harm had been done to their potential relationship.

"All right," he said. "I would have traded you two off for concessions from the Church, but they won't behave decently. You two are not our enemies. You helped us and we can help you.'' Jak studied the battery and pocketed it. "We have these batteries."

"Can we stay down here for the time being?" Chayn asked.

"Sure. As you've probably noticed, we have plenty of room. Follow me."

Villimy retrieved her coveralls. Chayn gestured for her to put them on. Despite the discomfort, Villimy already understood their cultural sensitivities to nudity and complied. They followed Jak to the main aisle and to a brightly lit and lightly populated section of the underground level. As they passed increasing numbers of pedestrians, a considerable crowd followed.

Jak showed them to an apartment. "This is my place. Stay here until I get the battery for your coveralls. Nobody will bother you."

Jak left and Villimy began pacing about the apartment, beginning to pant again. Hand-painted art work covered the walls, scenes of the planets and their landscapes. Potted plants crowded beneath ultraviolet lamps. Knickknacks covered every flat surface, small carvings, statues, electronic devices and small works of art made by children. The apartment reflected the personality and life of Jak Tellord. He obviously lived alone, this leader of these reclusive people. Chayn hadn't heard much about them topside, but obviously a considerable portion of the population lived in the lower levels, maintaining the environment that the topsiders took for granted.

Jak returned and handed Villimy several batteries without making eye-contact with the woman. Villimy snapped a battery into place in the device on her shoulder, flopped onto the couch and breathed a sigh of relief as the air-conditioner hummed and blew hot air into the apartment.

"What do you two need?" Jak said. "There's plenty of room down here. We've already put up a number of refugees from the surface."

"Won't that cause more trouble with the Church?" Chayn said.

Jak gave him an odd look. "Are you kidding? Look, the surface people conduct their commerce with the other colonies and play their political games. That's never affected us down here. This is a whole world in itself and we're happy with it. We run the place, surface and subsurface alike. We control the temperature, provide the air, purify the water, keep the food processing and sewerage plants running. They'd die within a day topside without someone to run their world for them."

"What was Kraken trying to accomplish behaving like that?"

Jak stuffed his hands in his pocket and wandered through the room, comfortable in his own environment. "Throw some weight around, intimidate us. From what I heard, Ed getting killed was an accident. Both sides overreacted. We probably would have already received an official apology if it hadn't been for you." Jak grinned. "Not that we'd prefer an apology to watching Kraken fed some of his own medicine. It wasn't up to me to offer you refuge. I reported your presence to my supervisor and got an official okay."

Chayn took a seat next to Villimy, amused by Jak's indecision on how to relate to the woman. Jak pulled a chair around and sat down.

"What happens now?" Chayn said. "How does Reylaton react to Kraken?"

"I suppose there'll be a low-keyed civil war going on topside. Nothing to get excited about. I am more worried about the talk I hear of an invasion by the Blackstar aliens. Do you know anything about that?"

"It's a problem you all share in common. I don't know what can be done about it. It would be a destructive encounter regardless of how it's handled."

"Do you have any idea how vulnerable these colonies are? A hundred pounds of thumbnail-sized gravel dropped in our orbit could shatter the skylights beyond repair. A

131

hundred pounds of explosives could destroy the air purification and recyling plant. Imagine what a thermonuclear
weapon could do.''

"You share your fears with the Church," Chayn said.

"I admit that I'd rather not fight with them," Jak said
with a shrug. "It's stupid to kill over a difference of opinion
on how to stay alive."

Villimy leaned forward. "Do you know who we are,
citizen Tellord?"

Jak blinked at her in silent confusion. Chayn liked the
way Villimy asserted herself, already suspecting that Jak
would prefer to ignore her existence. Maybe he thought
those huge, golden eyes would go away if he didn't look
at them. Reylaton simply appeared not to have the energy
to cope with Villimy Dy. Under normal circumstances, her
appearance in the city, even more than Chayn's, should
have been widely publicized and the center of a great deal
of speculation and discussion as Rashanyn adapted to the
idea of non-Rashanyn humans.

"I heard about an alien spaceship that was said to travel
faster than the speed of light. The Church says you're agents
of the Dark Stargod. Some people think like that. Why is
it important? Is there something you can do to help?"

"In the course of handling our own affairs," Villimy
said, "perhaps there is something we can do. Chayn, what
could you learn of the Blackstar aliens if you had your
starcraft?"

Chayn gave the question serious consideration as long
as Villimy wanted to bring it up again. "It's an obvious
solution to everyone's problems, isn't it? If we were trusted,
we could probably learn enough about the aliens to give the
military a fighting chance of coping with the threat."

"Where is your ship?" Jak asked.

"The military took it to the base orbiting Jasper."

Jak relaxed, the ship far beyond Chayn's reach as far as
he was concerned. "That base is the size of a small moon
and armed to the teeth." He stared into space, lost in

132

thought. Chayn let him drift, content to pick up what information the man might offer.

"I don't understand how Kraken figures on coping with the military," Jak said. "They've always stood firm behind the idea that attacking the Blackstar aliens is too risky, but I sure the hell doubt if General Pak will let Kraken get away with insurrection."

Chayn looked at Villimy. "If I had that interface equipment we'd have a better chance of keeping on top of things. Without Trenton, we're stumbling around in the dark."

"What equipment?" Jak said.

"When that military bus in the tunnel was attacked, we were on our way to the Hub with some people and equipment from Reylaton Electronics. It would be difficult to explain, but I could make good use of it right now."

"If it's all that important, we have the stuff. A bunch of suitcases? They must have been forced to abandon it. It was found when our crews investigated the damage and stored in case it was of value."

"Do you have computer terminals down here, anything tied in with the system topside?"

Jak gave him a tolerant smile. "The entire governmental network originates in the sublevels. The hardware is down here where it's shielded. We handle the hardware, Reylaton Electronics and the others the software."

Chayn laughed, a thousand possibilities surging through his imagination. "Then we have Reylaton by the balls," he said. "We have access and ultimate control of the entire city."

"Could you use it to stop the military?" Jak said with suppressed enthusiasm, not inclined to accept Chayn's claims at face value.

"The military?"

"Look," Jak said, shifting forward in his seat to outline the point he wanted to make. "We can handle Kraken easier than the military. They have control of the hub and I've heard they're preparing to storm the city. If that happens, we're going to be mighty busy down here trying to patch things back together. If we had the opportunity, we'd stop the military from entering Reylaton and let the city handle Kraken in its own way. They won't tolerate him indefinitely. And if a few suitcases of equipment gives you that kind of access to a data processing facility, maybe you could get your ship back with it.''

"Jasper's a long way from here," Chayn said. "But you'd better show me the equipment. We can have a good look at what's going on in the city.''

Jak made arrangements for Chayn to see the equipment. By the time they were ready to leave and meet a group of maintenance technicians who were to observe and report on Chayn's use of the equipment, Villimy had crawled into Jak's bed, her air-conditioner humming softly in the quiet apartment.

"Let her sleep," Chayn said. "She manages to get her two cents worth in where it does the most good.''

Jak escorted him by electric cart to a large, bright computer center bustling with activity. Jak, a section foreman, joined a group of other foremen and a supervisor named Obrian. Chayn couldn't provide any guidance for the several technicians to set up the unfamiliar equipment, but when it was ready for use, Chayn pulled a chair in front of the screen and donned the set of earphones.

"Unlikely-looking gadgets," Jak said as the group gathered around. "What do you hope to accomplish?''

"I'm not sure. I'll take a look at traffic control and see what General Pak is up to.''

The technicians spent a moment discussing the mesh helmet that provided Chayn with direct control of the computer network, worried that Chayn would distort and damage computer programming. Once they relinquished the item, Chayn had no trouble plunging into the depths of the nonphysical world of the computer network. By the time he floated suspended in a void observing masses in space, a wide assortment of spacecraft trailing behind in Reylaton's orbit, he could ignore the vital role the Watcher played in translating a complex visual and audio pattern into intelligible, sensory information. Most of what he saw was translated from radar images, but this time, there were visual images as well, both converted from analog signals to the digital form. Chayn recognized battleships and fighter carriers, but had to search for information on a giant craft that turned out to be a troop carrier preparing to dock at the hub. Reylaton was under seige.

Chayn broke interface and pointed to a nearby screen. "Does that connect with the phone system topside?"

"No," Jak said. "It's just a data readout screen for local use."

"Keep an eye on it. I'll have to demonstrate what I can do to get any cooperation. You have a few problems and I might be able to help."

Chayn remeshed and took on a challenge he didn't know for certain to be possible. Data processing cores were connected with others by magnetic fields rather than conducted, electrical current. He could modify programming fields. Without physical impediments, he infiltrated into areas of the computer system otherwise inaccessible from the equipment with which he worked. Chayn searched through the local equipment and located the screen he had pointed out to Jak. He overpowered a magnetic switch and turned the screen on, then slipped his way into the communication network, searching for the information that would locate and connect him with Kraken. He finally narrowed the man down to one particular output, a wallscreen in a government office somewhere on Reylaton.

In order to use the visual material he wanted to work with, he had to run it through a system to convert analog signals to digital coding. Once he had accomplished that and overpowered another switch, Chayn could literally see into the government office.

Kraken sat at a desk alongside a window, dictating into a recorder. Chayn adjusted the audio system until he could hear the man speaking. When the screen came on, Kraken looked up in surprise. Chayn fed the visual from Kraken's office to the small screen in the computer center for the benefit of Jak and his associates.

"Kraken!"

Kraken stood, color draining from his face. In all his fifty five years, he had never seen a wallscreen come to life of its own accord. Chayn used an image from a camera set up by one of the technicians to record his own use of the interface equipment, feeding onto Kraken's screen an image of his face, a close-up, eyes closed, lips compressed. Chayn repeated Kraken's name several times, encountering difficulties in having the end product sounding human.

"Kraken, what do you hope to gain by civil insurrection!"

"Who are you!" Kraken cried out. "What do you want?"

Chayn shifted his strategy to take advantage of Kraken's unexpected panic at the spectral image on the screen and its inhuman voice. "Do you not claim that supernatural forces intervene in the affairs of men? Decide for yourself the nature of the force that demands explanation."

Kraken backed against the window, knocking over his chair. He tripped over a cord, pulling the recorder from the table.

"Kraken, you risk the lives of millions. At this moment, the military forces of Rashanyn assemble beyond your city, prepared to undo by violence that which you have accomplished by the use of violence. Explain yourself. What do you hope to gain by this strategy?"

"The rest of the system must know!" Kraken cried out. "They must know that men cannot live in fear for unending centuries! Fear cripples our very souls, saps our enthusiasm for life itself! We cannot continue like this!"

"You refer to the threat of the Blackstar aliens?"

"Legions of the Dark Stargod! They know we're too powerful to fight! They sow fear and sap our strength century by century, weakening us permanently! We must re-

136

gather our strength and resolve to end forever the threat that lurks at the black hole!''

''You speak of gathering strength when you yourself split the forces of Rashanyn into warring camps.''

''We are only one city of fifty million in a civilization of twenty billion!'' Kraken pleaded. ''We are a democracy, but the military still rules like a tyrant, balancing the debilitation of fear with the risks of annihilation! But they have no empathy with the masses who awaken in the morning, fearful for their wives and children and a future they may not have! They weigh risks dispassionately, like things on a scale, choosing the lesser evil, but evil nevertheless! It's time for us to show them that we are afraid! It's time to show them the violence born of fear!''

Kraken shook so badly, his knees gave out. In abject terror, he sank to the floor. ''It's time,'' he shouted. ''For Rashanyn to choose between life or a death that rots us from the inside!''

Chayn withdrew, guilt-ridden and saddened. Breaking interface, he looked around at the stunned, silent men in the computer center. He could imagine the impact that Kraken's hysteria must have had on them, especially considering that Chayn, in their eyes, had accomplished something technically impossible.

''I hate to say it,'' Chayn said. ''The man's a fanatic and maybe insane, but if you people have lived with this for two thousand years, he may be absolutely right.''

Fourteen

Jak was a foreman of the maintenance personnel in his section, each section a self-contained social unit with children growing to take the place of their parents. The chain of command worked in reverse to what Chayn would have expected. An impartial department of employment hired and fired employees, their decisions based strictly on the abilities, qualifications, and performance of each employee. A section of individual employees were expected to see to the smooth functioning and coordination of their work area. Therefore, they elected their foremen. A group of elected foremen, in turn, elected an area supervisor. Supervisors elected a board of overseers, an organization called the Guild. Villimy Dy used the resources of the wallscreen to understand thoroughly this strange underground world of Reylaton before Chayn and Jak Tellord returned.

When they returned, she could tell that Chayn had performed his miracles once again, moving an inexorable series of events forward one more step. She needed no details of the incident that had transpired to follow their conversation.

"I cannot act alone," Jak said. "One section doesn't have the authority or the resources to be of much help. But there were enough witnesses. We made video tapes. Obrian can apply to the Guild for a coordinated effort in this. If you want to get into the hub, we could arrange that, but once there, you'd be pretty much on your own."

"That won't accomplish anything unless there are ships leaving for Jasper."

"If you stopped the military from entering Reylaton, a few of the high command vessels in the area are bound to return to Jasper until the situation is normalized. I have no idea how you'd board one, remain undetected, and gain access to the base at Jasper. Military security is too tight to play those kind of games with them."

"Security systems can work for me, not against me," Chayn said. "A little bit of confusion and the entire system collapses. If you can find a way to get me into the hub undetected, I'll stop the military from boarding Reylaton. Our cooperation needn't extend beyond that."

"I'll speak with Obrian. The Guild will have to approve our plans. I'll check with you later on what we come up with based on what we've seen you do with the computers."

When Jak left, Villimy said, "You plan on going alone."

Chayn hadn't consciously faced the fact that he intended leaving Villimy behind. "Maybe that would be a mistake. What do you think?"

"I am quicker than you," Villimy said, "but you have more stamina and perseverence. You require less sustenance." Villimy tensed and held her head high. "I would prefer to leave with you, but you stand a better chance alone, so I will remain behind."

"There's more to it than that," Chayn said. "If I manage to stow away aboard a military ship, they can't have any doubt as to our whereabouts. You can keep Kraken busy. The military will think we're organizing an active underground here. And if you can keep Kraken busy searching for us, if you can cause enough trouble to keep his mind off larger issues, you'd be doing Reylaton a considerable favor."

"What will you do if you recover your starcraft?"

"I'll have a close look at the Blackstar aliens. They have to be rational beings. I'll communicate if I can. There has to be some basis for mutual cooperation between the two species. I think the starcraft has the capacity to resolve the crisis."

"Then you come back for me."

"When we are finished here, I'll take you home," Chayn said.

"That is correct."

"I took for granted that we'd be spending the rest of our lives here," Chayn said. "I settled that in my mind when we first arrived."

"No," Villimy said. "You justified your behavior. You did not want to admit that you sacrificed your freedom for my life. You did not want to face the alternative of letting me die. You didn't have the time to consider other options, but they're always available, even now."

"You're not a burden to me, Villimy."

"I survive," Villimy said, "as long as that is true."

Jak did not return immediately. Chayn turned the thermostat down to its lowest setting, doubting if he'd be able to catch much sleep during the night. Villimy catnapped endlessly, rousing from her light sleep from time to time, the movement of her body against his igniting in Chayn an insatiable desire for her slender body. Gazing into her surrealistically large eyes, he knew his hunger went beyond physical need, as if he sought to merge more than just their bodies into an indivisable unit. His slow, ponderous lovemaking stressed her nervous system to the breaking point, but she sought him again and again, riding an ecstasy of lust in the security of Chayn's strong arms.

Jaklin Tellord returned in the morning with three other men. Chayn recognized Obrian. "We have formulated a plan of action," Jak said. "I'll outline it for you. You modify it as you choose."

Jak gestured for Chayn and Villimy to be seated on the couch. He paced in front of the wallscreen as he talked.

"The military has isolated the hub, but traffic control is still tied in with some of the computers that provide orbital parameters for the city. You'd have some access to the computers there. There is an item of equipment, that, if damaged, would necessitate a complete replacement. You can arrange for that to happen. Politically, we have always been neutral, so General Pak will rely upon us to replace the unit. It will be little more than a mock-up. You will be inside with as much life-support equipment as you might need. Once the unit is connected, your access to the computers of the hub will be unlimited. The rest is up to you."

That left an enormous amount of detail and vital information hanging in limbo, but its potential seemed feasible to Chayn. ''When could we start?'' he asked.

''Immediately. We verified what you told us, that a carrier is to dock with Reylaton. Over fifty thousand troops are to restore order in the city. Your value to us is to prevent that from happening. Right now, millions of people stand behind Kraken if for no other reason than to let the military know that they want something done about the Blackstar threat. The damage a civil war would cause will stress our resources to their limits. The topsiders rely on us blindly. We cannot let them suffer the consequences of their foolishness without suffering ourselves. Reylaton is a holistic entity. It's not an independent collection of people and machines.''

''I'll have to leave Villimy with you,'' Chayn said.

Jak looked at her. ''We will care for her.''

Chayn grinned. ''More than likely, she'll care for you. Don't underestimate her. She's quick as lightning—physically and mentally. Keep her on ice and well fed and she'll be one hell of an asset to your people.''

Chayn meant to chastise Jak for continually talking around her, but it bypassed him completely. Obrian stepped forward and introduced himself.

''I've assigned my best technicians to take a look at that interface equipment you were using. We managed to steal some memory storage from Reylaton Electronics to supplement our efforts. They assure me that it can be microminiaturized.''

Chayn had worried about the clumsiness of the equipment. ''You mean reduced in size?''

''More than that. The mesh helmet that detects the neural field of the brain for amplification and feedback can be replaced by electrodes directly inserted into the brain. The electronics can be reduced to a small chip implanted under the skin. The physical hook-up to a piece of hardware can be replaced by a field antenna, a fine, wire mesh, embedded, let's say, in the palm of the hand. You'd only need proximity to interconnecting field plates in order to interface with a system.''

"How long would that take?"

"We're working on it. It's probably finished already. It requires surgical implantation, you understand.''

"When?"

"Now, if you'd like.''

"You're not wasting any time,'' Chayn said.

"There's none to waste. We doubt if you can achieve what you claim to be able to do, but it's worth the effort at least to try.''

"And we're ready to move now?"

"Immediately.''

Villimy sat in close physical contact with Chayn during the long journey a quarter of the way around Reylaton, but took an interest in the scenery as they sped down the familiar aisle on a monorailed transport. She brought up the observation that the features of the aisle duplicated themselves every few kilometers. Obrian explained to her that Reylaton was built in self-sufficient sections. Theoretically, the huge torus could be broken into pieces. Except for the vunerable surface level, each section would seal itself off and provide emergency life support for the population.

"Has it ever happened?" Chayn asked.

"Once to a city orbiting one of the satellites of the outer worlds,'' Obrian said. "They were rammed by a damaged freighter. Three million died, but over forty million survived. The city had to be rebuilt.''

They entered an open area directly beneath the two kilometer wide spoke that rose through the skylights of the city to the hub fixed in the center of Reylaton's torus. A well-organized group of technicians led them to a series of interconnecting laboratories. Chayn was shown the completed device to be implanted in his body. A plastic case contained the barely visible, ultra fine filaments of wire, a piece of delicate mesh and a small, flat square of plastic.

"That's it?"

One of the technicians smiled knowingly. "A computer typically operates in the millivolt range with field strengths that are barely detectable. That's why our equipment requires such extensive shielding. This microminiaturized equipment uses a voltage supplied by the brain itself. We leave it up to the hardware, the field plate that we'll be showing you, to amplify the output to a useful level."

"How extensive is the surgery to get that spaghetti into me? I don't know if I like the idea of being stitched from head to foot."

The technician shook his head with bemused superiority. "Within twelve hours, you'll see no evidence of surgery. You'll never know you have this spaghetti, as you call it, inside you."

"It stays in permanently?"

"It has a useful lifespan of only two years. It's designed to be absorbed eventually by the body."

"Even the electrodes in the brain?" Chayn said with a grimace of distaste.

"Those too."

Chayn conceded to the operation. Conducted with local anesthesia, Villimy kept him informed of the progress as he lay naked on his stomach in a small, sterile operating room.

"They're using a device that cuts a trench in the skin, buries the wire and seals the wound behind it," she said. "You're beginning to look like an electronic schematic, Chayn."

"Thanks."

Chayn particularly resented having his skull bolted to immobility for the electrode implants in his brain. Villimy watched with dispassionate interest, her attention split between the procedure itself and a fluorescopic image of his brain on a nearby screen.

"Your brain shows evidence of evolutionary differences in comparison with Rashanyn physiology," Villimy informed him. "You've just convinced them that you are really not of Rashanyn. They're using a scanning technique to implant the electrodes by function instead of location."

"Do they know what the hell they're doing?"

"If they don't, they're not about to admit it."

Chayn arose after the operation, expecting to feel twinges of pain here and there. The electronics had been implanted in his armpit. His right arm had a brownish line running down the inside to his palm. His palm itched.

"The discomfort will pass in a few hours," the technician informed him blandly.

They led him to a computer console. "This is an off-line access device," another technician said. "These connecting cables are universal. The field plate of the cable connects to the field plate of the unit. The cable end contains amplifies and transforms complex, electromagnetic fields to signals of coherent light transmitted by fiber optics. Place the palm of your right hand over the field plate of the cable, please."

Chayn grasped the end of the cable. It sucked his mind from his body. He flowed, split into a million, discrete pieces, his psyche joining the mathematical precision of the computer. Alarmed, Chayn reflexively jerked free and staggered back.

"You appear to go into a catalytic trance," the technician said. "There doesn't seem to be much risk of loosing your balance if you happen to interface in an awkward position."

But Chayn suspected there was a hazard. The device inside him was more sensitive than the equipment Jarl had introduced to him. If he wasn't careful, he could lose his sense of identity in the enormous complexity he had encountered.

"That's the first part of our strategy," Obrian said. "The second part is getting you into the hub undetected."

"You've got that ready to go also, of course."

"Of course. Follow me, please."

Chayn took Villimy's hand and followed. They entered another part of the lab. Obrian consulted more technicians. They led the party to a computer console centered in the room.

"This is a duplicate of the unit in the hub we hope you can damage by distorting the core fields. That necessitates replacing the entire console. This is what they'll get back. It doesn't function at all."

"Won't that mildly upset them?" Chayn said.

Obrian grinned. "They shouldn't have time to notice." He opened a front panel. The interior was padded and contoured for a human figure and crammed with equipment.

"Roughly, it's a pressurized container. If you're trapped in here for any length of time, you have food, water, air, and power, even sanitation facilities. There's a biomed unit to reduce your metabolism and provide some isometric stimulation to your muscles. You could survive in here for three months."

"Why that particular length of time?"

"Have you given any thought to how you'd manage to stow away aboard a military transport to Jasper?"

"No."

"We have. You wouldn't be able to mingle with the crew. Most equipment is stored in vacuum in the cargo holds. Once you get into the hub, you can overpower programming and manipulate commands fed to the computers, even originate your own. If you could arrange to have this unit with you inside transferred aboard a military craft destined for Jasper, you have a chance of accomplishing what

145

you want. We see no other way. A passenger transport makes the run in three days. A cargo transport in three months."

"I'm letting myself in for more than I figured."

"I don't know what you could have accomplished on your own," Obrian said, "but you're not leaving unprepared with our help."

"Are we ready to move now?"

"Anytime you are. The sooner the better, but we've tried not to rush you."

On Chayn's request, Jak showed him and Villimy an office where they could talk alone. He left them in haste, disturbed by the heavy emotional atmosphere emanating from the alien couple. Despite appearances and in Villimy's case, because of them, Jak recognized them as truly alien, qualitatively different from anyone he had ever known.

"Will you be all right on your own?" Chayn asked Villimy.

"Jak will care for me. Jak collects unusual things."

"So I've noticed. But you'll have your hands full with Kraken. I've frightened him twice and he'll be after us with one hell of a vengeance. I should be back within a week. I don't intend spending three months in the hold of a freighter."

"You will succeed," Villimy assured him.

"You have an odd relationship between your intellect and your emotions. They're not at war with each other. That's not true of the kind of people I've known."

"Right now, that's an asset. I suffer, but it will not show."

"I don't intend a farewell, Villimy. I wouldn't be doing this if I didn't think I could pull it off. It isn't me. It's the starcraft and other things in me put there by people that must be stargods. I'm learning to use what they provided."

Villimy slipped her arms around him and dropped her forehead onto his chest. "I know."

"You go back with Jak from here. Okay?"

She nodded.

Obrian watched the two of them emerge from the office. Without looking back, Villimy went to Jak. Obrian nodded discretely to his foreman. Jak and Villimy turned and left the laboratory.

"We'll take this console topside to the elevator docks," Obrian said to Chayn. "Then we'll see what you can do about damaging its counterpart in the hub. It shouldn't take more than an hour for them to send down a requisition. They won't know for certain if we'll cooperate, but if we're ready to move, they won't question our cooperation. It's an important piece of equipment. But once you're in position, you'll have to analyze the situation and act fast. Arrange for a major breakdown or an accident of some kind. High ranking officers will return to Jasper immediately if they assess repairs to take more than a week."

"You're sure of that?"

"I'm sure."

They left the laboratories and were walking along a brightly lit cavern alive with pedestrians when the sirens began screaming. Foot traffic stopped for an instant, then broke into an orderly stampede. Groups of a common destination began forming. The open areas emptied of personnel. Obrian continued an unhurried pace toward a cluster of offices standing in the open.

"What's happening?" Chayn asked.

"Kraken probably. There must be a security force headed down from topside."

"For what purpose?"

Obrian looked at him and grinned. "Topsiders trust our loyalty to Reylaton, but in no way could Kraken appreciate having Reylaton's maintenance facilities infiltrated by agents of the Dark Stargod."

"What will they do?"

"Search," Obrian said. "Topside security is mostly sympathetic toward us. They'll just go through the motions. Are you worried about the woman?''

Despite his anxieties, Chayn shook his head. "No, I'm not worried about Villimy. If Kraken believes in demons, he's got an especially formidable one to cope with in her."

Fifteen

They were more than just patterns of light and sound. They were a part of his psyche, an integral part of his being. He made no effort to translate the experience into sensory terms. And it felt like a crime to destroy their mathematical precision. But with an effort of will, he distorted, initiating the kind of discordance that Jarl had been so enthusiastic about him repairing. Apparently, it had never occurred to Jarl that interface could be used to destroy. Without making the sabotage obvious, Chayn waited long enough to be sure that the harm would spread, then broke interface.

"Are you certain?" Obrian said with an anxiety that gave away the intensity of his desire to have the military block-aded.

"It's not pleasant having to take someone's word for something important," Chayn said, grimly amused. "Like those military ships you say will be leaving for Jasper."

Chayn paced the length of the small, barren chamber, anxious to be on his way, but not at all anxious to make use of the mock console. One way or another, he intended to paralyze the hub and be on his way to Jasper within hours, not that he believed it would work out that easily. He looked forward to none of the excitement that lay ahead, wanting nothing more than to regain possession of his star-craft and the freedom he had given up by relinquishing control of it to Rashanyn authorities. He vowed that he'd never pull a stunt like that again.

A small communication station called for someone's attention. Obrian answered the call, then turned to Chayn. "You're on your way. They demanded a replacement console immediately. They sounded like they would have sent an armed detachment down to confiscate it if necessary."

Two grim-looking technicians who thrived in an environment of color-coded electronics aided Chayn. He climbed into the cabinet and fitted himself into the foam contour. The technicians connected the special coveralls he wore to the equipment stowed inside the cabinet with him, an arrangement that would make it unnecessary to leave in urgent search of a men's room. They strapped him down and Chayn slipped his right hand into a glove that interfaced with a small data processor controlling the surprisingly complex life support facilities. Most of it was self-regulating.

When they shut the panel on him, a small light came on automatically. Air pressure stabilized and the air conditioner began humming. Chayn tried out the biomed unit also built into his coveralls. It worked groups of muscles against themselves, a provision that would prevent cramps over long periods of inactivity. Twitching muscles felt like they were having harmless spasms. He ignored the electrosleep circuits for the time being. Those would enable him to pass over long periods of time in medically safe sleep. The food concentrate and water canisters were above him with two dangling tubes to suck on as needed.

The technicians plugged the fake field plate cable of the console into a general computer access system. The field plate connected to the glove on his right hand. Chayn entered the system, exploring at random. Computers were being used to organize Kraken's search of the sublevels. The troops were moving casually, marking progress too evenly to be making more than a token effort to carry out Kraken's orders. Chayn switched over to ground traffic control and located the transport carrying Villimy Dy and Jak Tellord back to his section. Already a dim anguish and nostalgia disturbed him. Only the most absolute necessity forced Chayn to leave her behind.

When they disconnected him, Chayn didn't like being sealed off from the world, deprived of his senses with his destiny in the hands of blind fate. He kept watch on the temperature and pressure gauges, waiting for some sign of change that would indicate he was being moved. His imagination provided all the premature sensations of movement he'd ever experience in actuality. But after a time, he did feel motion, figuring the rather bumpy ride to be in the rear bed of an electric cart.

At no time did the pressure or temperature gauges waver, but within an hour he felt his weight lessening, proof that he was on a freight elevator, on the way to the central hub. Weightless and disoriented, he recalled with a queasy feeling having vomited in his pressure helmet aboard the derelict. That already seemed to have occurred an age ago. But the nausea passed as he waited expectantly for the interface with the hub computer systems that would occur when the hub technicians unwittingly plugged the unit in. He felt slight sensations of acceleration and deceleration as the unit was guided down corridors, around corners, and bumped against a wall to be latched in place.

Despite his anticipation, the interface still took him by surprise. The vast, inhuman spaces of an electronic environment swallowed his psyche and spread it thinly across mathematical infinities. His greatest fears were realized. Helpless, he waited for dispersal of himself, but despite the incomprehensible complexity pulling him in all directions, his sense of selfhood remained intact. When he realized that he would not lose track of his sense of identity, he began thrusting outward with a discriminating will.

A thousand different systems gave him a varying perspective of the physical and social organization of the hub. Vague ideas of how to accomplish his task formed and solidified. He went directly to the regulatory systems, focused on the most densely populated regions of the hub, and warped core fields. Emergency circuits sprang to life as air pressure and temperature began failing. Chayn disabled enough of them to keep the emergency alive and spreading.

He infiltrated traffic control and saw with countless eyes. From the bridges of the battleships and the control tower of the hub's docking facilities, Chayn absorbed the environment, aware of the position of every craft within a hundred kilometers of Reylaton. The troop carrier had already docked, but thousands of mercenaries were filing back aboard as the life support system of the hub failed. Chayn invaded security circuits and blocked access to emergency equipment lockers, forcing large numbers of Reylaton personnel to abandon the hub for the elevators of the spokes.

Knowing that it wouldn't take long for the military to regain control of the situation despite the damage he had caused, Chayn searched for a way to compel the military task force to abandon its mission. The key lay in the massive docking bays. There were three of them, one filled with the gargantuan bulk of the troop carrier. A civilian transport lay just off a second bay, moving in on automatic for docking.

Chayn took control of the docking sequence and sent the huge craft yawing to one side. He fought a losing battle with the sheer quantity of emergency shut-down commands and the lightning-swift efforts of other computers coming on-line to take over the mass insanity spreading to the navigational system. Chayn withdrew when he realized it was already too late to stop an imminent collision between the hub and the careening transport.

Chayn anticipated minor damage. The cargo ship was moving less than a meter a second and decelerating rapidly. He watched in horror as the megatonnage of the cargo transport passed through the hull of the hub as if its construction were the most delicate, fragile structure in existence. Hull plates and girders glowed red hot, buckled, and sprang loose. The cargo transport itself appeared to disinigrate in a cloud of twisted and torn superstructure.

In the hub itself, within the torus of Reylaton and aboard counless military ships, a thousand sirens were wailing, tens of thousands of men mobilizing to rescue the trapped and the injured. The elevators of all three spokes were descending toward the torus. Judging the resources of the military fleet to be sufficient to handle rescue operations, Chayn overpowered regulatory circuits and burned out the motors of the largest elevators, effectively isolating the torus of the city from the hub.

Chayn backed off and studied the destruction he had caused. No ship could dock with the swiftly rotating torus of the city itself. Only through the hub did the military have an effective route through which to funnel troops and supplies sufficient to quell a disturbance among fifty million inhabitants. Until the hub was rebuilt, Reylaton was now an isolated social entity within the Rashanyn Empire. Kraken would be pleased. So would Obrian and the sublevel world.

The gauges registered a vacuum outside his cabinet. Now his exit from Reylaton depended on access to a military ship leaving for Jasper. Chayn had not damaged enough of traffic control to render it useless. Most of the computers remained on-line and were reorganizing the mass of spacecraft in the area. Chayn began his search of those craft. He had access to the identity of most of them and, in some cases, a detailed list of passengers and cargo. Within an hour, Chayn detected evidence that the military was conducting rescue, salvage and clean-up operations before abandoning the damage to Reylaton's construction crews for repair.

Chayn fixed his hopes on a ship called the Betafax IV. He could sense the enormous influx of data transmitted to the craft from various military command centers and the orderly patterns of data flowing from it. The craft hung in the void against the backdrop of stars, a monstrosity of exposed hardware designed for speed and power in the airless vacuum. Six massive fusion engines sprawled across the stern bulkhead. The Betafax flowed like a jewel among the stars, a thousand portholes blazing with light, bristling with laser turrets, particle accelerators and launch tubes for missiles ranging in size from millimeters to meters in diameter. Electromagnetic defense shields glimmered like a curtain of light around it and ablative shields gleamed in the golden light of Rashanyn.

His opportunity arrived in the form of a request for a list of priority salvage. Core memory storage units classified secret or higher were included. Chayn searched for a fake identification and location code for his console. Three times the Betaflex rejected his code as he slipped it into transmission. In growing desperation, Chayn duplicated an already existing identification code and tacked on his own location number. It went through. Chayn breathed a sigh of relief.

Physical discomfort began interfering with his interface. Chayn used the muscle stimulators to remove the cramps in his legs and back. Watching through security systems, rescue teams worked their way through the hub at an excruciatingly slow pace. Nuclear powered tugs latched onto the hull of the troop carrier and backed it from the ruined docking bay into space where insect-like repair craft clustered around to fix the superficial damage. But torches flickered around the cargo transport embedded and welded in place, its nose buried deep in the ruined docking bay. When tugs pulled it away, it trailed debris like clouds of dust, small craft moving in to sweep through the area with magnetic fields, clearing the immediate area of the deadly garbage. The tugs glared like stars, guiding the huge craft into a lower orbit about Gilderif for repairs at Reylaton's convenience. Only then did the salvage teams move into the hub.

When they disconnected Chayn's console, he went blind. Trapped within his tiny cocoon of air and heat, he used the electrosleep device to quell the panic pouring from his unconscious. Only when the pressure gauges returned to normal could he hope to escape his self-made prison. Still, unless unknown and uncontrollable factors intervened, he was headed for the Betafax IV and a world called Jasper almost a billion kilometers across Star Rashanyn's planetary system.

He set the electrosleep control for twenty minute periods of unconsciousness, but lost track of the number of times he reset the controls. He set the control for hourly periods, keeping track of time by making finger smudges on the metal over his head. Ten of them accumulated before he awakened and almost triggered the unit for another hour's sleep before noticing the needles of the gauges rising slowly. He waited them out. Two hours passed before the pressure gauge showed normal. Anxious to be free of his confined quarters, he ignored the rising temperature gauge.

Chayn cracked open the pressure seal and opened the panel a fraction of an inch. An ice breeze washed across him. His first breath shocked his lungs to momentary paralysis. His eyes watered and he lost his hold on the panel latch. He grabbed the lip of the panel to pull it closed until the temperature rose to tolerable levels. The flesh of his fingers froze to the metal. Grimacing in pain, he noticed the intense, infrared radiation washing through the cargo hold of what he hoped to be the Betafax IV. Ruddy light reflected from cargo stored in zero G grapples. With the flesh of his fingertips frostbitten, the back of his hand reddened with superficial burns. When his fingers came free, Chayn pulled the panel shut and lay back in the foam, his heart pounding.

Moments later, he heard voices echoing in the cavernous cargo hold. There were two of them, male and female, speaking in low monotones. The voices rose in volume, then faded in the distance. Chayn stuck his head outside the cabinet. The infrared lamps had been turned off. He looked between his console and another close item of equipment through a space of twenty meters to another wall of cargo. He couldn't tell in the zero gravity if he looked up or down. His perception vacillated from one perspective to the other.

He released the straps holding him in place and disconnected his coveralls, floating free in the confined space. The numbness in his fingertips became intense pain.

"This console over here," the woman said, her voice drifting and echoing from nearby.

"It couldn't have been a mistake," the man said. "It had to have been a deliberate falsification."

"It's no priority item. Mark it off inventory. We'll have it moved later."

Minutes later, Chayn heard an airlock thud open and clank shut in the distance. After a moment, he had a horrifying thought. What if they evacuated the hold again?

Chayn resealed himself in the cabinet. An hour later, the gauges still showed an atmosphere outside. The pain in his fingertips became a throbbing. The surface layers of skin were peeling, but it wouldn't be anything serious.

It would be safer to remain in the console. If he tried exploring this strange enviroment, he'd be risking stumbling over his own ignorance again. Still, he had no idea of where he was. He could just as easily waste his time if he wasn't aboard a craft that would be soon accelerating to Jasper. If he could find a computer input device, he'd have access to all the information he needed. Then, if everything was going according to plan, he could return to the cabinet and lay low for the duration of the journey.

Chayn decided to risk it. It wouldn't do any harm to look around the cargo hold.

Chayn opened the panel and let himself float out, a number of other potential hazards occurring to him. What if the ship accelerated while he floated in free fall several tens of meters from a direction that might suddenly become down? Chayn reached for a nearby strapping band and pulled himself into an open aisle. He looked downward through a hazy distance, awed by the size of the cargo hold. The personnel and cargo airlocks were a quarter-kilometer away. The vast amount of cargo around him blocked his view in most directions, making it impossible to determine the size of the hold. He was in a three-dimensional maze without any up or down perspective. Chayn thought that perhaps he had some free fall experience in his amnesic past, but not much. The lack of perspective disoriented him.

Braving the risks involved, Chayn pulled himself forward, toward the airlocks. He gained speed and missed a handhold. Tumbling through the air, he calmed himself out of sheer necessity. His trajectory was diagonal across the aisle. He glanced back to fix the location of his console in his memory, then concentrated on braking his velocity against a wall of cargo without mangling himself in the process.

Chayn grabbed hold of a cable, spun around, and slammed his feet against a metal sided crate. He pulled himself hand over hand the remaining distance to the end of the aisle and looked across a fifty-meter abyss to a landscape of metal one hundred and fifty meters in diameter, the apparent width of the ship itself. The slightly concave bulkhead had a number of smaller, personnel airlocks scattered across its surface littered with equipment, conduit, plumbing, and air tanks. The airlock he had seen from the console was still closest to him, but he balked at having to launch himself across the intervening space.

He aimed carefully and launched himself, keeping his eye on the airlock gradually slipped off to one side. Air friction slowed him to where he could break his momentum by simply reaching out and grabbing onto a length of pipe. He walked on his hands to the airlock, avoiding looking back at the yawning abyss.

He peered through a rectangular, glass pane and through a second one in the inside hatch. Beyond, he saw a row of consoles, computer equipment for inventory control. With a growing elation, he squeezed together two handles to open the outer hatch. He pulled himself into the small chamber, closed the outer hatch and opened the inner one.

He stuck his head inside the room. There were no side corridors or doors, just a long space and another, single hatch at the end. He moved into the room. Now that he was inside the ship, he had little intention of ever returning to the cramped, confined coffin of the fake computer console. Somewhere aboard a craft this size he ought to be able to find a comfortable place to hide.

A sudden, whooping siren startled Chayn into paralysis. Rising from a low, throbbing tone, it reached ear-shattering frequencies, tearing through his nerves. Chayn clutched the sill of the inner airlock in panic, noticing the photoelectric security beam he had broken far too late to do anything about.

"There is an intruder in the cargo area," a soft, feminine voice said over the rise and fall of the siren.

"There is an intruder in the cargo area."

Sixteen

Villimy Dy sat silently beside Jak Tellord on the transport, slicing through the tunnel at high speed, returning her to a strange place and separating her from the only man she trusted. She had grown use to these white-skinned aliens with the small eyes dominated by their need to control their environment and each other. She sympathized with the plight of Rashanyn, but without Chayn felt isolated, lost, and insecure. She functioned entirely upon her intellect, waiting for the day when Chayn would return to give freedom to the other half of her life.

She had paired with Chayn, grown to complement him. It hadn't been by choice and Chayn did not yet understand the ways of her people or the needs of her body. Possibly he would never understand them. These humans lived as autonomous units even when mating and bearing children. Pairing for her people meant much more, possessing a physiological basis that went beyond the usual affection and sexual attraction that these people knew. To behave spontaneously, to give freedom to her emotions would probably be to act possessive in Chayn's eyes. The closest Chayn could ever come in fulfiling her emotional needs based on his imprint within her psyche would be for him to desire her presence on a permanent basis. And that she could not demand of him.

Until then, she would fit into the structure of life around her. She would do what Chayn expected of her and Jak Tellord might, in the end, come to regret her presence in his world. She would still have to give way to the pressures inside her, express and vent tensions. Chayn had tagged Kraken as their advesary. Therefore, Kraken would bear the brunt of her need to express herself, her aggression, her frustration.

"I don't know anything about you," Jak said to her

finally. "If you have anything you need to make life comfortable other than what we normally provide for ourselves, you'll have to let me know. If we behave toward you in ways that you find insulting or annoying, you'll have to let us know. We can't minimize the differences between us unless we know what they are."

Jak could not maintain eye-contact with her for very long. She smiled at the effect she had on him. She had been right in suspecting that Jak would take a perverse interest in her as a collector of unusual things. His mind roamed a larger universe than the sublevels of Rashanyn. It took a great deal of understanding for him to say what he had said.

"I will let you know what I need," Villimy said, wishing she could match the exaggerated curve of the mouth that passed as a smile for these people. "And you will not cause me discomfort. I know Chayn Jahil. He is like you in most ways."

"Where does he come from?"

"From another time and space. He lives a life of decades, but scattered over an eon. Or does that sound unbelievable to you?"

"It does, but at the same time, I know you're not lying to me. How about yourself?"

"From a world I may have lost forever. I am lost, like Chayn."

This time, he did look at her. "Your relationship is close?"

"We have only each other."

Villiny felt him shift gears. If he could not possess her in the way he wanted, he would satisfy himself caring for an orphan. Jak had not paired. That could not be important to him. But he had invested much of himself in the care of the people around him, making their needs his needs and ignoring the reason for the rejection of his own personal needs. Remembering their encounter with Jak's streak of violence, Villimy felt secure in his care.

Villimy heard the sirens first. Jak did not hear them over the hush of engine noise until Villimy brought the matter to his attention.

"It's a new security arrangement," he explained. "We'll have warning when topsiders are entering the sublevels."

"This cannot be a local warning. We have passed through more than one section."

Jak nodded with a worried expression. "It must be a large scale mission. It can't be anything other than a search for you and Jahil."

When the transport reached Jak's session, he used his personal communicator to avoid the search parties and drove Villimy to an apartment next to his own. "This will be yours," he said, escorting her inside. "There are some storage areas behind it. I'm planning on having them sealed off permanently and connecting them to this apartment. We'll stock it with supplies so that you can stay out of sight when necessary, but you'll have to remember not to leave any personal effects lying around, especially spare batteries to your coveralls."

"Batteries, the thermostat setting, things that would be a dead give-away." Villimy smiled at him, aware of this thoughts of her strangeness.

Jak glanced at the device riding her shoulder; it issued a flood of warm air, a constant reminder of the odd qualities of this perceptive, alluring creature. "I'll have a spare made up for emergencies, maybe something more attractive to wear. Will that be okay with you?"

"I will be appreciative."

Villimy paced her barren apartment after Jak left to monitor the search in progress. He returned and introduced her to his section leaders. Without exception, they were fascinated by her, although the full intensity of the awe and wonder they would have displayed toward an alien from the stars was blunted by the burden of fear and its consequences, a low-keyed, chronic depression that neither she nor Chayn had first noticed upon their arrival. They adopted her more as an attractive pet and a symbol of their defiance of Kraken's arrogance than as an individual in her own right, but Villimy understood the difficulties that could arise between peoples of substantial physical differences. She fixed their names and faces in her memory, knowing these men to be important resources toward her continued survival.

Late the next day, Villimy watched recordings of Chayn's escape from Reylaton on the newscasts. Backed against the far wall of the apartment with involuntary shudderings of fear running through her, she watched the massive transport careen out of control into the docking bays. Reylaton authorities attributed the damage to wholesale computer failure, possible due, they explained, to a freak storm of high intensity radiation from somewhere in the galaxy. It had never happened before and would probably never happen again, but Villimy gave a nervous laugh in her empty apartment. Even Chayn did not understand or realize the extent of his powers. They were gifts of the stargods. Even her own people had legends of humans who roamed the universe alone, tools of the stargods intervening in the affairs of scattered races of humanity. Villimy had never believed such stories before. Among her own people, they had been stories told to and believed by children.

Home, a place lost among the stars and down through corridors of time that could never be retraced. If he could, Chayn would find her world, but not her time nor the people she had known. They were both like fossils brought back to life, remnants of the past, nomads of the present. If Chayn chose to pair with her, it would be there, among the stars and the realization that they were both orphans of time and space sharing that bond if little else.

During the night that followed, the dimming of the lights in the corridors of the sublevels, Jak Tellord burst into her apartment and into her bedroom. Startled from her sleep by the noise, Villiny leapt from her bed in terror, barely suppressing an instinctive attack upon the intruder. Jak backed away from her with stark terror in his eyes. Villimy shuddered and relaxed. These people were so slow that it sometimes exasperated her. They plodded through life on a straight line course of easily-deduced motivation. They were powerful, but she could dance circles around them. Villimy noted the hackles rise on Jak's flesh, but envied him in a way. She made her errors also, wasting energy on vacillations between mistakes and their compensations. Perhaps neither had the advantage over the other. Jak would have a long life and she a short one by his standards, but in the end the quantity and quality of their experience would be the same.

"I'm sorry, Jak," she said. "You startled me."

"I'm sorry, too," Jak said, thoroughly shaken. "Damn, I thought you were going to tear me to pieces."

"It's a difference in metabolism," she explained.

"Yeah, so I noticed."

Villimy sat on the edge of her bed to give Jak's adrenalin a chance to drain off. "What did you want?"

Jak nodded toward the living room. "There's something on the screen that I thought you should see."

Villimy followed Jak into the living room. He picked up the remote control from an end table. The screen swelled to life with the larger-than-life image of General Pak. Snow and audio static made it difficult to understand his words.

"Kraken is jamming. Listen to this."

". . . competent authorities declaring the Church of Rashanyn of Reylaton . . . violating basic tenents of separation of church and state . . . excommunication proceedings . . . appeal to the people of Reylaton for . . . rationality . . ." The picture faded completely.

"He's been broadcasting for an hour, probably a tape on rerun to work its way through the jamming for those who want to piece together what he's saying. Pak is saying that

Kraken is paranoid and that the public is being duped by rumors, coincidence and mass hysteria. Kraken is getting to be more fanatical by the hour. The antiKraken forces and the Church are firming their stands and preparing to take each other on. There's bound to be a great deal of civil disturbance topside."

"Down here, too?" Villimy said.

Jak gave her a wry grin. "We were born and raised on mechanical engineering and the virtues of level-headedness and common sense. We have our fanatical loyalties, I suppose, but not that kind. Maybe I gave you and Chayn a taste of what it takes to anger us. I did think you two were dangerous criminals when we discovered you wandering around down here."

"Is that an apology?"

"It took time to slip it in and word it right."

"I think we understood." Villimy nodded to the static ridden screen. "How will Kraken respond to that?"

"We'll see a little bit later. I'll have a video recording made in case Pak tries to jam Kraken. I hear he'll be leaving soon for Jasper. It's a shame. I'd rather see someone around keeping Kraken just talking like a fanatic instead of behaving like one."

Jak hadn't taken personal offense by Villimy's reaction at having been awakened abruptly. She could feel him trying to be close, to establish a rapport with her. He walked to the door and turned, visbly suppressing something he wanted to say.

"You're wondering how Chayn managed to awaken me from sleep."

Jak nodded with a sheepish smile.

"He did so very carefully."

Jak knitted his brows. "Are you psychic? How did you know what I wanted to say?"

Villimy shook her head patiently. "Not psychic. Just very observant."

Jak left and Villimy sat on the couch and turned to a station that the Church used for its programs. She listened to a pedantic clergyman explaining the rationale behind Kraken's emotional behavior. She wondered how anyone could believe Reylaton to be the center of a universal, raging war between forces of good and evil. And yet, she had seen enough of human behavior to understand how emotion could form its own intellectualizations. After all, General Pak did not understand the effects of chronic fear on a population.

Finally, Kraken did appear on a news special. He sat behind a desk wearing a black robe, his fingers interlaced on the desk before him. Dark, piercing eyes focused on the unseen audience behind the camera. Villimy smiled. He had gone to great lengths to put forth a composed, rational appearance.

"Fellow citizens, members of the Church and believers in the Word. Many of you have just viewed an illegal broadcast beamed into Reylaton from military forces hovering about our ancient and great city. Because of the destruction of the hub, it is General Pak's only access to the city, an accident the general terms coincidental and freakish, he is unable to use our studios in a conventional manner, nor is he able to bring into our city his guns and storm troopers to depose the new civilian government of Reylaton. The general stated that authorities in touch with the situation on Reylaton and aware of the events that have transpired, have declared me paranoid, claiming that I have behaved in an irrational manner in accordance with outmoded beliefs in the supernatural. He claims that the Rashanyn Supreme Council does not recognize my legitimate seat upon the Reylaton Council and that the Church of Rashanyn is considering excommunication proceedings against me because of my crimes in inciting riot, bloodshed, and civil disobedience."

For the first time, Villimy saw Kraken smile. It looked more like a snarl. "I am honored. I am honored to be accused of believing in the Stargods, the foundation of belief for the Church of Rashanyn. I am honored that the Rashanyn Supreme Council believes that a single man has the strength to overthrow the government of a city of fity million inhabitants. I am even honored, although saddened, to hear that the Church considers excommunication on the basis of data presented to it by General Pak and his military forces who are no longer with us to dictate our beliefs and our civil behavior.

"I grieve that you, the people of Reylaton, have not shared in my honors." Kraken opened the palms of his hands and held them out in question. "Does it matter? Do we seek honors or truly resent injustice based on the destruction of truth? In the name of the Word, we do not seek honors nor return hatred for hatred. In these enlightened times, who bothers to question the value of the Church when men no longer believe in good and evil, in the Stargods and their foes, the legions of the Dark Stargod? And if there is no belief, who bothers to question whether events are merely coincidental and humanly inspired or whether perhaps we live on a stage upon which the last battle will be fought between forces of light and forces of darkness?

"Are the onrushing events of recent days coincidental? Am I a mad tyrant playing upon the fears and the hopes of fifty million gullible souls? In earlier programs, we have attempted to demonstrate that these events began the very day that two inhuman creatures arrived upon Reylaton from the darkness of interstellar space. They arrived in a mysterious craft that the military claims to travel faster than the speed of light and to be indestructible. And yet they claim the visitors are merely human, helpless refugees from the stars."

Emotion began playing on Kraken's face. "In taped documentaries confiscated from government and military files here in Reylaton, you have seen and heard these creatures for yourself, one of great strength and the other of mysterious beauty. Their arrival coincides with the probe incident from the black hole and a determination by the military that invasion by the Blackstar aliens may be imminent. The aliens arrived the day turmoil charged through Reylaton, destroying forever the guarded tranquility of our fair city. Rest assured that we are not alone. Rebellion, dissent, and protest rage throughout the system of Star Rashanyn. The Word of Rashanyn tells us that we were exiled from the Galaxy of Man for our sins. It does not say that we were exiled to another galaxy of men. It says that we were sent into realms of the inhuman, losing forever the grace of the Stargods. We lost not their love or support, but only their divine protection.

"Can you really believe, fellow Citizens, that the destruction wreaked upon the hub that so conveniently isolates us from harm is simply coincidental? Can you really believe that the alien creatures at large in our city are simply random visitors to be taken at face value despite all that has occurred? Reylaton is one small city in a civilization spanning many worlds. Our role is a small one, but it must be an honorable one. We demonstrate to the Supreme Council our needs and demonstrate to the Church of Rashanyn our faith. We shall also demonstrate to the Dark Stargod our eternal vigilance. The aliens shall be found. They shall be made to confess their identity and their purpose in our world. When we uncover their subterfuge and their guile is no longer effective, we shall broadcast to the universe at large, to General Pak and the Supreme Council and the Church hierarchy, the truth. And the truth shall be spoken by agents of the Dark Stargod who have failed in their dark mission. I speak of the military as our enemies, but they are our brothers. Misguided as they may be, in the end they shall be our salvation. We shall feed the Blackstar aliens to the abyss from which they arose. And Rashanyn shall be at peace once again."

Villimy switched off the screen. She sat in the silence with her feet tucked beneath her and her arms held against her breasts. She tried to span the void with her longing, to search out Chayn Jahil and be secure in his safety or prepare to die with his destruction. But she had no psychic powers, only a knowing of the way of men. What the Church of Rashanyn did not understand was that their colony ship had not been the only one to span the void between two galaxies. They did not understand simple faith to be what it could not be, a longing for a secure and comprehensible life in an insecure and incomprehensible universe.

Villimy waited an hour for Jak Tellord to arrive. Kraken's speech had been much to effective for the sublevel populations to ignore. When he arrived, she burst out laughing. "Jak, please enter," she called out to his soft and tenuous knocking.

"Is something wrong?" he said, closing the door behind him.

"Nothing is wrong with me. Something is wrong with you."

Jak looked puzzled.

"Kraken has frightened your people."

"If his control topside becomes absolute, we have no defense against him. You can't fight fanatics when they're perfectly willing to be martyrs."

"Will you abandon me?" Villimy said softly.

Jak stiffened in silent protest. "We have not chosen to abandon you and we will not be betrayed by our own people. But Obrian has told me to prepare for intensive, sublevel searches for you and Chayn. We have to make immediate plans for your defense. Kraken must not believe that we give aid to you. Our only means of defense is to make you as much of an adversary as he wants others to believe."

Villimy smiled, knowing the effect it had on these people. "Do you doubt that he has a real demon to fight?"

Jak grinned and shook his head. "Not me. I don't doubt it for an instant."

"Then let us conspire to pit Kraken against his own fears."

Seventeen

The paralysis triggered by the whooping sirens lasted an eternity. A flood of panic finally galvanized Chayn to action. He launched himself toward the first of the line of computer consoles, braking his dive neatly against the side of the nearest machine in the zero-gravity environment. He yanked loose the interface cable and slapped his right hand over the field plate.

The consoles were inventory devices as he had suspected, keeping track of the contents of the cargo in the holds. Chayn rushed through the mathematical structures, searching for access to the other data processing functions of the spacecraft. Bursting through to them felt like squeezing through a tight and dark tunnel to broad daylight. He fled through sophisticated levels of programming, locating the security system, and overrode the alarms. They did not retrigger themselves. He erased memory of the intrusion, but had no other way to cover his tracks. Technicians would search through the circuits without locating the source of the problem. It would be an anomaly that would keep them on guard.

Chayn spent a moment absorbing navigational data. They would launch soon. As he feared, it would be a high acceleration run, ten gravities at launch for a brief period followed by a full gravity for a good part of the trip. Deceleration would be another, constant gravity until the ship's arrival. In three days, the Betafax IV would be orbiting the military base at Jasper.

Chayn went over the technical readouts of the ship. He committed a few potential hiding places to memory, but the ship was too well organized for random factors to drift about without detection. Unless he chose to return to the fake cabinet in the holds, he would have to find a place to hide and stay put. He chose the passenger section. The lists were low, but not so low that a newcomer would be noticed. And the passengers would not be wearing military uniforms.

Chayn disengaged and dived headlong down the corridor to the hatch at the end. There was a rotating wall showing through the small pane of glass. Chayn glanced back down the corridor, ensuring he hadn't left something undone or any evidence of his passage, then turned his attention to the mystery of the rotating wall beyond the hatch.

He opened the hatch, swung himself outside and closed it behind him. He hovered inside a huge, flattened drum thirty meters in diameter and nine meters thick. The one stable bulkhead contained many hatches, probably other inventory control centers. The rotating wall had ladders radiating from the center just across from him outward to the three meter wide, circular rim of the drum. There were hatches set at intervals along the rotating rim. Chayn quickly figured out the setup. This was the transition point between the zero-gravity areas of the ship and the rotating section that provided the psuedogravity of centrifugal force.

Chayn pushed across the space, grabbed hold of a ladder, and began moving down it. Now, the bulkhead with the hatches to the inventory control centers rotated from his new perspective. As he moved outward along the ladder toward the perimeter, an increasing feeling of gravity gave him a satisfying sense of up and down. At the bottom of the ladder, he could stand on the bottom of a huge, shallow drum standing on end. One wall turned. He stood a few steps and discovered that any location along the walk with the circular hatches at his feet would suffice. He felt like an animal in an exercise cage and tried to pin down a memory of just what sort of animal he had in mind.

The hatches at his feet were numbered and would lead downward to corridors running the length of the rotating drum of the Betafax's passenger section. He knew that one hatch led to safety, but could no longer orient himself as he had in the computer system to choose the right hatch.

Suddenly, a hatch opened overhead. Looking directly up, Chayn watched a woman drop through the opening head first. For an instant, his mind told him that she would fall directly onto him, but she stood, hanging upside down. She didn't see him at first. She began climbing a ladder. From Chayn's perspective, it appeared as if she climbed down toward him.

She saw him. They both looked directly overhead into each other's eyes. "Sir, civilians aren't allowed in this area of the ship."

"So I've noticed," Chayn said, desperately trying to decide which hatch led to the corridor he wanted. "I seem to be lost."

The woman looked confused. "Who are you?"

Chayn grabbed hold of a ladder and began climbing toward her, his weight diminishing. He slowed when she tensed. "Could you tell me which hatch leads to the passenger area?"

"Look," she said in protest. "You can't even get in here without a voice print on record. How could you be lost? Who are you?"

She had big, blue eyes, not as impressive as Villimy's, but attractive in a more conventional way. She had a conventionally beautiful face. Black curly hair billowed about her head. Her body beneath snug, blue coveralls would have done a goddess justice.

Chayn had knuckled down to worrying about one day at a time for the journey to Jasper. Now, he worried about each passing second, one after the other. How would he escape this perdicament? "I was given permission to check on some equipment in the hold," he said.

"But, sir! We'll be launching in forty minutes! No passenger is allowed out of the section! You'll be killed if you're not secure in your acceleration bunk!"

Chayn grinned. "Would you believe I'm a stowaway? I'm a follower of Kraken. I have a two-kiloton nuclear device on board.'' Chayn held up a fist containing an imaginary triggering device. "If I push this button, the infidels die!"

Chayn tried to make his grin as maniacal as possible. Only the energy of his desperation projected the illusion of fanaticism he tried for. Chayn felt like a complete idiot.

The woman began backing away from him. Chayn felt gooseflesh on his arms. It looked as if she were climbing her ladder upside down and backwards to boot.

"Oh, my God!" she gasped.

She began scrambling back down the ladder. Chayn climbed up after her and past the center point of the drum. Suddenly, he did find himself climbing head first down the ladder. He began losing his grip, but instead of taking a fall toward the rim of hatches, he let go with his feet and pivoted through the air, striking the woman across the back with his knees and pinning her against the ladder. He grabbed the wrist of her right hand.

"I'm sorry. I have to take you hostage. I don't want to have to blow up this ship.''

With a look of pure horror, she gazed at Chayn's clenched fist. Chayn did not know what she imagined to be in it, but her imagination had saved the moment. Oddly, she didn't seem to be personally frightened of him.

"Please!" Chayn begged. "I have to find a safe place to hide! I think this may all have been a mistake from the beginning! I need time to think!"

The woman looked from Chayn's genuine expression of desperation to his fist. "Don't push that thing! I can help you! I'll call security!"

"No!" Chayn bellowed, then softed his voice. "Just you. Help me until I have time to think. I don't want to see a uniform. I mean it. If I catch sight of a uniform, I'll blow this ship apart!"

Chayn had never seen such courage in a person before. She literally sweated with the stress of decision. She didn't panic and fear for her own safety did not overpower her. She licked her moist red lips with the pink tip of her tongue, her eyes locked onto his. He could almost see the gears turning inside her head.

"Okay," she said. "We have to get strapped down for launch." She glanced at a watch built into the arm of her coveralls. "We have about thirty-five minutes."

"No tricks," Chayn warned.

She glanced at his fist. "No tricks. I promise. We'll talk about this after initial acceleration has passed."

"I'm not letting you out of my sight," Chayn said. "I won't talk with anyone right now. Can you handle it?"

She nodded eagerly. "I was just checking on an error in inventory. It's not important now. As long as my crew chief knows where I am, he won't be needing me right away."

They climbed down to the rim of hatches and walked around the drum. The woman stopped and nodded to a hatch at her feet. She touched a disk set in the bulkhead. The hatch irised open. A ladder led down through a shiny tube to a deck some ten meters below. Chayn led the way. He doubted that the woman would try to escape. Her loyalty was to the Betafax. That much was obvious.

At the bottom of the ladder, Chayn looked down a deserted corridor stretching into the distance. He could no longer feel the rotation of the ship. It felt like a normal gravity field. But the interconnecting corridors would have a pronounced, upward curve to them. Chayn didn't take well to an environment of curved floors. He suspected he had been raised and born in an envirnment like this, but his roots were on the surface of a long lost world. Villimy had painted him beautiful word pictures of the flat landscape of a planetary surface, an open sky, and light flooding from a single sun. Rashanyn had never known such an environment.

Chayn tried to keep his eyes off the woman as she descended behind him. Contaminated by his deceit, he didn't want to add lascivious conduct to his growing list of crimes. He respected this woman more than she'd ever know.

She led the way down the corridor. A door opened ahead of them and a man in a crimson robe bordered with metallic gold emerged and walked just ahead of them. Chayn's nerves screamed, but the woman strolled along, her hips swaying, without visible indication that she had problems of any kind. The man turned into another door and several more later, the woman turned and gestured to a closed door.

Chayn gestured for her to go in first. They entered a dark room. The woman turned on the lights. It was a cramped cabin containing little more than a pair of bunks, sanitation facilities partitioned off by a sheet of metal, a small desk with a viewscreen and a nearby food and drink dispenser built into a wall.

"There's no one assigned here." The woman looked worried. "Someone might find out. They might know you're aboard when they launch. The extra weight, you know."

"On a ship this size?"

She nodded. "Your weight will make a difference in fuel consumption."

Chayn glanced again at the desk. The surface contained a keyboard. He glanced down at the side of the desk and breathed a sigh of relief. The inevitable cable curved from a field plate to the wall. "What's this?" he asked.

"Data retrieval. General information for the passengers."

Chayn couldn't interface with the girl watching. "What happens when we launch?"

"A steward sees to the passengers." She nodded to the bunks. Chayn noticed the straps. "A sedative is administered automatically. There's a biomed unit built into one of the straps. The crew takes care of itself, but the setup is the same."

Inspecting the cabin, Chayn opened a panel and found

himself looking at packaged utility coveralls. He ripped open the package. They were tailored for a smaller physique, but were constructed of a stretch material to fit all sizes. Chayn wondered if they'd stretch fifty percent beyond their capacity. He still wore the special outfit that Obrian's technicians had provided him with and he found the plumbing necessities uncomfortable. He started stripping the coveralls off.

"Sir! What are you going to do?"

Chayn grinned at her and shook his head. "Nothing like what you're thinking. Turning your head doesn't require much effort."

Chayn partially turned his back, but could feel the woman watching as he changed, the both of them aware of his massive build in comparison with Rashanyn norms. The fresh coveralls were snug, fitting the contour of his body like a second skin, but they were elastic enough to avoid restricting full movement of his limbs. Chayn shoved the old pair of coveralls down a disposal chute, severing his ties with the fake computer console in the cargo hold.

Chayn opened another package of coveralls. "Get into the lower bunk."

Reluctantly, the woman did as she was told. She strapped herself in, knowing that to be Chayn's intentions. For the first time, he sensed her worrying about her personal safety.

"I'm not going to hurt you. I need time to think and I don't want you watching me. I'm going to put these coveralls over your head. You aren't helpless. Just promise that you'll be still and won't cause me any trouble."

She nodded acquiescence. Chayn laid the coveralls over her upper torso and head. "I know this is demeaning," Chayn said. "It can't be helped."

She didn't bother arguing the point.

"By the way, what's your name?"

"Joan."

"I'm Chayn. Nice to know you, Joan. Just lie still, don't

ask questions. I don't even want to know you exist for the next few minutes. Will we have some warning before launch?''

"A horn will sound ten minutes before ignition. A siren will blow one minute before and a countdown will be sounded during the last thirty seconds."

"When do you have to report in?"

"Within another five or ten minutes." Her voice quavered now.

"It'll be all right," Chayn said.

He didn't dare comfort her further. Fear was his only weapon no matter how reluctantly he wielded it. Enough desperation still came through to convince Joan that she didn't dare take heroic measures to cope with him, but if he relaxed for a moment, she'd be apt to change her mind.

Chayn sat at the desk, pulled loose the field plate and dropped into a simple realm of the processers that drove the screen display. He could feel the detail of their neat, perfect logic. It occurred to him that the human brain functioned in much the same way. A neuron passed a bioelectrical impulse or it didn't. From the binary code arose the enormous capacity of the human brain. Chayn wondered about the nature of the mind, human consciousness, the realm of reality that seemed to lie beyond the physical. He could feel the amused presence of the Watcher, feeling secure in the powers of that advanced entity helping him translate the more involved processing in the main computer network, even if answers to his ponderings weren't forthcoming.

He searched for information on a crew member named Joan. Joan Losa, age 28, native of Illitulan, an atmospheric mining colony orbiting one of the gas giants, assigned as stock clerk and weapons crewperson, CP fourth class, on the five megawatt laser. The computer kept a constant tracer on every passenger and crew member aboard the Betafax. Most identities were tagged with a green code in Chayn's mental analogy of the data. Joan's had a yellow code. Chayn replaced it with green. He assimilated the manner in which crew members were assigned their tasks. Chayn provided Joan with a special missions assignment by order of a randomly chosen, high-ranking officer. Chayn went over the passenger list, paying little attention to individual names, but wondering if he'd be able to fake an entry. He decided not to try, but discovered that Joan had been right about his weight being detectable. The total mass of the Betafax could be calculated down to the kilogram. Chayn altered the passenger mass listing by the appropriate amount. If they detected the increased mass of the vessel, Chayn wanted them looking for an inanimate object, not a person.

Chayn broke interface. It didn't appear as if he'd escape detection during the entire length of the journey, but if he managed to hang loose for another few hours, he doubted the Betafax would alter trajectory for his benefit alone. He'd still be headed in the right direction. If it hadn't been for Jarl, Jak Tellord and Obrian, he wouldn't have gotten this far. Chayn flexed his hand. He could no longer feel the wire buried in his palm.

Chayn removed the covering from Joan's face. "You won't have to report in," Chayn said. "The screen shows you to be on special assignment for some captain."

Chayn gestured for her to check for herself. With a puzzled expression, she rose and moved to the desk, keying in a data request with amazing skill. "I don't understand," she said. "What did you do?"

"Will anyone be checking on you now?"

"I don't know what this is all about. I don't even know Captain Mallory."

"If it's a mistake, will he know?"

"It can't be an error."

"But if it is?"

"He won't know about it."

Chayn decided that her frown didn't detract from her

beauty at all. He gave her a disarming smile. "Don't worry about it for now."

"Look," Joan said. "I don't know who you are, but you're going to have to explain yourself."

Chayn clenched his right fist, hoping Joan hadn't noticed his empty hand. He held the fist out to her and by the expression on her face, he still had her convinced that he held some kind of firing mechanism for a two-kiloton nuclear device stowed away aboard the ship.

Joan slumped in exasperation. She turned away from him. "They'll catch you when we arrive at Jasper. What are you going to do?"

"Maybe just blackmail them into taking me back. Do you suppose they will?"

"Yes, perhaps you can bargain for your freedom. But you'll have to be firm and not panic or appear frightened. They won't risk the ship on principle."

Chayn's desperation had slipped. He couldn't maintain the facade for much longer. He was a lousy liar and had never considered acting as a career. Of that, he felt certain. Without the element of fear holding Joan at bay, he'd have to resort to physical force to prevent her from escaping to give warning of his presence.

"What do you know about Reylaton?" he asked.

"Nothing."

Chayn sat on the edge of the lower bunk. "I'm not going to be offended by any personal opinions, but I need to know the military's policy toward Reylaton. What do you know about the situation?"

Joan responded to the firmness in Chayn's voice. "Some religious leader assumed power," she said. "We were to give support to a General Pak to go in and arrest the man and return the Council to power." Joan's pupils dilated as she relived the destruction of the hub. She had been close enough to watch it happen. "Some kind of break down damaged life support in the hub of the colony. A transport rammed a docking berth.''

''What's happening now?''

She looked directly at him. ''The brass is returning to Jasper. It'll take weeks, maybe months to rebuild the bays. But there's more going on than I know about.''

''What do you mean?''

''I've heard talk about aliens, invasions, rumors of that kind. General Pak is taking some people from Reylaton to Jasper for a high level conference. That I know for sure.''

''Do you know who they are?''

''Some people from an Institute and some electronics corporation.''

Odd that Trenton and Jarl hadn't suspected him of the strange things happening to computers. Chayn hadn't encountered any evidence that they knew of his ability not only to interface with, but manipulate, data processing systems.

''How much longer to launch?'' he asked.

She glanced at her watch. ''Twenty minutes.''

''What do you think has been happening lately? I mean about the probe incident, the rebellions, the rumors about the aliens. Those things.''

''I have a family,'' Joan said, no longer reluctant to speak with him. These were issues that disturbed everyone. ''They fear an attack by the Blackstar aliens. They've lived with it longer than I have, the fear, I mean. The military doesn't want to start anything, but I understand why people want something done.''

''It's an intolerable standoff. Is that it?''

She nodded.

Chayn didn't dare say anything more. She spoke to him politely, calmly, but he sensed the tension seething below the surface of her composure. She hadn't as yet recognized him as a human being, probably as nothing more than a dangerous object to be handled with care until the nearest opportunity for disposal presented itself.

Chayn began worrying about the launch. He had no idea what ten gravities of acceleration would feel like. He did know that the Rashanyn were a wiry and tough people.

"What can I expect when we launch?" Chayn asked with renewed grimness.

"This entire cabin pivots on gimballs. The pressure of acceleration and deceleration will always be a downward pressure to you. You'll notice the hesitation sometimes that allows the cabins to swing around and orient itself to inertial forces. Ten gravities is a strain on civilians. You may black out, but it will be only temporary, a matter of seconds."

"What about the full gravity of acceleration afterward? How long does that last?"

"This is a high-speed run. It will last one day. Right at the moment, we are in a large, drum-shaped compartment that rotates when we're not under power. During acceleration, the rotation is stopped and the corridor outside becomes a vertical shaft. Down will be toward the stern of the ship. There will be a hydraulic lift in operation. There will be a day of free fall afterwards, then another day of deceleration."

Chayn nodded, anticipating lots of trouble.

"We'd better get strapped in," Joan told him minutes later.

Chayn clenched his fist, trying not to forget about his imaginary triggering device.

The horn sounded through the cabin, a low-pitched, foreboding background of sound coming from a speaker on the desk screen. Strapped into the upper bunk, Chayn wondered how much he had overlooked in his ignorance of this primitive form of space travel. Perhaps Joan had already sabotaged him in some way, guaranteeing his death during the first few seconds of acceleration by loosening a strap of keying in an overdose of sedative on one of the straps crossing his shoulders.

Then, a siren grated on his nerves, the familiar whooping sound of dire warning followed by absolute silence.

"Acceleration will commence in thirty seconds," a husky woman's voice said over the speaker, the same voice that had warned of an intruder in the ship, the voice of Betafax's computer.

"Acceleration will commence in twenty-five seconds."

Villimy couldn't be more than a few kilometers away from him, a mere, short walk given a flat surface, some gravity and atmosphere. The airless void that separated them could easily have been light years. The imminent launch separating them made the chasm unbridgeable. To the human mind, there could be no difference between a million kilometers and a million light years. Both were incomprehensible distances, measured only by artificial yardsticks and the cold symbols of mathematics.

"Acceleration will commence in ten seconds."

Chayn listened as the pleasant voice counted him down to potential disaster.

"Three, two, one. Ignition."

Nothing happened.

"Launch."

An invisible hand shoved Chayn into oblivion.

Eighteen

Villimy inspected her new quarters. Jak Tellord followed her around anxiously. There were four rooms with low hanging ceilings, well furnished, but showing haste in preparation. Plumbing and conduit ran along the walls. The floor consisted of metal grating in places, masses of wiring and switching boxes visible in the subfloor. The rest was covered in rugs of varying patterns and colors.

The living room contained a wallscreen, the bedroom a closet filled with a wardrobe made to Villimy's proportions and specifications. The kitchen contained a food and water dispenser, the bathroom complete with a refrigerated shower. And she had a small, fourth chamber. It contained a control console tied in directly with one of the disused drone stations.

"This isn't a prison," Jak said, eager for her compliance. "But this console gives you considerable freedom to move around as well as complete security. You can open and close the garage doors by remote control. You have access to fifty robot units. Radio control antennae run everywhere in these sublevels. Your frequency can't be traced back to here."

"This apartment isn't located on any schematic," Jak said. "Topside doesn't know it exists. Only the team that constructed it knows you're here." Jak's breath gave forth billowing clouds of water vapor in the frigid air. Villimy had the temperature down to her satisfaction. Jak was freezing, eager to leave, but more eager for her approval.

"We have to appear innocent to Kraken. We can't be implicated in a conspiracy. From time to time, we'll give false reports of sightings of you and Chayn in the sublevels. You'll appear to be moving around the circumference of Reylaton and we hope to lead Kraken away from this section. But for your own safety, you should stay out of sight."

Villimy turned quickly enough to startle Jak. "Why do you fear my disapproval? I appreciate your support, Jak. I will refrain from harming your people, directly or indirectly."

Jak sighed and nodded. He sat down on the couch, throwing his arms across his chest in a futile effort to keep warm. He looked up at her. "You're not going to sit passively by and let events run their course," Jak said. "That has me worried."

Villimy paced in front of Jak. His eyes followed her quick, graceful movements. "I am a stranger in this land," she said. "I follow Chayn and support him. He is my only connection to life. Now, Chayn is elsewhere, but I act in his behalf."

Villimy faced Jak, looking down at him. "Does Chayn ignore your plight while he fights to regain his starcraft? He is a man like yourself. I am not quite human by your standards and I find your culture and your environment alien. But Chayn's mission is also mine, even when he is not conscious of the things he desires. Perhaps Chayn can help solve the larger, more serious problems of your people. Kraken is a negative influence in Rashanyn. When Chayn returns, Reylaton will be at peace once again. That will be my mission. Kraken is not evil. Men are not evil. But some beliefs and some emotions are destructive. Those I will destroy by a power that Kraken alone has given me. If I am accused of being a demon, then I will behave as such, but I'll demonstrate in the end that we are not really enemies. I am offended that I must defend my honor again and again."

"That's exactly what has me so worried."

Villimy put her hands on Jak's arms and pulled him to his feet. Thrown off-balance by her abruptly intimate behavior, Jak stood and faced her with a surprised expression.

"Perhaps I make you very nervous." She kissed Jak on his cool cheek. "But I am honored by what you feel for me. Besides, all that adrenalin is good for your nervous system."

Jak walked to the apartment entrance in a daze. "It's your show, Villimy. If you can pull it off, I sure won't object. Just don't let Kraken catch you. I don't want to see that happen.''

When Jak left, Villimy went through the apartment once again, ensuring she had everything she'd need to hold out on her own for the next few days. She refused to think beyond that.

She turned the wallscreen to the Church channel and the continuing marathon in progress for the search for the two aliens infesting Reylaton. Villimy recognized two aspects of the psychology behind the focus on that particular issue. To begin with, she gave Kraken credit for more intelligence than he seemed to display. She suspected that Kraken used the issue of dangerous aliens to keep the crisis alive in Reylaton. Others seemed to be going along with the momentum to keep the population from confronting the consequences of the rebellion and the economic impact of the damaged hub. As the hysteria caught on, the search through the sublevels took on the aspect of a solemn, religious ceremony. The screen showed armed black-robed troops moving through the sublevels, clearing out a section and moving through with devices that could detect a single human body in the area. As each section was secured, the population moved back in if the area was inhabited and guards stationed at critical locations to monitor passing traffic. Villimy spent the next hour studying the Church of Rashanyn in depth, its beliefs, social and political structures, correlating what she learned with events in progress.

She went into the small room with the control console and studied camera views of the drone garage Jak had given her to use. One machine in particular caught her attention, a small, multi-armed device that moved about on treads. Each pair of mechanical hands were easily as agile and flexible as human hands. Then she noticed a larger machine equipped with a laser cutting torch. Villimy decided she wanted the torch mounted on the smaller, multi-armed drones. She could use other drones to transfer the device. The only delicate modification necessary would be to neutralize an electronic circuit that prevented the cutting torch from being activated unless aimed at a target not more than a meter away, a precaution that prevented the tool from becoming a weapon. Villimy wanted a weapon.

She napped and snacked on protein cakes on and off for the six hours it took to complete the task. Then, she welded pieces of heat-resistant shielding onto the drone, enough to offer protection from laser beams without impairing camera views or the flexibility of the arms.

The drone had six arms. Any two could be operated manually. The other four were programmable. There were eight cameras on the machine. Early the following morning, the drone spun and twisted about the inside of the garage with amazing rapidity, four of its arms waving about just for the psychological effect, two under Villimy's direct control. With her hands in the gloved master unit and her feet controlling direction and speed with foot pedals, she practiced moving about, picking up tools from the floor at top speed as she passed, tossing them against imaginary targets against concrete walls. The lasers scorched the walls black. In four hours of practice maneuvers, the battery level fell only twelve percent.

Topside, the polarity Villimy had anticipated became apparent. The hysteria intensified among only a minority of the population. Reylaton was possessed by Dark Stargod agents programmed to sabotage the city during the invasion of the Blackstar aliens. But the majority of the city, the silent majority, increasingly recognized that Reylaton had fallen into the hands of a fanatic. They would tolerate the situation as long as Kraken behaved in a manner reasonable enough to reflect to the Rashanyn government, military and Church authorities, their discontent with the chronic reign of terror the Blackstar aliens imposed upon them. They would remove Kraken from power if he became unmanagable. Chayn had convinced Kraken that he dealt with superhuman powers. That also would be Villimy's strategy. The topsiders would see little of her antics. If Kraken didn't quite believe in his own doctrine, he soon would. Kraken would be plagued by Villimy Dy.

Villimy drove the drone from the garage in the evening, selecting a main corridor and driving for three hours before parking it for a rest. She drove for another three-hour shift, then another, interspersing the ordeal with naps and meals. Within a day, she moved the drone halfway around the torus of Reylaton, attracting little attention during the journey. She parked the drone in an abandoned, unlit garage and waited for the next wave of searchers to pass through that area.

Villimy met them at dawn, a party of ten, black-robed figures passing through a main aisle on foot. Villimy wheeled the drone around ahead of them to block their path.

"For whom do you search?" Villimy said, her mechanical voice echoing through the silence.

The group stopped dead at the sound of the inhuman voice, bewildered by the strange creature of metal blocking their path. They knew perfectly well the function of the drones. They had not expected to be confronted by one in this manner.

"Identify yourself!" The leader of the squad stepped forward, swinging his rifle down toward the drone.

"Villimy Dy."

She fired, a pencil beam of crimson light, detonating the rifle in a ball of white hot plasma. The man fell backward, throwing his arms across his eyes. Villimy shot through the group, grabbing two rifles as she lunged through the wall of bodies. Her treads bounced on the pavement as someone fell across the drone. Villimy drove into the clear, turned and fired twice in rapid succession at rifles lowering to fire on her. Others scrambling to their feet made a mad dash for cover. Villimy fired upon them, striking the men in their knee joints. Despite the pain of the injuries, Rashanyn medical technology would have no difficulty reconstructing knee joints. The public would hear of minor wounds incurred in battle, but Kraken's witch hunters would suffer. The air filled with screams. Villimy turned and drove rapidly away.

An hour later, Villimy watched a group of black-robed figures firing upon harmless drones approaching in formation down the main aisle. Exploding batteries sent gouts of flame bursting through the plastic and metal bodies. The drones spun out of control crashing into the wall, each other, careening onto their sides and rolling in coils of black smoke. Angered men in blue coveralls converged on the scene. Villimy laughed aloud in her hidden apartment. Any complication would heighten Kraken's difficulties.

The next group of searchers did not attempt to fire on her. As she passed through their midst, she grabbed two rifles, turned and fired on others as fast as they were lowered toward her drone. Ten men were no match for her reflexes, nor those of the drone. She fled into a side corridor, sought out a darkned and isolated area, and shut down for a nap.

Villimy routed occasional guards stationed at their posts, but the larger search parties were more difficult to track down. In order to conserve her batteries, Villimy studied a schematic of Reylaton for the location of the nearest elevator shafts from topside, planning for a major ambush. Already, the public broadcasts were reporting incidents involving a rogue drone routing search parties and the harassment maintenance crews suffered in performing their vital duties. Church newscasts reported a demon disfiguring the righteous and holy. The rift deepened between the Church and the general population.

Villimy took up position in front of a main elevator shaft, hidden in the recesses of a nearby corridor. An hour later, the doors slid open. Twenty to thirty of the armed figures in black emerged—wearing laser armor.

Villimy opened fire on the rifle barrels, still a highly

vulnerable target. The exploding power packs caused more injury than Villimy intended inflicting. Two or three of men fell dead of facial burns. Villimy ducked behind the cover of the corridors and fired at exposed feet.

The drone took a laser hit from behind, the image on the screen dancing. She swung around and switched the cameras from visual to infrared. Three men rushed her in the darkness, her shields glowing red hot from the assault. Villimy fired three times and the men fell screaming, curling into fetal positions. Unable to retreat down the corridor blocked with their bodies, Villimy moved back into the broad aisle, taking a rapid succession of laser hits across her shields. Two of her cameras went dead. Villimy switched to others, firing at the source of the quick red beams with unerring accuracy. She swung the camera turret around, rolling at top speed down the aisle, but no one dared follow. Three kilometers away, she pulled into a darkened recess in one of the corridors and shut down.

Villimy stood and stretched tight muscles, moving out from behind the console. She ate alone in the silence of the apartment, feeling an almost sexual excitement and recognizing anger satiated by the destruction she wreaked through the sublevels. The crisis would grow as Kraken desired, but it would soon grow beyond his capacity to control it. Eventually he'd destroy the drone. But there'd be others.

Villimy heard Jak approaching long before he entered the apartment. The hollow sound of his feet against the sheet metal of the air vents outside carried from a considerable distance. Still, he stood in the open doorway to ensure she recognized him before entering.

Villimy sat at the kitchen table in Jak's line of sight. He joined her, swinging a chair around backward, folding his arms across the backrest. "You've been busy," he said.

"Isn't that what you expected of me?"

"What do you hope to accomplish except to infuriate Kraken?"

"Nothing but just that. His fury makes people uneasy."

"Me included," Jak said. "He'll just bring in larger weapons and more armor. That laser of yours isn't much of a weapon."

"Larger weapons and more armor will slow down the search parties. I don't need much of a weapon to stop them. I want to be small and relatively harmless, an underdog taking on the best Kraken has to pit against me. Besides, how do you suppose Kraken will react?"

"I don't understand what you're getting at," Jak said. He pulled together an insulated jacket he now wore. With a smile, Villimy rose and fetched the man a cup of hot beverage. Jak accepted it with an appreciative smile.

"Kraken is a megalomaniac," Villimy said. "He will take my success as a personal affront. I insult his stargods and his concept of a good that should reign victorious over evil. It's part of your religion, Jak. You were expelled from the Galaxy of Man because you sinned. You are doomed to fight evil until you win over it. Many religions have the same symbology. The psychology of man is the same wherever he is found. Much religion of this type is based on guilt. If Kraken cannot cope with my behavior, eventually he will experience guilt and fear. And nobody appreciates such emotions of weakness in a leader of men."

"So what will Kraken do?" Jak said.

"He depends upon others to act for him. He will beg for more support and will begin losing what support he has."

After an hour's worth of pleasant small talk, Jak left uneasily. He relied heavily upon Villimy's assessment of the situation. For the first time, he forgot about their differences and had talked to her as another human being, one for whom he felt concern in his helplessness.

Kraken spoke in the evening.

"The demons turn our own technology against us," Kraken said, his eyes boring into the camera. He sat at his desk, his composure unsteady. "They grovel in the darkness from which they sprang. They remain in a position to sabotage Reylaton the day the forces of the Blackstar attack Rashanyn. And yet, I hear rumors that the so-called aliens are merely defending their lives against the forces of the Church. Many have dropped away from the old ways and the old beliefs upon which our civilization is founded. What will you be saying the day the demons destroy vital equipment in the sublevels and endanger the lives of your mates and children? Do you believe the demons fight a selective war upon Reylaton? Do you believe they differentiate between the Church and the neutral citizens of Reylaton?

"My people, I beg of you! Support our cause! We are not your enemy! The Church is our life, our only hope! Let me not find citizens of Reylaton siding with these creatures against the Church! Let me not find forces of the Dark Stargod infiltrating the loyalty of our sublevel citizenry! These creatures can be apprehended if we receive the cooperation we need from you. Reasonable men cannot object to having these noncitizens, these aliens, these demons incarcerated, interrogated, and incapacitated from causing any more injury and destruction. What sense does it make to turn the unknown loose upon Reylaton and have faith in their good will and no faith at all in your Church, your civil government, and in your own people?"

Villimy shut off the wallscreen. She knew what Kraken would do next in desperation and she had to block his move. She went to the console and cut in the screen. The screen showed only darkness. Villimy cut in the infrared filters. Still, only darkness. More curious than concerned, Villimy sat at the controls and switched to other cameras.

Darkness.

Villimy tried to move the drone.

"It's no use," a deep voice said over the speaker. "We have located your drone and deactivated it. The drone will be turned over to Kraken. Speak with our leader if you dare, demon. Our technicians will identify the origin of this machine. You will not be difficult to locate after that."

"I will speak with Kraken," Villimy said.

"Then, you will die," the voice returned.

"On the contrary. You have struggled long and hard to sign your own death warrants."

Villimy leaned back in her seat and waited. Soon, the face of Kraken would invade even this screen. Perhaps they could trace the origin of the drone, but the small accelerometer in the drone would also provide Villimy with the location where she would speak with Kraken.

Soon, the battle they fought would be on a very personal level. Villimy did not like the role of a demon. She'd correct that bit of misinformation eventually, given half the chance. It would be Kraken's undoing.

Nineteen

Chayn awoke and focused his eyes with difficulty. Something touched the end of his nose, a transparent, cylindrical object. A hand grasped the contoured grip of the weapon. Chayn ran his eyes up the arm to a face. Cold, blue eyes were locked onto his. An expression of outrage distorted the young man's face.

"Who is he?" the man demanded, his voice grating through suppressed anger.

He wasn't speaking to Chayn. Joan stood behind the man, a look of pure panic on her face. "I told you, Karl! We knew each other a long time ago on Illitulan. I didn't know he was aboard! Now put that damned thing away before he has you arrested! You can't just barge into a private cabin and intimidate civilian passengers!"

The expression of grim confidence wavered. Karl backed off and shoved his pistol into a shoulder holster. Joan shoved her way between the two men. Chayn looked up into her own expression of outrage. "Where is it!" she demanded in a harsh whisper while undoing Chayn's straps.

"It has a timing mechanism. I set it for an hour and hid it before we strapped in."

Joan fell for the unlikely story, Chayn's imaginary triggering device for his nuclear warhead secure for the moment.

"Who the hell is he?" Karl demanded. "If he's from Reylaton, it's sure the hell unlikely you met him on Illitulan. Joan, what the hell is going on?"

"I'm on special assignment, Karl! Check for yourself! Then, please, get out of here! I told you it was over between us!"

Karl sneered at her. He spun around and ran his fingers over the keyboard to the desk screen, stiffening when he encountered the reassignment Chayn had slipped into the computers. "What the hell's going on, Joan! Captain Mallory is in engineering!"

Joan shook with fear and anger. "I told you, Karl, he's a friend of mine. My mission assignments are none of your business. Now get out of here!"

Chayn sat up and tried standing, shocking Karl by his size and bulk. "You don't know that man," Karl said. "I know you better than you think. He's not your type."

Joan unzipped her coveralls and slipped them over her shoulders. The single piece garment slipped down her slender torso, hanging up around the well-rounded curve of her hips. She stunned both men, but her behavior had special significance for Karl.

"I told you that we know each other," Joan hissed, her voice ice. "What the hell do you want from us? A demonstration?"

Karl's face reddened. He turned and left the cabin. Chayn

191

noticed with a twinge of concern that the corridor outside the cabin no longer existed. Karl, the rejected lover, entered an elevator he had placed on temporary hold.

When Karl closed the door behind him, Chayn glanced once at the alluring, finely sculptured torso of the girl, forcing his eyes to focus on something of more neutral emotional content. A wall sufficed. Joan pulled the coveralls back over her shoulders. She zipped up, walked to a corner of the cabin and began crying.

Chayn kept his mouth shut. He paced the room, eyeing the desk screen, curious about the progress of the ship. Without most of the three day journey still ahead, he walked the narrow edge of disclosure, arrest, imprisonment. Joan spun on him suddenly.

"Damn you! What right do you have to do this to me! What right do you have to threaten the lives of five hundred people!"

Chayn tried to look determined. He clenched his right fist. "It'll be over soon."

"And we'll all be dead! Is that it?"

"I don't think so," Chayn said. "Just hold things together until we reach Jasper."

"What's that going to accomplish? What do you hope to gain? Jasper's the biggest military base in the whole system!"

"Let me worry about that," Chayn said. "I know what I'm doing."

Joan didn't bother to reply. She joined him, pacing the cramped cabin from wall to wall. In the stillness, Chayn could hear the elevator passing their cabin.

"Who do you stand behind?" Chayn said. "In the privacy of your own thoughts, do you sympathize with the civilian populations of Rashanyn? Shouldn't the military make some preparations for at least an adequate defense against an attack by the Blackstar aliens?"

She spun on him again. Somewhere in her experience,

she had found it a very effective gesture. She didn't move as quick as Villimy, but she communicated her anger quite well. "Yes! Yes, I think the military should be doing something! They've been gearing for war for over a century!"

Chayn forced himself to sit down and appear calm. "Explain that to me."

"I don't have to explain anything to you! It's classified information! They'll court martial me for talking to you!"

Chayn shook his head. "Think about it. You're trying to talk a religious fanatic out of blowing up the ship and killing five hundred people. Why not give me any information that'll help me to reconsider my stand? What am I going to do with it? Are they going to let me go back to Reylaton to tell everyone?"

Joan remained expressionless for long seconds. "The military doesn't want the Blackstar aliens to know about the mobilization. The probe incident would have revealed that to them. They want the civilian population to remain in the dark so that the aliens won't detect any social changes. We don't know how far advanced the aliens are or what they learn or can deduce from the information they gain by the probes."

"Then Kraken's rebellion is a waste of time?"

"All of the rioting and rebellion! All of the pain and suffering! All of it is a waste of time! Do they think we're stupid? Why in the name of Rashanyn do they believe the military would refrain from a military solution to an invasion?"

Chayn felt suddenly depressed. "Things sure do get complicated."

The desk screen began beeping. Joan gave it a look of horror. "It's Karl. It must be."

"Answer it," Chayn said. "Use your own judgment."

"You trust me, I suppose," Joan said.

"Emphatically."

Joan slipped into the seat before the desk. The screen

bloomed to life. "Captain Mallory knows nothing about a transfer," Karl said. "I checked the passenger lists. There's nobody from Illitulan aboard this ship except you. The stewards say there's nobody missing from their assigned quarters. Who is he, Joan?"

"Let me handle this, Karl. I'm warning you. Stay out of my affairs." She switched off the screen.

"Will he?"

She shook her head. "We've been together for over a year. He's jealous."

"You're one hell of a woman to lose," Chayn said, regretting the compliment.

She turned and gave him an odd look.

"Just an observation."

Joan continued to stare at him. Chayn figured he was rapidly losing control of the situation.

"What if he tells?" she said.

"Can we hold out here until we dock?"

"Probably. But they'll get you in the end. They can evacuate the atmosphere, drop the temperature to absolute zero, gas you or burn you out."

"With you in here with me as a hostage?"

Her eyes widened. She glanced again at his right fist, this time with doubt in her eyes. "I don't think they'll risk the ship."

"I don't want to have to use it," Chayn said, holding his fist out for effect. "It's not what I want to accomplish. Like I said, maybe this mission isn't necessary after all."

Joan nodded. "Okay. I can still help, but they have to believe that you mean me harm. They have to believe you can't be reasoned with."

"You don't believe I'd blow up the ship?"

She gave him a sharp, doubtful look. "No. I think you're bluffing."

"Joan, don't back me into a corner."

"No, I didn't mean it like that," she said quickly. "I

just mean you're not a fanatic. You're not deranged or anything like that."

Chayn leaned back on the bunk. "But you thought so at first?" He grinned.

"I thought you were going to rape and kill me and blow up the ship, damn you! Now stop teasing me!"

"I'm not teasing. I just thought the military consisted of fanatics and cold-blooded. . ."

"You thought *we* were fanatics!"

The screen beeped. Joan answered. A different face stared over her shoulder. Chayn didn't bother moving from view. Joan tensed in recognition of the uniformed officer.

"CP Fourth Class Joan Losa?"

"Sir!"

"What's going on?"

Joan glanced back at Chayn with an expression of hopelessness. Now the fun and games commenced, Chayn decided.

"I have a man here who claims he has a nuclear warhead smuggled aboard the ship. He's got some kind of triggering device in his hand. He's holding me hostage."

"I see."

The screen went blank.

Joan slumped. "It's the only way."

"I know. Tell them I won't talk with anyone. You handle public relations."

The minutes dragged by. Chayn kept an ear perked for the elevator passing the cabin. He didn't want a direct confrontation, but decided they wouldn't try it so soon.

The screen beeped. Joan responded.

"I would like to speak with this man in the cabin with you, Joan."

"He says he won't speak with anyone. He says he wants to go to Jasper. He says he won't harm anyone if we don't interfere."

"I see. Are you okay?"

"I'm fine. He seems reasonable enough, but I'm sure he means business."

"We'll assume he does, Joan. I'll be back to you in a few minutes."

The screen went blank.

"How long will they take to search the cargo?" Chayn asked.

"Twelve hours," she said after a moment's thought. "They won't be certain even then. They'd have to disassemble everything down to individual components to be sure. How well hidden is it?"

"They won't find it," Chayn said with absolute confidence.

Minutes dragged by in silence. Joan stretched out on the upper bunk with an arm across her eyes. She surprised Chayn by dozing off. The constant pressure had drained her.

Chayn slipped over to the desk and pulled loose the field plate. Deciding to risk a few minutes of interface, he entered the computer network, searching at random for anything of interest. He discovered a general alert in progress and large numbers of personnel reassignments to the cargo hold. Communications were working hard translating information into binary signals transmitted to Jasper. Nearby civilians were being moved and the lifeboat bays had been activated for immediate use.

Chayn broke interface.

Joan was turned onto her side watching him. "What were you doing?"

"Nothing. Just curious."

"You looked like you were in a trance of some kind."

Chayn bunched his right hand into a fist again, but Joan had to have seen his hand over the field plate. By now, she knew there was more to the situation than met the eye. She lay back down and pretended to rest again. Chayn returned to the bunk and stretched out below her. He felt like dozing himself.

"The cargo hold was in vacuum," Joan said. "How did you survive?"

"A phony computer console, the one you were checking on when we ran into each other. There's a life support system inside it."

"This has been a well-planned operation, then," she said.

"I've had a great deal of help."

"They'll believe there really is a warhead when they find the console. They'll leave you alone for now."

Chayn sighed. The game was up. "There's no warhead?"

"I saw your hand. You had nothing in it."

Chayn flexed his fingers. "Good. I don't like lying to people anyway."

"Do you expect to continue this charade?"

"I'd sure like to."

"What were you doing with your hand over the field plate?" There was a distinct edge to her voice.

"It would be hard to explain. I was interfaced with the computer, trying to find out what they're doing. They've assigned a lot of people to search the holds. They've activated the lifeboats for immediate launch and they're communicating with Jasper for instructions."

Silence followed.

"How can you do a thing like that?" Joan asked finally.

"Like I said, it would take awhile to explain. It's how I escaped Reylaton and Kraken. It's how I damaged the docking bays at Reylaton's hub. I prevented the military from boarding Reylaton and enabled myself to escape."

"Why?"

Chayn decided to tell her. It felt good to speaking the truth for a change. "I helped the sublevel maintenance people keep Kraken and the military from tearing up the city. In exchange, they constructed the phony console to help get me to Jasper. I'm headed there to pick up my ship. The military confiscated it when we arrived."

"We?"

"You've heard rumors of the aliens on Reylaton?"

"Yes."

"I'm one of them. The other is still on Reylaton."

More silence passed.

"You don't have a bomb, but you can harm the ship just as you wrecked the hub at Reylaton."

That had never really occurred to Chayn. He had lied to Joan, manipulating her into cooperating with him. All along, he really had the same destructive potential.

"That never occurred to me," Chayn said. "I'm not interested in damaging this ship."

"You'd let them come in here and take you into custody?"

Chayn sighed, backed into a solid corner. "I wouldn't harm the ship to stop them."

"I've heard about you," Joan said, her voice calm and unconcerned on the surface. "They were just rumors. What do you want to do? Just leave if you get your ship back?"

"It has a faster-than-light capability. I've made friends on Reylaton. A few are on this ship. I want to visit the black hole and learn something about the life form there. It might help. But I'm not trusted. Kraken's ready to burn me alive and the military wants my head on a platter to dissect neuron by neuron for information on how to operate my ship. I don't intend cooperating with anyone on that basis."

The screen beeped. Joan slipped off the bunk, dropping past him to answer the call. She sat before the desk and touched a key.

"Joan, are you okay?"

"Yes, sir, I'm fine."

"We've found the console. We know how he entered the ship. Do you have some idea of his identify?"

"No, sir."

"Is he letting you talk openly with me?"

"Yes, sir."

"Do you have any information on the warhead?"

"No, sir."

"Can we ask a few questions through you?"

She looked over her shoulder. Chayn took note of her alertness, her intelligence, and composure. He nodded.

"You can ask questions through me, sir."

"Ask him if his name is Chayn Jahil."

Chayn wondered if it would confuse them to deny it. He set the thought aside and nodded.

"He responded in the affirmative, sir."

"Ask him if he will speak with General Pak or Trenton. He knows both individuals."

"Trenton," Chayn said. "Tell him he can send Trenton down."

"Did you hear that, sir?"

"I heard." The screen went blank.

Joan began pacing.

"Don't worry," Chayn said. "They're more afraid of me than any old two-kiloton bomb. And they'll consider you a genuine hostage. When this is over, you'll damned well get a medal and a promotion. When Trenton gets here, you can leave."

Fifteen minutes passed before Joan said, "Can I stay if I want?"

Chayn sat up. "Why would you want to stay?"

She gave him a nervous smile. "I'm scared. I know what's happening here, but if I go back, they'll interrogate and isolate me. I don't want that right now."

"Then you're still a hostage and I'm still a terrorist. You can be my press secretary."

"Who is this Trenton the Commander spoke of?"

"A friend. Was that the Commander of the Betafax IV you were speaking to?"

"Yes."

"Well, Trenton and General Pak are friendly enemies, so to speak. I don't have anyone I'd consider a real enemy except Kraken and maybe not even him in the end. I seem to be surrounded by people who'd simply prefer to see me dead, missing, incapacitated or a bit more cooperative. Fear does funny things to people."

"To a whole civilization."

Chayn agreed. "Some can handle it and some can't."

"I can."

"I know damned well you can."

Trenton finally arrived. Chayn rose to greet him as he entered the apartment. "I never thought I'd see you again," Chayn said. "What are you doing here?"

"I'm on my way to Jasper to give the brass a briefing on you and Villimy Dy. I never thought I ad see *you* again."

"We both thought wrong."

"Why didn't you stay with Jarl when the shooting started?"

"Dropping down that manhole was Villimy's idea. It turned out to have been for the best."

"It looks to me like you're in the same position you would have been in if you had cooperated. Is Villimy with you?"

"She's back on Reylaton with friends and stirring up trouble for Kraken."

"I'm glad you found a few friends who could do you some good," Trenton said. "I take it you're after your ship."

"I decided to take a crack at getting it back. Right at the moment, it doesn't look as if I'll succeed."

Trenton remained by the door, glancing at his watch from moment to moment. Chayn empathized with the man's plight, but they had lost the rapport they had shared on Reylaton just after their arrival. Trenton had lost his Institute and had been caught up in the turmoil of events.

"Chayn, the military is too powerful. They won't allow you to have the starcraft back. Right now, you're openly challenging their authority. They won't allow that."

"Are you here to talk me into giving up?"

"What else is there, Chayn? They know you don't have a nuclear warhead on board."

Trenton looked around the cabin. Chayn knew he searched for evidence of Jarl's interface equipment. By now, he probably suspected that he had been responsible for the destruction of the hub. He would have had to use the interface to gain access to the Betafax IV. Without it, he posed no more threat to the ship than Joan Losa.

"It's a bad situation for you, Chayn. General Pak is happy to have you aboard. It's what he wanted from the beginning. There's no hard feelings, though. You won't be mistreated, Chayn."

"It's not over that easy," Chayn said. "I'm still a terrorist. I even have a hostage."

Trenton was startled by Joan's sudden smile.

Trenton gazed at him with an open, puzzled expression. "You have something up your sleeves."

"I must have," Chayn said. "You know I'm not stupid."

"That won't stop them from trying to roust you out of here. They won't harm you or Joan, but you must know they have ways to regain control of the situation."

"That's a nice way of putting it, Trenton. I can't stop them from trying."

For the first time, Trenton offered him a weak smile. "Why do I get this depressed feeling that I'm not going to be able to talk you out of this?"

"Go back, Trenton. Tell them that you failed. Let them play their games. If they don't intend to harm us, what difference does it make?"

"They want your cooperation. I know they won't get it. I don't think they deserve it, but there's nothing I can do to help."

Trenton turned back to the elevator. "When it's over, Chayn, we can talk some more. Maybe there are options we haven't considered yet. The military is bound to be cautious, but concessions can be made in time."

Chayn let Trenton leave without saying anything further. They all knew about his interface capability, but they had no way of knowing about the microminiaturized equipment embedded in his flesh.

Joan moved to stand beside him. "Will they take you that easily?"

"No."

"They're going to try something any second now."

They waited, standing in the center of the cabin.

Chayn's ears popped. "Oh, damn," he said. "I think they're going to take away our. . ."

There wasn't enough air left in the room to finish.

Twenty

Villimy stayed within hearing range of the console, waiting to see who might care to speak with her through the captured drone. An hour passed before she heard background noises from the speaker. They had, for a time, disconnected the audio circuits. They had not disconnected the drone's transmitter. The drone's accelerometer had sent clear data all along. Villimy slipped into her seat and waited.

"Are you still there?" a timid voice asked.

"No," Villimy said. "I am not."

"I am Kraken," a much louder, recognizable voice stated. "I wish to speak with you."

"Out of simple curiosity, I will listen."

"What do you hope to gain by your continual attacks upon my men?"

"Self-defense," Villimy said.

"We will find you in the end."

"That is your personal opinion. You are welcome to it."

"Who aids you in the sublevels?"

"I am unaided," Villimy said, not at all regretting the lie. "I do not find your technology difficult to handle."

"I find it difficult to believe that you have avoided the notice of sublevel maintenance personnel."

Villimy smiled. "Why? Am I not supposed to be a demon?"

"Are you?"

"I think the idea is rather silly. I think you play upon the fears of your people."

"I have no choice in what I believe. The Word of Rashanyn provides me with the truth."

"You speak garbage," Villimy said. "A book does not contain enough information to program a small computer. How can it program a man's behavior? Words are symbols for ideas and concepts. Any language allows for only a vague guideline of association. How a book is interpreted is more indicative of the psychology of the reader than the content of the book."

Villimy waited out the silence, wondering if she could trap Kraken into a philosophical debate.

"Give yourself up. You shall be treated with respect."

"No, thank you."

Villimy cut off the drone entirely, knowing better than to try to argue with Kraken. She inspected the data provided by the accelerometer, noting that the drone had been moved in a two-dimensional plane. It hadn't been taken topside. She selected one of the larger drones, wheeled it out of the garage and down the dark corridor, twin headlights casting more light than she needed to see. When she turned into the main aisle, she spotted black-robed figures ahead and decided to play it safe. She pulled off against the wall and shut down except for the cameras and audio.

The men were not on a mission. They sauntered along

slowly, conversing among themselves, their rifles dangling from shoulder straps. A drone approached from the distance, silencing the group. Villimy watched with acute interest. Kraken's men no longer trusted any drone and yet the machines were essential for routine monitoring. How had they arranged to handle the predicament?

The drone spoke. *"Sidula,"* a man's voice sounded. And the search party relaxed, resuming their conversation, the drone continuing on its way, unmolested.

A password. Villimy smiled. Sidula was the name of a stargod famous for a battle against the Dark Stargod during creation. Villimy continued on her way, slowing a half hour later when she sighted three dark figures ahead. With forty-eight drones left in the garage, she risked little by testing out the password.

"Sidula," Villimy said, stopping before the tense group.

Their weapons lowered. She saw a glimmer of light. The screen went dead.

Her voice! They had fired at the sound of her voice!

Villimy switched back to the garage and selected a third drone. It used a memory unit designed for programming the drones for simple tasks to record the password. Slowing the recording down lowered her voice so that it sounded like a man's, but it slowed pronunciation. It took an hour to record digitally the sounds and bunch them back together without raising the tone. When she finished, the password sounded masculine.

She took the third drone back into the main aisle, but Kraken had won a small victory. They had destroyed the second drone only a kilometer or two from the garage. Villimy decided to make a practice of swinging around any other group she encountered to attack from the rear. She'd be helpless if Kraken discovered the garage from which she operated.

Villimy passed the same group of men that had destroyed the second drone. She gave the recorded password and moved on. Moments later, she passed the smoldering wreckage of the second drone and moved off to one side to allow a truck right of way as it stopped to clean up the wreckage. Villimy continued without pause, watching with her rear cameras as a crane lifted the machine onto the back of the truck.

She located the spot where she had last parked the first, laser-armed drone, and began reciewing the accelerometer data. She had no trouble retracing the route Kraken's men had taken in moving the drone to wherever Kraken had spoken to her through it. She encountered search parties with increasing regularity, but her male-sounding recording got her through without incident.

She entered a large, open area. The roof of the sublevel stretched so high above her, the haze of water vapor blocked her view. And yet light as bright as sunlight shone through. Offices and garages clustered in the open, single story structures, probably a dispatch-location for heavy equipment. Drones steered clear of the buildings. Guards were stationed every few meters around the area. Villimy couldn't be certain that Kraken would still be inside, but there were tens, perhaps hundreds of the black-robed militants inside the glass-walled buildings.

Villimy laughed when she saw a nearby train of small, low, flatbed trailers. They were just the right size for her drone to pick up and hold in front of itself as a blast shield. She couldn't resist the opportunity to retaliate.

Several guards were watching as Villimy turned the drone aside, rolled over to the trailers and extended its arms. She twisted its mechanical hands down and explored for a firm grip, then lifted the trailer into the air, hydraulics whining in protest. Villimy swung around toward the cluster of buildings, positioned the trailer as a horizontal shield in front of the drone, and accelerated at full speed.

The trailer blocked her forward view and her other cameras were shot out in the first few seconds, but she knew the drone to be under heavy attack when the metal before the camera began glowing red hot, then emitting white sparks. The drone veered abruptly to one side. Villimy lowered the shield to realign the drone on the building, compensating for a damaged front wheel. At fifty kilometers per hour, the heavy machine careened into the glass wall of an empty office. The screen went dark in the next instant, the controls dead, but she had little doubt that the machine had scattered the wreckage of the offices over the entire area. Villimy chalked up one minor victory for herself.

Villimy went to her bedroom to rest. She stared up at the ceiling, a vague depression setting in, a growing feeling of listlessness. Chayn's absence darkened her world. She shuddered, her thoughts drifting back far enough to recall the eternity she had spent aboard the starship among the dead and decomposing bodies of people she had once known. Villimy Dy hadn't survived that experience, not the person she had once been. The memories of tha launch of the starship were memories of another lifetime, centuries, perhaps millenia, in the past. The ship had been shiny and new, hanging in the void of stars above a bright and green planet. Her people had been alive, their dreams burning like the stars. Even then they had known of the risks of crossing the abyss, but what mind could bother with something as incomprehensible as a four-hundred-light-year rift of blackness and a sleep lasting for centuries. They had left their home world forever, confident of success. Another world awaited them, traded from space-faring aliens for the knowledge of their civilization, a virgin planet in exchange for the contents of their data banks.

Villimy remembered the awakening. Relay panels had shorted and were burning. Others awakened prematurely, dying of frostbite without regaining consciousness. And others thawed, but the impulses to reactivate heart, lungs, and brains never awakened them from their long sleep. Villimy alone survived to find the starship a derelict hanging motionless in the abyss. And then the crypts began to fail, one by one. Corpses rotted, the air turning to a miasmic stench. Perhaps she had gone insane at that time. Perhaps earlier, but probably when the giant, pasty-white, and beady-eyed alien entered the chamber.

These humans did not pair as her people did. To them, mating and childbirth were psychological rather than biological factors of life. Trenton had not known that she would die without Chayn. Chayn did not know. In her madness, her insides had stirred and she had paired with an alien.

And yet, she had a life of sorts to live. If Chayn returned, she would find joy in his love. Together, they would leave for the stars, find her home world, and return to it. She desperately needed to know what had become of her people. She didn't want to be the last of her kind in the universe. If it turned out to be so, she would survive as long as Chayn would have her. For he would be the last of his kind as well. They would know a life beyond the surrealism of dreams and die fulfilled.

Until Chayn returned she would fight to survive. Perhaps Kraken meant not to kill her, but only to imprison her and in doing so, imprison some of his fears. Jak reacted to his fears as well. Violence was not his way. It had not been her way either. Not in those uncountable years in the past on a world that had never known war. Violence there had centered on the strife and stress of pairing, defense and offense against competitors for a mate. Jak would never understand that she fought to defend her life for Chayn, that violence to do so was a deep, psychic drive for her. To explain that to Jak would make her even more alien in his eyes.

Rashanyn would not understand. Chayn might someday.

Villimy sent out another drone to reconnoiter the damage to the cluster of office shacks. The first group of black-robed figures she encountered opened fire on the drone. That meant that they had destroyed two drones in the same general area, headed from the same direction. The search would be narrowing soon.

A running documentary on the wallscreen showed searches being conducted all over the sublevels of Reylaton. Reports were pouring in of the blue-skinned alien sighted in dark corridors from one end of the city to the other. Villimy would have enjoyed some of her infamous reputation if it hadn't been for the apathetic response of the depressed population of the city. But more important than the games she would have enjoyed, Kraken's popularity had fallen off in the atmosphere of anxious, but helpless watchfulness. The documentary stressed the need for more volunteers, chastising the disloyal dropouts who were exchanging their black robes for civilian clothing by the droves. Kraken had already worn thin on the city's preoccupation with the treat of invasion coming from so many different directions.

Villimy recognized Jak's footsteps in the airducts beyond her apartment, stumbling occasionally in the darkness of the maze. It would be, Villimy admitted, difficult for Kraken's forces to find her hiding place built in the complexity of ducting above the floor levels of the sublevel. When he entered, she sat on the couch in the living room and waited for him to say whatever he had on his mind.

"Why don't you lay low for a while, Villimy? The searches are becoming more efficient. They're beginning to pay more attention to air ducts, conduit, and runoff sewers from topside. We've had three searches in my section in the past twenty-four hours and they have devices that can tell if anyone's passed through a little used area recently. This place is not as secure as it was in the beginning."

"Chayn will be back soon," Villimy said. "Kraken is a thorn in the side of Reylaton right now. I want to keep it that way. If Reylaton tolerates Kraken's rule, when Chayn returns, he might not be able to get back into the city."

Jak sighed and sat down in a chair facing her. "If Kraken

finds you here, he'll arrest everyone in this section. At the very least, we'll lose our jobs and be exiled topside. The sublevels are our life, Villimy. You and I must find a way for you to continue with your strategy without risking the welfare of innocent people."

"Has Obrian given you any orders to fulfill?"

Jak shook his head. "His reasoning is still similar to yours. The more noise Kraken makes now, the less tolerant Reylaton becomes later."

"I can leave, Jak."

The optimism in his eyes didn't escape her. "I'm concerned and the idea sounds good to me," he said. "But there's nowhere for you to go. You're my responsibility. You stay. We just have to bat a few ideas back and forth and take some of the pressure off this section. I'm not asking anything more than that from you."

"How tight is security topside?"

Jak leaned back in his chair, refraining from trying to outguess her. "Not very. But you'd be noticeable. Your flesh tone is noticeable. Your sunglasses are too dark. You'd have no elbow room.

"Can you suggest a place for me to stay?"

"I know a few people with apartments topside who are working down here during the emergency. You could steal their ID cards. But you'd better explain what you're up to, Villimy. I'm not cooperating with you if you risk your neck on a foolish scheme."

"What are ID cards?"

"Keys to the city. They operate vending machines and open locked doors. They function as currency on Reylaton as well as identification."

"Arrange for me to steal an ID card, Jak. I want to go topside. I have ideas. When I'm done, I can return here to wait for Chayn."

"Explain yourself, Villimy."

Villimy stood and walked to the wallscreen controls. She

keyed through channels until she encountered an interview in progress between two men.

"Who is he?"

"A former government official."

"Many of the public stations are neutral, aren't they?"

"They're not large enough to get involved with controversial subject matter while Kraken is in power. They can't afford the political pressure or harassement. Unless they corner a really good story, they keep a low profile."

"Reylaton is very quiet," Villimy said. "Kraken is the only colorful, living personality in the whole city. They'd like panel discussions on the possibility of other human civilizations in the galaxy. They don't dare. They want to discuss Kraken's competence as a political leader. They don't dare. But it seems they avoid controversy simply because it doesn't accomplish anything. Talk is just talk. There are so few alternatives to action, doing something about the problems that exist. Everybodies attention is on the Church and Kraken, just watching events unfold."

"So? What's your point?"

"Would they interview me?"

Jak tensed. "Are you serious? Are you just going to walk into a public broadcasting station and ask them if they'll interview you on video?"

"How would they react, Jak? Would they call the police? Would they arrest me on sight? Would they shoot me?"

"They'd be more apt to ask you to leave, close shop for the day, and hide under their desks. You're too hot to handle, Villimy."

"They'd be shocked, but I'm a political refugee as far as they're concerned. The only thing that keeps their ratings alive is following my progress on the sublevels during their newscasts. It's worth a try, Jak. They wouldn't have to ask anything controversial, just what I think of the weather, the latest fashions. Mundane and boring things. But I know they're curious about me. How could the city not be curious about me?"

"You're serious about this?"

"It takes the pressure off you. It throws Kraken off balance and provides me with a new strategy to work with. Reylaton is an emotionally depressed city. Anger is the best release for depression. So far, Kraken has cornered the market on anger, directing it toward me. Those who are secretly supporting me will do so more openly if they see and hear me speak as I am, a human being like themselves despite the differences between us."

"This is something you've been planning very carefully?"

"No, it's just something I came up with. Does it meet with your approval?"

"If you're careful."

Jak left the apartment smiling and Villimy laughed in joy at the depth of her deceitful tact. It seemed like a viable idea, but she had, in fact, made it up on the spur of the moment. Better than Jak, she could foresee the problems she might cause the people of the sublevels. To harass Kraken, she could spread the effects of private war around a little more democratically.

She selected a tunic and trousers Jak had supplied for her. Topside, it would be unnoticeable except for the small blower on the right shoulder necessary to keep a reasonable temperature against her skin. She had adapted somewhat to the excruciatingly high temperatures these humans enjoyed and swore at times that the energy-sapping heat would eventually slow her down to their level. She donned the sunglasses that dimmed the blinding sunlight of Reylaton and decided she would pass for their version of humanity. Standing before a mirror in the bedroom, she smiled at the curve of her body. Back home it had been nothing exceptional, but was considered an unusual asset here. Even Jak had trouble with the conflict between his suppressed lust for her and his repulsion toward her more alien qualities. She would pass for a citizen of Rashanyn, but not upon close examination.

Jak returned two hours later. Villimy had napped. Despite the late hour, her senses were keenly alert.

"I called Obrian," Jak said. "He arranged to have a few people call in to report a simultaneous sighting a ways from here. Kraken won't be able to resist. He's pulling his search parties out of this area."

Villimy left the apartment with a few regrets. There were forty-seven drones left in the garage, the most direct way to deal with Kraken's witch-hunt. Jak led the way. Villimy followed though the air ducts and the hidden panels to a ladder that led to the floor of a dark and deserted corridor. An electric cart awaited them, driven by two armed maintenance personnel. They drove down the main aisle for more than five minutes without seeing one of Kraken's men, then pulled into a dark side corridor. Villimy had little trouble seeing in the dark. The headlights blinded her.

"This is a supply elevator," Jak said. "It leads directly into the first floor of the building where you'll be staying. It was a travel agency a short while back. The building is pretty well empty."

Villimy finally made out the doors of the elevator set into the concrete wall. Jak handed her a small, plastic card. "Do you know how to use this?"

"No."

Jak added a sheet of paper. "Some friends of mine had a quick, brainstorming session. These are instructions on the things you might need to know. Do you know your way around the city?"

"Yes."

"Stay away from people," Jak said. "That means public transportation. If you have to move around, do it in the early morning hours."

Villimy nodded.

"There's a diagram of the building on the back of the instructions."

Villimy climbed out of the cart.

"Villimy, are you sure you're doing what's best for you? You could live in the sublevels forever if you'd keep a low profile. You might not accomplish as much as you'd like topside. The things that are happening are too big for one person to influence. Even Kraken."

"Even Chayn?"

Jak said nothing. Villimy sensed his doubt. But Chayn lived and he would return.

Villimy palmed a disk on the wall alongside the elevator. When the door swung aside, a bright light flooded into the corridor. She stepped into it and turned. Jak and the two men were a gray silhouette against a black background. The doors swished shut and the floor pressed against her feet. Villimy grasped a handrail as the elevator accelerated and gasped as her weight diminished suddenly, then returned to normal. The doors swung aside to a brightly lit, but empty corridor.

Before leaving the elevator, Villimy read the instructions and appreciated the concise and detailed thought that had gone into them. She studied the diagram of the building on the back, then wadded the paper up in her fist, slipping the ID card into a shoulder pocket.

To her left in the corridor, she could see the main entrance to the building. She turned to her right and walked to the end of the corridor. It branched both ways. She turned left and walked diagonally across to a numbered apartment. She slipped the card into a slot in the door frame. The device beeped once.

Many sublevel supervisors maintained topside apartments, not for the sake of the environment, but to be close to the business aspect of their positions. This one belonged to a friend of Obrians, Jak had informed her. The man and his wife were living in the sublevels during the duration of the emergency generated by Kraken and his antics. Villimy had the place to herself, undisturbed.

She wandered through the three basic rooms, able to deduce the kind of people who lived here by the furnishings. There were charts on the walls, a bookcase of technical manuals and a wallscreen set up for considerable microfilm storage.

The man was all business, but the woman's touch here and there told of suppressed dreams, artwork of imaginary landscapes of green forests and blue skies, portraits of children and young people, sculptures of small animals and winged creatures that might have existed somewhere, sometime. It reminded her a lot of Jak's place.

Villimy checked the time. Reylaton wouldn't awaken for another two hours. She fixed herself a snack, then napped for a while. She paced the empty apartment for the last hour, trying to block the flood of fears and worries for the future. Too much could go wrong to give it any useful thought.

She checked a pictorial layout of Reylaton from the city directory, verifying that Reylaton Broadcasting, Channel One, lay only a short distance away, a ten minute walk along the pedestrian ledges of the stepped buildings rising on either side of the pavilion. She made no plans on how to approach the people there. Again, there were too many unknown factors to contend with.

There were few pedestrians in Reylaton's artificial dawn. Rich golden light spilled through the concave skylights arching overhead, although down the length of the torus the skylights curved upward, meeting the upcurve of the landscape in the hazy distance. In the relatively cool, early morning air, she would have enjoyed a panoramic view of mist-shrouded forests. She shared a deep need for green living things with these species of humans. There were forests above the city, but now she doubted if she'd ever have the chance to see them.

She stepped into an elevator that would take her to a plaza below, a commercial center where the central river ran beneath the pavement. When she stepped out into the sparse crowds of people, many of the shops had already opened for the day's business.

She walked straight across the plaza to Reylaton Broadcasting. A plaque in the entrance identified Tedd Ilotin as programming director. She walked into a main office and stopped before a reception counter.

A woman glanced up from her desk, startled by the strangely attractive person looking down at her. "May I help you?"

"I would like to speak with citizen Ilotin, please?"

"Your name, please?"

"Villimy Dy."

The receptionist didn't seem to recognize the name. She rose and vanished into a rear office. Villimy scanned the large office. Several tens of persons sat at consoles, brightly colored screens dancing, fingers racing across silent keyboards.

The receptionist returned with a vague smile. "I'm sorry, citizen Dy. The programming director cannot see you without an appointment. I can arrange one if you'd like."

"There's been an error," Villimy said. "He does want to see me. He has forgotten who I am. Would you deliver a brief message for me?"

The woman balked, but nodded, growing increasingly ill at ease in the presence of the woman with the siblant whisper. She wondered what the dark sunglasses were for. There were no chronically ill people on Reylaton, no crippled or genetically defective. "Yes, all right. What is it you want me to tell him?"

"Tell him I am Villimy Dy, not citizen Dy. I am not Rashanyn."

The woman tensed, her lips parting in astonishment. She remembered the name now. She turned and fled across the floor. A minute passed before the woman reemerged with a look of frightened determination on her face. A man followed her out of the office, breaking into a trot to catch up with her.

"Tedd asks that you leave immediately before he calls the authorities."

The young man coming up from behind put his hand on her shoulder. "It's alright, Dev. I'll handle this." He gestured for Villimy to follow him, retracing his route to the back office.

Villimy moved around the counter, aware of the many eyes following her. She caught sight of herself reflected in the glass front of the office. She had taken her white downy hair for granted. She looked just fine, but she stood out like a crack in the skylights of Reylaton.

The young man held a door open for her. Villimy stepped inside and stopped. An older, balding man looked up at her from behind a desk with an expression of barely concealed anger. The younger man moved to the side of the desk.

"Just listen to her, Tedd. It won't do any harm."

The older man gave a reluctant nod, studying Villimy for a moment before speaking. "What is it you want, Villimy Dy?"

Villimy tried a smile. "I thought you'd be interested in interviewing me."

The seated man reddened and glanced up at the calm composure of the younger man. "Jas, get her out of here. She'll have us all arrested for harboring a criminal."

"I'm not a criminal," Villimy said. "No legal charges have been filed against me or my friend, Chayn Jahil. I am not a citizen, not legally human. In fact, I am classified as an animal, falling under the jurisdiction of the Exobiology Institute and, indirectly, under that of General Pak."

"What is it you want to say on a public broadcast, citizen Dy," Jas, the younger man, said with a smile.

"Nothing specifically. I just thought you might have a few questions you'd like to ask me. After all, it isn't every day that you have aliens dropping in for a visit."

"It isn't every day that we mistreat them," Jas said. He looked down at Tedd Ilotin. "It isn't every day that we sit back and let a maniac run the city. Tedd, we can't bypass the opportunity. I'll check with our attorney's first, but for Rashanyn's sake, we can talk about the weather and what she had for breakfast. We'll fake the entire interview, treat her like a guest and visitor to the city. Think what it would do for our ratings!"

Tedd nodded. "Okay, maybe I jumped too quick. Citizen Dy, if this looks like it might work out, we have very little in the way of compensation we can offer you right away. And we will have to reserve the right to edit anything you might want to say."

"My purpose in coming here should be obvious," Villimy said. "I understand the position I'm in. It's not the fault of the people of Reylaton. But showing them what I am like might help to throw some light on what Kraken is like. That needs to be done."

"We can tape the interview now and broadcast this evening," Ilotin said. "Jas will take you to the studios. Jas, drag it out for at least an hour. We're down to three percent audience, but it'll pick up and we'll rerun it until we peak and drop back down to three percent. Tell Baxter to increase security during broadcasting. We'll vacate the offices tonight. Kraken will try to stop us, but if he can't stop us by force, it'll be too late for a court injunction. Make sure we clear with the legal department before you start."

Villimy followed Jas from the office, her heart beating furiously. This would be her final victory. She'd not be able to hide from Kraken so easily in the days to come. But Chayn would be returning soon.

He'd have to return very soon.

Twenty-one

Chayn's lungs collapsed. Internal body pressure triggered a sudden mass of aches and pains, sharp ones in his ears. Regardless of whether they intended killing both him and Joan or to just render them unconscious, Chayn had only seconds to act. And he acted from the first awareness of trouble, diving for the cable of the desk screen. He pulled loose the field plate, clamped a hand over it and drove with blind desperation into the electronic wilderness, searching frantically for the life support system. He found the monstrously complex system and forced himself to organize his perception in order to break down the mathematical structure into blocks of logic. He located the atmospheric regulatory circuits, discovering each cabin to be individually monitored. When he found the interference from some overriding input console, Chayn destroyed it, short-circuiting every core field in sight. He readjusted the interference and searched for more indication of trouble. His thoughts abruptly cleared, proof that his body breathed once again.

Chayn spent another few minutes analyzing the life support systems. They were incredibly complex, but his interface ability filtered through the ever present Watcher included an expansion of consciousness that allowed him to be aware of more information than he'd normally be able to keep track of and to reason his way through computer logic at lightning speed. Some of it, perhaps, was his own intelligence amplified by the capacity of the computers themselves, a more literal blending of human and machine intelligence than anyone could have imagined.

When he broke interface, confident that they were secure for the moment, he kept his hand over the field plate, holding himself away from interface by an effort of will. If his attention slipped for an instant, he'd interface. Which meant that an odorless, anesthetic gas wouldn't take him by surprise. Little of anything would.

Joan picked herself up off the floor, making funny faces to equalize pressure between her ears and the repressurized cabin. "That hurt! Damn them!"

"They failed," Chayn said. "If it makes you feel any better, I think I just destroyed some valuable equipment."

"You stopped them?" Joan stole glances at his right hand over the field plate.

"I'll explain when we have time. But I don't think they'll try that again. Not anything quite that obvious."

Joan's backlog of anxiety overwhelmed her. She slumped to the floor, crossed her legs and put her head between her hands. "They could kill us, you know. They could kill us in a fraction of a second."

"They wouldn't try it unless they were certain of success, unless they were certain I couldn't retaliate in half that amount of time."

"Are you just going to sit there like that for the next three days?"

"Do they have any surveillance on this cabin, any way to eavesdrop or detect our movements?"

Joan shook her head, her halo of curly hair flying. "No, nothing like that."

"Then how about something hot to drink? What's the menu like?"

Joan looked up at him and forced a smile. "Are we setting up housekeeping already?"

"Maybe, but without the fringe benefits. We can't afford to be preoccupied."

Mocking disgust, Joan climbed to her feet and busied herself at the food and drink dispensers. "I suppose I'm going to remember this as one hell of an adventure. If it gets any worse, I might take you up on your offer and part company. What if they know I'm not really a hostage anymore?"

"They know nothing. That's what makes them so nervous. They depended on what Trenton knew about me. His information is no longer reliable."

Chayn left the cable disconnected from the console and lying on the floor, the cabin too small to allow him to move more than a second or two from contact with it. He joined Joan at a small counter built into a wall. They drank a hot beverage and ate protein biscuits in silence.

"They'll get us during transition," Joan said.

"What's transition?"

"Once when the engines cut off and we go into free fall and once when the engines reignite for deceleration. They'll try something during one of the transitions."

"Tomorrow."

"Tomorrow's not that far away," Joan said. "We've been busy a good part of the day."

Chayn agree. They would act soon. The military wouldn't allow him near Jasper. They wouldn't dare chance it. And Chayn knew he couldn't keep tabs on the operation of the entire ship, or even a small fraction of it during interface. There were multiples of billions of individual factors to handle. And if he pushed too far, convincing the military that he was invulnerable, Jasper might decide to write the entire ship off as a loss. Possibly, they had arrived at that decision already, but first the commander of the Betafax IV would take whatever actions he could to rid his ship of Chayn's infestation. Chayn couldn't see Trenton, Jarl or General Pak cooperating in plotting his death, but neither would they have much to say about the strategy to neutralize him. Jasper would probably determine that in their orders to the commander. Chayn considered cutting off communication between the Betafax IV and the military base orbiting Jasper, but suspected the base would destroy a ship approaching in complete radio silence.

Acutely aware of Joan's presence beside him, Chayn wondered about Villimy. He ached for her. Nothing that Joan could add to his life would intrude upon the special place Villimy held in his very soul. He found Joan desirable and Joan increasingly scrutinized him in return, attracted to him as well, but studying him at odd moments with an almost objective focus, as if he had some special significance for her that arose from her attraction to him, but at the same time was irrelevant to it. As for Villimy, she would survive as least as well as he might manage to accomplish that feat. That's what worried him. Chayn had sensed some deep and vital attachment to him in the woman. Chayn did not want to see Villimy suffer anymore. No living thing deserved to experience the nightmares Villimy had survived. Chayn felt as if their very souls had intertwined, so intense had the rapport between them grown. Neither would survive without the other.

Joan glanced at him. "I'd be flattered if you were looking at me like that and thinking about me. But you're not. The other person you came with. She's a she, isn't she?"

"I'm not going to ask if you're psychic. I think I've been underestimating a woman's intuition. Yes, she is most definitely a she."

"Does she look like you?"

Chayn laughed. "God forbid!"

"What a strange expression."

"A memory that doesn't stand up to be counted. I don't want to go into that either. But my partner is a woman, quite unusual and she doesn't look a bit like me. She's human, but not genetically compatible with the Rashanyn. You look more like me."

Joan smiled. "God forbid. You're built like a fortress, like the base at Jasper itself. Men wouldn't find that attractive on me."

"Yeah, but your eyes are the right size and color."

Joan let that pass. "Are you genetically compatible?"

"With who?"

"With me."

That embarrassed Chayn. "Yes, we are. Supposedly, I'm of another species caused by what your genetic engineers call genetic drift, but we happen to be drifting in the same direction. Either that, or I'm of the original strain.''

Joan dropped the subject. They passed an hour in uneasy silence, engaging in small talk for few minutes at a time. They had too little in common to express the rapport that had developed between them. Chayn could sense it, but he couldn't define it. Neither of them grew restless. A part of Chayn's thoughts kept their focus on ways to avoid the rapidly approaching crisis. The intermittent conversation eventually arrived at the question of Joan's motives for staying with him.

"I'm a stock clerk," she said. "I joined the military for adventure. So far, my adventure has amounted to an overly possessive boyfriend and a cargo hold to keep organized. And it's just not an adolescent kind of hunger for adventure I'm talking about. There's no challenge in life anymore. Rashanyn stagnates. Most of the exploration missions to the nearby stars have been cancelled. The colonies have become reclusive and the military has nothing to do but shuffle diplomatic missions around the system. I don't want to settle down yet. I was searching for something first. But I guess it doesn't exist anymore. I'd go with you if you'd have me.''

"I'd take you if I could."

"I believe you." She glanced at him, but avoided eye to eye contact. "I don't even think you're just saying that to make me feel better. But it's not possible and I'll leave when I'm not of any use to you anymore. I know the difference between my fantasies and reality.''

"I could tell you to go after what you want in life, but I'm having trouble following that kind of advice myself."

"Later on, when things quiet down some, if they quiet down, I might ask a favor of you, Chayn Jahil. I might. Is it okay if I ask? I don't want an answer now, just permission to ask.''

Chayn nodded. "Sure."

They managed two hours of fitful sleep. Chayn slept on the deck, his hand inches from the cable and the interface plate. Dropping into the computer network occasionally, Chayn kept tabs on the lifeboat bays, suspecting what the commander of the Betafax IV might be up to, but unwilling to interfere with the functioning of the spacecraft. The first day passed, the first third of his journey.

The husky, computer-synthesized voice warned of free fall conditions commencing within thirty minutes.

"Won't they rotate the passenger section for centrifugal gravity?" Chayn asked.

"They won't bother. There aren't many passengers and most are employed by the military, accustomed to traveling on high speed runs. Besides, free fall is a change of pace. It lasts nineteen hours. It's a good time to save time in port, check over the condition of the hull and perform other, routine maintenance checks. If they try something during transition, can you catch them at it?"

"I'd better."

Chayn failed. The moment the engine was cut off, the ship's complement of lifeboats launched manually. Twenty of the small craft carrying over twenty passengers apiece ejected at right angles to the Betafax IV. Less than eighty persons remained on board. Chayn searched through the computer system for further signs of trouble, but found nothing. The commander of the ship had learned his lesson well. Anything out of the ordinary would be done manually if at all possible.

Chayn explained the situation to Joan.

"That was a desperate measure to take," Joan said. "We're at maximum velocity. It'll take a small fleet to retrieve those lifeboats when they pass Jasper. Chayn, what are they planning to do?"

"The question is, what can we do to stay a step ahead of them. We obviously don't have much time."

"We'd better move," Joan said after a moment's consideration.

"Explain."

Weightless now and growing accustomed to it, Chayn held on to a cable protruding from the wall. Joan dived to the cabin door and glanced up and down the elevator shaft-turned corridor once more. "I don't see any guards, but there are surveillance cameras in all the corridors. We're at level one, corridor five. Can you take care of them?"

Chayn remembered the electrical schematic of the Betafax. Computers regulated varying power supplies to equipment. He could overload and damage the cameras. "All right. I can do that, but what do you have in mind?"

"I know where there's an emergency access tube leading from a supply room just down the corridor to the level above this one. And just above that, there's a maintenance crawl space just outside the core. It runs most of the length of the ship."

"What's the advantage of hiding in a crawl space?"

"They can't locate us. And there's quite a few field plate cables you can use. It's a damn good idea. Take my word for it."

Chayn interfaced. Knowing roughly where to look, he had no difficulty locating the simple cluster of components that fed the security camera. He didn't perceive them as components. He had to experience the effect they had on an electric current to deduce their purpose. He selectively overloaded two of the cameras.

Joan led the way from the cabin with an excitement bordering on euphoria, diving down the corridor with an expertise born of long experience in free fall. Chayn rebounded from one side of the corridor to the other, forcing Joan to backtrack and give him a hand when he found himself floundering in midair. Joan sailed inches from a plastic mesh covering the lights on what had been the ceiling, using the mesh for traction. Once Chayn caught on, he could duplicate Joan's smooth maneuvering with only occasional blunders that sent him cartwheeling through the corridor.

Near the end, Joan swung around, dived for a door and

entered a small, unlit room, pulling Chayn in behind her. A light came on automatically. Joan pointed to a rectangle of metal set flush in what had once been the ceiling. She kicked it in, revealing a metal tube just large enough for Chayn to fit through if he set his mind to ignoring the potential for acute claustrophobia.

"It's never been used," Joan said. "You first."

Chayn guided himself up the tube. Joan gave him a shove and followed. The panel contained a handhold on the inside, allowing her to pull the sheet metal pack into place. It latched into place, obviously designed to be kicked in.

Another supply room slowed them down, forcing Joan to cope with two more panels as they passed through, but beyond, other exit points were set into the walls of the tube and posed no restriction. Approaching the end of the tube, they moved into darkness.

The tube intersected with a rectangular tunnel wide enough for the two of them to progress down its length side by side. A catwalk designed for traction in weightless conditions ran down one broad side of the tunnel. The other sides were thick with hardware, plumbing, and conduit. Joan moved on ahead, rapidly outdistancing him, but Chayn pulled himself forward cautiously, not about to build up enough momentum to mangle himself in these confined quarters.

Joan stopped ahead. When he caught up with her, she pointed between two junction boxes. Cables emerged from the wall of the tunnel and were attached by field plates to the boxes.

Chayn pulled one loose and interfaced. He entered darkness, unable to move. He backed out and tried a second plate. He nosed his way through bright and complex passages into the heart of the Betafax IV. He plied his way into navigation. A countdown was in progress for a deceleration rate of ten gravities. Once ignition commenced, ten gravities would be straight down the narrow tunnel toward

225

the stern of the ship with enough force to rip their arms from their sockets if they chose to resist such a crushing force.

Chayn entered the input areas of the computers, the bridge of the ship. He searched for ways to establish communication, locating visual and audio circuits open between the bridge and engineering. He commandeered them, running the visual through a digital analysis unit in order to see whomever he might be speaking with. Looking into the bridge felt he was seeing with his own eyes, but with damaged sight. He saw in only two dimensions and the detail looked grainy.

The commander sat on a dais overlooking several control positions in front of a curving control console. Chayn had a three quarter view of the man.

"This is Chayn Jahil," Chayn said softly, trying to avoid startling anyone. "We have to talk before someone gets hurt."

The man swung around in his seat to face the direction of the voice coming over the speaker. "I am Commander Domnivion. What do you wish to say to me?"

"I don't know. None of this is really necessary, but I don't expect you to know that. Is there anything you wish to say to me, Commander?"

"Only that we cannot allow you to reach Jasper. I've been ordered to self-destruct this ship if such a risk exists. And I can accomplish that regardless of your influence over our data processing facilities."

"If I used the same logic, Commander, I'd drain the bridge of air this very moment. The ship would then be mine. I'd have two days to isolate or murder the remainder of the crew and to assimilate the functioning of this ship. I could deceive Jasper into thinking the Betafax to be manned and under proper control."

"If you can accomplish that, why do you bother with threats and warnings?"

"I'm neither threatening you nor warning you. I don't intend to murder to accomplish what I must. I'll defend myself, but only within certain parameters of reasonable and decent behavior, Commander. People have died because of my blundering, but it won't happen again. I'm after my ship."

The commander did not answer immediately. "I have my orders. I've made my decisions and have initiated steps to have them carried out. This conversation serves no useful purpose."

"Give what I've said some consideration, Commander," Chayn said. "I may be a bit hard on your pride, but I'm not your enemy."

Chayn broke interface.

"It doesn't take eighty people to pilot this ship," he said. "The commander probably has search parties combing the ship. And we're on a countdown to a ten-gravity deceleration period. They're not going to let me get close to Jasper."

"What are you going to do?"

"I'm thinking of giving up. I can't wreak havoc through an entire civilization to lend a helping hand. It might be better to give them the upper hand for a change, to let their fear of me be neutralized."

"It won't work," Joan said.

"They still won't let you near Jasper and this ship can't simply turn around and go back. You won't like the alternatives."

"There are over eighty armed people after us and we have about an hour and a half to find a very comfortable place to be when the engines ignite. What do you have in mind?"

"There's a place where we can hide," Joan said.

"We have to go outside."

"Outside the ship?"

"It's a bit risky."

227

"No kidding."

"It's the only way to get back to the cargo hold. There's a supply of construction shed back there."

"You're in charge."

Chayn concentrated on keeping up with Joan. He didn't like this constant subservience to women, but under the circumstances, he wasn't about to protest.

"This won't work if the commander has all the airlocks under surveillance," Joan said, turning down anothe tube and vanishing within its depths.

"Does he want to keep us in?"

"That's just the point. If he's not wasting men keeping us from going to where we wouldn't pose any threat to him, there's an emergency manual airlock toward the stern I don't think he know about. The commander can't know every section of the ship as well as the people who work in them and he hasn't the time to be studying technical readouts right now."

They exited the tube into another supply room, the broad, well-lit corridor beyond empty for the moment. The airlock Joan had in mind consisted of little more than a hatch in what would have been the deck had the Betafax been rotating, an emergency affair for a quick, wholesale exit from the ship.

"I didn't think they'd be guarded," Joan said. "The commander isn't overlooking anything, though. We can get out, but we couldn't get in without signaling the bridge for assistance."

"What about the airlock in the cargo hold?"

"That's entirely manual," Joan said. "Even if the commander knows about it, he still has the cargo hold sealed from the inside. And the chances of him knowing about the construction shacks is just about nil."

Joan shoved off and floated across the corridor, jumping off the far wall in a bank shot that took her to the entrance to a chamber near the airlocks. Chayn managed to duplicate the maneuver. Inside were rows of pressure suits and lockers for personal storage.

"I don't know if there's a pressure suit large enough to fit comfortably," Joan said. "You might have to force yourself into one."

Joan took for granted that he'd not encounter serious difficulties. The suits, like the coveralls, turned out to be quite elastic. Turning slowly in midair, Joan kicked off her coveralls. With boots built into the uniforms, she wound up wearing nothing at all. Captivated by the sight, Chayn was startled to self-consciousness by her laughter.

"It's unavoidable," she said. "Now it's your turn."

Chayn noticed a white, square bandage taped beneath Joan's left arm. Then she vanished inside the bulky pressure suit, the halo of tight curls stuffed into an opaque helmet. Chayn assumed it to be transparent from the inside. She watched in silence as he stripped off his coveralls and fought to don the tight-fitting suit. The opaque helmet turned out to be transparent from the inside.

He joined Joan inside the inner chamber of the airlock. She closed the inner hatch, then opened the outer one, and Chayn drifted out into the stars.

Joan grabbed him by his foot and pointed out the handholds welded along the hull. The outside of the Betafax looked like an engineer's nightmare, a forest of hardware and naked superstructure.

Letting the lower half of her body drift free, Joan pulled herself along the handholds, moving rapidly along the hills and valleys of the hull. Chayn followed for what seemed like hours until Joan pointed in excitement. She stopped, planted her feet on the hull, and tugged at a handle.

Chayn motioned her back. He planted both boots onto the hull and put an increasing amount of pressure against the handle. The airlock was designed to unlatch with an upward pressure against the handle. Chayn wondered about his chances of retaining his grip should the hatch opened suddenly and throw him backwards.

Joan reached out, grabbed his helmet and brought it into physical contact with her own. "I feel vibration! I think they've moved engine ignition up a bit! Chayn, it's vacuum-welded! But you have to break it free!''

Chayn felt the vibration. He closed his eyes and put every last ounce of strength into one last, superhuman effort to break the airlock hatch free of its seat.

The blackness overhead flared into incandescent white. Blinded by the soundless glare, Chayn knew that the thermonuclear engines were burning, sun-hot fireballs contained in their magnetic bottles. Chayn didn't feel Joan reach out to him to bring their helmets together, but he heard her voice conducted through the plastic.

''Two minutes! Two minutes!''

Two minutes. And at ten gravities the landscape of metal stretching before him would be yanked out from beneath his grasp. The two of them would not suffer, not in the brief instant they'd spend in the thermonuclear fireball burning on the stern of the Betafax IV.

Twenty-two

Villimy sat before the wallscreen and watched herself on video. Her voice sounded so mellow coming from the speakers, her manner so shy. At one point, on the screen, she pulled off her glasses to massage the bridge of her nose and at that moment, happened to have glanced into the cameras. So used to seeing these people of Rashnyn, the sight of her huge, golden eyes startled even herself. Gold eyes, pale blue skin and a halo of white down that glowed with a life of its own in the bright studio lights. She remembered each moment of that interview, but not like this, not from this perspective.

''Your eyes are the color of Star Rashanyn,'' the man

who had interviewed her had commented at that point and she had given him a weak, quivering smile in appreciation for his gentle, sympathetic treatment.

"The sun of my world is much like Star Rashanyn," she heard herself say. "My world is tilted on its axis ninety degrees. There is a season where the sun circles the horizon once each day and another when a sunrise that never ends circles the horizon once each day. Before my people were civilized, we took to the forests for protection against the light of two summers."

The interviewer had encouraged her to talk about herself. The beautiful but strange creature on the screen appeared to be so sad and lonely. Villimy had never recognized the depth of that sadness or loneliness. Not once did the interviewer speak of or even allude to events transpiring in the sublevels. He never mentioned Kraken or even Chayn Jahil. He worked entirely with what he had on hand, an unusual person, and he explored the depths of that person's feelings, letting the audience react as it chose. But they hurt Kraken badly when the man asked for her parents and her childhood. The tears in her eyes reflected in patterns of color across the screen.

When the broadcast ended, Villimy watched the rioting outside the broadcast studio. Tedd Ilotin had placed cameras on the outside of the building to show the black-robed figures breaking their way into the empty offices. Kraken's rioting came off as distasteful, crude, and futile.

Broadcasting from somewhere in Reylaton from tape, the interview repeated itself over and over during the night, interspersed with increasingly detailed shots of the viciousness of the fanatics making fools of themselves. Villimy finally turned the wallscreen off.

Unable to sleep, she left the building, its only occupant, and stood on the pedestrian walk, leaning against the railing and looking out over the city. She could hear the sounds of the rioting in the distance, but the distant sounds of anger barely disturbed the tranquillity of the night. Overhead, the stars shone through the skylights. They glimmered on the canal running below through the pavilion. A breeze passed, caressing her face, the constant hum of her air-conditioning unit drowning out total silence. On impulse, she reached up and turned it off. The stifling heat invaded her clothing instantly, but she had learned how to relax, not to fight the claustrophobic pressure of the heat. For a moment, even the sounds of the rioting subsided and she listened to complete silence.

Her eyes scanned the dark canyon of stepped buildings across the way. She tensed when she saw the black-robed figures scattered over the face of the buildings on the pedestrian walks. She looked down on the walks directly below her and saw two other dark figures. Kraken had a search under way for her topside. His men were entering and leaving the buildings, conducting a methodical, well-organized search in the early morning hours of the new day.

Villimy heard a sound off to her right. She glanced in that direction. Two figures ducked into a recessed elevator station. They had already seen her.

She could see better in the dark than they. She could hear better. She turned her air conditioner back on. She started to walk away from the two men, away from her apartment, intending to lose the two before returning to the security of the apartment. She stopped. It would be futile. Others would be converging on the scene already.

Villimy turned back to the railing, deciding to pretend that she hadn't seen them. They stepped back out onto the walk, assuming they were hidden in the darkness and unobserved. Villimy could see the pistols they carried in their hands in her peripheral vision. Alive with tension, eager to attack to dispel the anger surging inside her, Villimy smiled.

When they reached out to take her by the arms, the pistols all but nudging the alien in the back, they saw a sudden blur of movement and a glimmer of light from huge, golden eyes. Two streams of bright red laser fire vanished into darkness. Villimy shrieked her anger, lashing out with bare feet, her hands frozen into claws.

She left them bleeding and unconscious, backtracking to her apartment, a strange exhilaration coursing through her like an electric current.

Five minutes later, a knock sounded at the door. "Open in the name of the Church of Rashanyn!"

"You have no right to enter my apartment!" Villimy shrieked.

"The Word of Rashanyn is the only authority we need!"

Villimy ducked into the bedroom. She heard the front entrance swish open. She heard one man enter the kitchen, the other approaching the bedroom. Villimy turned out the lights. The man entered and Villimy pivoted once, the outer edge of a bare foot smacking the man beneath the chin. His teeth cracked together and shattered, the concussion of the impact sweeping through his brain. He dropped unconscious and Villimy grabbed him, lowering his limp form to the floor. She pulled him off to one side and retrieved the laser pistol.

The second man entered the room.

"You have no right," Villimy said from the darkness.

The man fired at the sound of her voice, but the return beam of deadly light came from another direction entirely. The robed figure stood frozen for a moment, then slumped to the floor, the laser wound through his chest neatly cauterized.

A beeping sound came from the communicators the two men wore. If the searchers were as well organized as she suspected, it would be only a matter of minutes before others arrived.

Villimy left the apartment, walking quickly around the corner toward the main entrance of the building and the elevators that would take her back to the sublevels. She froze. A man in black robes stood in front of the elevator, his lavender eyes locking onto hers the instant she moved into view. For a long moment, neither moved nor spoke.

"Let me pass," Villimy said, her pistol dangling in her right hand. "I have no wish to kill you."

The man raised his pistol. In the time it took him to do so, Villimy fired twice. The laser pistol in the man's hand exploded in a gout of flame. The second beam passed through the kneecap of his right leg. He collapsed in a high-pitched scream of anguish.

Villimy stepped over him and pressed the disk for elevator service. Nothing happened. Villimy shuddered in fear and anger. She had only moments remaining before the building crawled with Kraken's men.

She ran back to the apartment and keyed in Jak Tellord's number on the wallscreen keyboard.

A voice answered, the screen remaining dark. "Jak Tellord, section eight, sublevel foreman."

"Jak, this is Villimy. They've shut off the elevators, Jak. I want to come back down."

"I saw your interview, Villimy. Kraken's gone berserk. He's slit his own throat this time. Wait by the elevator. It shouldn't take more than three minutes to override the controls and clear the aisle down here of an ambush."

Villimy returned to the corridors. They were empty and she could hear sirens in the distance. The elevators were recessed in the wall a meter or so, providing a certain degree of protection. She waited and listened.

The doors to the main entrance burst inward in a shower of glass. Three men stepped through the empty frames of the door, light gleaming from laser shielding. Villimy fired at the leg joints in the armor. The men stepped confidently forward, looking down at the laser beams deflecting from the mirror-finished armor and charring the painted walls. One of the men collapsed screaming, the other two hesitating, astounded by the accuracy of Villimy's laser fire.

Another went down in a howl of agony, the third turning to flee, his back undefended. Villimy waited until he stepped through the door frame before firing through the calf of his leg.

Villimy punched for the elevator.

The moans of the three men on the floor grated on Villimy's nerves. She stared down at the writhing figure at her feet, wanting now to do something to relieve his suffering, but helpless.

Two suited men entered the building. They wore metallic radiation suits sealed at the joints and helmets with periscopes to prevent eye injuries. Each carried a bulky weapon connected by cable to battery packs carried on their backs. Villimy pressed into the shadows.

One of the men fired. Villimy screamed as the supersonic frequency shock wave passed within a meter of her. Spots of blackness flickered in her vision. Knowing what a direct hit would do to her, Villimy stepped into the open and fired twice at the only available target, the weapons themselves. They exploded in a shower of sparks, but enraged by Villimy's seeming invincibility, the two men threw the weapons aside and charged her unarmed in an effort to panic her and force her toward the rear of the building.

Villimy stepped into the open and fired carefully at the periscopes. One of the men spun and fell against the wall, the other ducking his head, neither injured, but both suddenly blinded by the laser melting through the glass of the periscope.

The elevator doors opened. Villimy leapt clear in a startled reflex, but the elevator was empty. She stepped inside and punched for the main sublevel. The doors closed and the floor all but dropped from beneath her feet. When it stopped, the sudden deceleration forced her to her knees. Already she weakened. Quicker than the humans of Rashanyn, she did not share their stamina.

But the action saved her life. The doors opened. Three

laser beams burned their way through the rear wall of the elevator. In the dimmer light, the laser beams left tracers of ionization in the air. Villimy fired at their source. Two men fell into the main aisle and collapsed directly across from her. The third shot detonated a rifle in a blinding flash of light.

Villimy fumbled along the wall for the controls to shut the doors. They slid halfway closed. An unseen, unheard laser beam struck with knowing precision from outside. Villimy heard the crackling of short circuits inside the walls. The doors failed to close. Sirens wailed in the distance, but she had no illusions of being rescued by Jak or the authorities in time. If they had a sonic rifle handy, they'd take her without another shot being fired.

Villimy forced herself to relax and to take a minute to regain her strength. The air conditioner whispering on her shoulder expelled the intense heat her body generated. Hunger and thirst gnawed at her, but given a chance to transverse the main aisle, she could lose herself in the darkness of the side corridors. Risking death, but relying on the slow reactions of her adversaries, she stuck her head into the aisle, looked both ways, and withdrew. She sank to the floor in sudden depression. There were many tens of black-robed figures outside, probably many more hidden in the dark recesses of the corridors.

"Demon!" a harsh, male voice called out. She recognized the voice as that of Hadak, the assassin who had originally accosted her and Chayn topside soon after their arrival.

"Fool!" Villimy called back. "Coward! I am a woman! My name is Villimy Dy!"

"Come out unarmed. You will not be harmed. You have killed many men because of Kraken's orders to take you alive!"

Kraken may have had a preference for taking her alive, but many of the shots fired at her had been aimed to kill.

"You have one minute, demon. We have enough fire-power to reduce the elevator to molten slag! You cannot survive!"

"I die only if I am a woman!" Villimy said. "If I be a demon, you die!" Let him mull over that for a while. Hadak was one of those who took the demon business seriously.

Villimy smiled suddenly. She leaned against the wall of the elevator and relaxed. She both heard and felt the subtle vibration of the monorail in the aisle. It grew in intensity until even the men outside heard it. They scurried for cover, but not soon enough. The cargo transporter roared up, braking furiously. The bulk of the transport blocked the elevator, armed men in blue coveralls running past the half open doors. Villimy heard men screaming in the silent battle that raged outside, crimson light flickering against the curved hull of the transport. She slipped through the elevator doors and around the bulk of the transporter. Kraken's men had ducked into the corridors and the maintenance personnel were in pursuit. Villimy considered waiting by the transporter for Jak, but sighted a cluster of electric carts parked in the distance. She ran to them, jumped into the driver's seat of the nearest one and took the cart at top speed down the empty and silent aisle of the sublevel.

She parked the car near the ladder leading up into the air vents. She hesitated on the ladder, ensuring that no one watched from the darkness, then vanished up into the vent. Exhausted, she could barely remember the locations of the hidden panels. She transferred from one vent to another until she stood before a blank wall. She felt for the hidden switch along an I-beam. The doors to her apartment slid open.

The sense of alarm didn't quiet within her. She stood in the open doorway, her eyes moving as she scanned everything in view. Stepping inside, the doors closed behind her.

She walked directly to the kitchen, pulled a cup from the dispenser, and drank three cups of water. She pulled a protein cake from its dispenser and wandered back into the living room, chewing slowly on the cake, her thoughts in turmoil. She turned on the wallscreen, turning from one news channel to another, and smiled, encouraged by the renewed vigor and excitement in the faces of the commentators.

Kraken had been removed for power by the Reylaton Supreme Court, charged with violation of the Rashanyn Constitution. The old Council had been returned of their former positions until new elections could be held to reestablish proper, civilian government. Kraken had not been located.

Villimy turned off the air conditioner unit on her shoulder. She walked to the bathroom, stripping off her clothing. She showered, returning slowly to a state of calmness. Jak would arrive soon. There would be no more need for her to hide. And within hours, Chayn would return successful. Rashanyn would be safe. Villimy wanted to go home.

Exhausted, she headed for the bedroom, leaving wet footprints across the floor of the living room. She reached around the corner to turn on the light—and stepped into oblivion.

Conscious when she fell, she didn't feel the impact. She didn't feel the black boot that slipped beneath her hip and rolled her over, nor the muzzle of the sonic rifle that touched the side of her face.

Wild, gold eyes stared unseeing at the ceiling.

Twenty-three_____

One last panicky effort broke the airlock free of its vacuum weld. Joan dove head first into the well of blackness. Chayn followed, escaping the flood of radiation and radiant heat of the fusion engines.

A dim red light came on in a small chamber as Chayn slammed the hatch closed behind them. Joan struggled with the controls to recycle the airlock. The controls were not functioning. Chayn pushed her aside and put his massive weight against the inside hatch. He would never have been able to open it against a pressurized interior, but the cargo hold had been vented of air. They dropped into an abyss lit by orange lights scattered thinly throughout the cargo hold. Joan skydived across the spaces between cargo anchored in endless rows. Chayn followed just as effectively if not as gracefully, constantly tumbling and battering himself against cables, straps, and crated equipment.

Joan turned occasionally to check on him. Chayn gestured her on, hoping she knew what she was doing in the few moments of safety left to them. The engines were on open burn, but if the Betafax accelerated, they would fall through these open spaces at many meters per second.

Joan pointed. Chayn saw nothing but a row of large, round ended canisters. Then, he noticed airlocks in one end and several ports down their twenty-meter lengths. Joan dived for the nearest of them and opened the outer lock. She vanished inside and Chayn dove neatly through from behind.

He struck his helmet on the inside lock, stunning himself for an instant. Joan shoved him aside to cycle the lock. Once inside the canister, Joan activated the power. Lights came on. Chayn heard the hiss of air, but Joan pointed out a gauge to him as a warning against breaking the seal of his pressure suit. The temperature gauge rose more slowly.

Without wasting a second, Joan pulled two nets from a compartment and stretched them the length of the cabin. Support cables anchored them against cabin walls at several points. She gestured for him to climb into his hammock, then shoved. She crawled into her own, bringing straps around to anchor herself, Chayn fumbling with his, trying to follow her example.

An enormous pressure pulled Chayn face down toward a corner of the cabin. Straps and webbing strained against his sudden weight, creaking in protest. Chayn cried out in pain at the enormous stress tearing at his limbs. In the next moment, he blacked out.

". . . almost killed yourself."

Time had passed. Chayn had no idea how much time. He struggled to regain control of himself. Every muscle in his body felt strained, every tendon torn and every bone close to breaking. But it was only his usual weight entangling him in the net. Joan worked to free him.

"That was a long two minutes."

"More like five. Something delayed acceleration. Otherwise, we would never have survived. Lucky you did."

"Don't jump to conclusions."

Chayn managed to climb free of the net. The deck beneath his feet felt level. "What is this place?"

"A construction shack," Joan said. "They're scattered around orbital construction sites. Workers sleep and take their breaks and meals in these shacks. We're safe as long as the commander doesn't remember that we have them aboard. They evacuated the air in the cargo holds to keep us from taking refuge here."

"How much air do we have?"

"Enough."

"Does that mean we've outwitted the commander?" Chayn decided to let Joan do the thinking for both of them. He tried supporting his own weight to ensure that none of the sprains in his joints were serious.

"For the moment. Ten gravities worth of acceleration is hard to take without proper equipment. They didn't find us aboard the pressurized areas of the ship. They probably checked the airlocks and found two suits missing."

"They think we're dead."

"They won't assume that," Joan said. She rolled up the hammock and stuffed it back into its compartment in the wall, then unfolded a conventional bunk. "The commander won't dock at Jasper. That's why we're accelerating early. Jasper will send out an investigative party. They'll have the ship thoroughly searched. We'll be found if we're still around by then. They're thorough."

"Where else is there to go from here?"

"Nowhere," Joan said.

Chayn welcomed the opportunity to refold and store his own hammock and unfold his own bunk on the opposite side of the cylindrical cabin. The aches and pains could have been considerably more serious. Chayn stretched out on the bunk with a groan, appreciating the feeling of weight despite the comfort free fall would have afforded him. Relaxing, he felt the accumulation of fatigue begin to flood through him. He treid to remember when he had slept last and fell asleep wondering. Sometime later, he awakened long enough to verify that everything was holding its own, then let sleep claim him for as long as it wanted. Or, as long as Joan allowed. He dreamed of sleeping, of dropping into tranquil blackness, letting it fold over him again and again, dropping deeper and deeper into a realm of serenity. But there were people waiting anxiously for his return and a soft voice urging him to consciousness. He couldn't sort out the faces and names of the people, but he struggled to consciousness.

He opened his eyes to a strange but beautiful face. Villimy's face would have been a familiar one, known to the deep levels of his psyche still dominating, but giving way to waking consciousness as sleep dissipated. But it was still a friendly face. He smiled back at it.

"Do you want to sleep longer?"

After a moment, Chayn felt surprisingly clearheaded. How long have I been out?"

"Twelve hours."

Joan went back to a small table and two seats she had unfolded from the wall at the other end of the cabin. Chayn joined her, sipping a cup of hot beverage she had fetched for him. It was a common drink, bitter and a stimulant, but was rapidly growing on Chayn. Joan set two plastic-wrapped biscuits in front of him.

"Joan, how do you manage to take this all in stride?"

"I might regret it all later, but I've enjoyed myself so far. Or does that sound suicidal?"

"Someone accuse you of being suicidal?"

"I like to move around a lot."

But she seemed quiet and tense. "Is something bothering you?"

She smiled. "Not really. It's just that it'll be over soon."

"A real dead end, huh?"

"I'm afraid so, Chayn."

"We've made a good team, Joan. I've made a lot of friends I'll probably never see again. I regret that, but we ought to find some ingenious way of getting you back to your old life style unharmed by all of this. If there's something you need from me, I'd appreciate it if you'd ask."

Her smile faded slowly. "I'll be okay."

Joan went to the rear of the cabin and stripped off her pressure suit, changing into a fresh pair of coveralls. Again, Chayn noticed the bandage under her left arm.

"Did you injure yourself?"

Joan turned and looked at him for a moment, then stripped off the bandage before pulling the coveralls up and over her shoulders. "There's a bathroom and shower through that hatch." She pointed to the hatch Chayn had assumed to be another airlock. "Zero-gravity equipment of that sort is a

242

bit complicated. I'll have to explain it to you if you want to make use of it.''

Joan handed him what turned out to be a plastic packet containing papers. She sat back down, sipping her beverage, nodding for him to look at the content of the package.

It contained a tube with a needle and a yellowish solution. Chayn unfolded the papers. They were documents. One was an application to the Population Board of Illitulan, the other labelled a Certificate of Allowance.

"Illitulan is a small and isolated colony," Joan said. "Most of us can no longer interbreed with our own people. One of the obligations of citizenship for a woman is to give birth to one child. Just one, to bring in as much genetic variety as possible."

"That's one hell of an obligation," Chayn said.

"Not really. All I have to do is to request a blood sample from a friend. Every cell in the body contains a usable chromosome pattern. Our genetic engineers can arrange for the rest, including a surrogate mother if I don't choose to bear a child myself."

"What sort of obligation do the men have?"

Joan smiled. "To father a child, of course. If not genetically, then socially. Each child must have a mother and a father, preferably a mated couple. There are enough of those to go around. If a man is not mated, then he provides financially and has certain legal rights to associate with the child until adulthood. It's an arrangement that has worked for over a thousand years."

"There are no orphans?"

"No, of course not."

For some reason, that touched Chayn. "Why do you carry these documents around with you on your person?"

"For the next few years, the choice of the father of my child is mine. Afterward, the choice belongs to the Population Board and he's chosen from a gene bank. I carry that around with me because the people I meet come and go so quickly. I thought perhaps I might find someone that would make a good genetic father in a situation a lot like this one, with you and me.''

''I see.'' Chayn hoped he didn't see as clearly as he suspected he saw, particularly in light of the mysterious favor Joan wanted to ask of him.

''I wish you the best of luck, Joan. Is that why you joined the military?''

''One of the reasons. Let's just say I intend returning to Illitulan. It's a pleasant place to live, Chayn.''

The hours threatened to pass in silence. He had too much time to think. He thought of Illitulan and Reylaton and thousands of other colonies he would never visit in this isolated segment of human civilization.

''Is that why you asked if I'm genetically compatible with the people of Rashanyn?''

''Yes.''

''Is that the favor you wanted to ask of me?''

''Yes. Of course it is.''

''Why haven't you asked?''

''I haven't the right.''

''Is it that much of a sacrifice on my part? A blood sample?''

''That's not the way I plan to work it. I want to go back to Illitulan carrying my child within me. That's why I had to let Karl go. He wanted to mate with me, but I have my own people to mate with. I only wanted Karl's baby. That and a blood sample. Because even if there are genetic deficiencies, they can be corrected during pregnancy as easily as before.''

''Oh,'' Chayn said, blushing furiously, his heart suddenly hammering.

And Joan refused to say anything more.

''That's why you helped me,'' Chayn said.

Joan was lying on her bunk when he spoke. ''I didn't want to let you go so easily. And you said you could help

244

Rashanyn. But I told you I don't have the right to ask anything of you. Chayn, you can offer, but you have no obligation to me.''

Chayn stretched out on his own bunk. ''When you go back, what are they going to do with you, Joan. They're going to know you helped me. I couldn't have survived without you.''

''They'll court martial me,'' Joan said.

''You knew that from the beginning?''

''Yes. It's not important.''

Chayn decided to keep his mouth shut until he figured out exactly what Joan was up to. She was an acutely intelligent woman. She had left no loose ends dangling in her behavior except one, the conflict between her own sense of honor and something she had wanted from him all along.

Joan dropped to the deck. Chayn looked over at her. She stood beside him and stripped off her coveralls.

''Joan, what are you doing?''

''I'm going to take a shower.''

''Why does that make me nervous all of a sudden?'' he asked.

''Because when I'm done, it's your turn. I know you find me attractive, Chayn. I've been dishonest with you, but I cannot undo my error now. It's too late.''

''I don't understand.''

''They'll send me back to Illitulan if I carry the seed of a man. Because we are a civilization of small, isolated colonies, that is a law that transcends all others.''

Joan closed the hatch to the freefall shower behind her. ''I see,'' Chayn said to the empty cabin.

Formalities consisted of a blood sample that went into the preservative solution and Chayn's signature on one of the documents. When Chayn stood before her in the silence and the isolation of their bubble of heat and air, Joan looked up at him, the largest, most massive male she had ever met. Her breasts rose and fell quickly with the dawn of arousal.

"God forbid," she said softly.

It felt strange to make love to Joan Losa. Chayn had no memory of any sexual experience except with Villimy Dy. And he did not betray Villimy. This was the same physical act, but performed with an almost solemn deliberation. Chayn could not forget for an instant that he would be leaving something of himself behind in the care of this beautiful creature willing to span worlds in search of the father of her child. Their almost simultaneous climax felt like an ending and a beginning at the same time. Joan cried and Chayn held her close until her sobbing subsided to a quiet joy.

"Thank you, Chayn Jahil."

"Take care of yourself, Joan. There's nothing else you owe me."

Chayn felt a sudden sensation of falling. Lying on his side beside the woman, he grabbed for the edge of the bunk. Joan gasped and held tightly to him.

"Free fall," she said. "We've arrived."

"Arrived where?"

"I don't know. There's a good chance we'll rendezvous with a ship sent from Jasper. Let's wait and see if we dock. We'll feel it when it happens. But I'm sure Jasper will have this ship dismantled piece by piece to make sure you're not still aboard, Chayn."

Chayn tentatively let go of the edge of the bunk, fascinated by the sensation of weightlessness with Joan still in his arms. She hooked one leg around his thigh and pushed against the wall, sending them tumbling slowly through the length of the cabin.

"Trust me," she said. "I'll know when it's time to leave."

Chayn held lightly to the woman. "And I suppose you're not ready to disengage just yet."

"Not yet. Are you?"

"Maybe we'll give it another minute or two."

Docking occurred an hour later. Chayn felt the vibration in the air and eyed Joan. She nodded.

"What now?"

"We get into the pressure suits and wait. If it's a search, we're better off letting them find us here."

The wedged themselves together in a corner, looking out through one of the ports for signs of movement. Joan explained the search procedure she anticipated. The ship would be evacuated of personnel. The search party would be equipped with devices capable of detecting the subtle environmental effects of a warm, living body within a certain area. Section by section, they inspected, secured and vented the atmosphere behind them.

Hours passed in total silence.

"Something is wrong," Joan said.

"Not as far as I'm concerned."

"I don't think there's a search party. I think they evacuated the ship."

"Just abandoned it?"

"Yes."

Restlessness began setting in. "Let's take a walk and see what's going on."

They donned their helmets, vented the construction shack, and opened the airlock. Chayn insisted on taking the lead. Moving into the main aisle, Chayn glanced down the abyss toward the airlocks to the inventory stations. The airlocks hung open.

Chayn launched himself between rows of cargo in the customary zigzag path to the airlocks, his final aim off less than a foot. He broke his momentum against the bulkhead, swung himself into the airlock, and kicked down the aisle before the row of consoles.

The life support section of the ship was not rotating. All of the hatches hung open. The entire ship was in vacuum, exposed to the airlessness and dead cold of deep space.

Joan slipped ahead of him, diving the length of the corridors in seconds. Chayn followed, knowing where she was headed. In the free fall environment, it took only minutes to reach the airlock leading to the bridge. Here, the hatches were closed, monitor lights indicating an atmosphere beyond. Joan waited for Chayn and pulled herself up to bring their helmets together for direct communication.

"It's a trap!" Joan said, her voice sounding hollow and distant. "They figure if we're aboard somewhere, we have to show up here sooner or later!"

"There's something more to it than that," Chayn said. "Let's have a look."

Joan complied. She reached out to activate the controls. The wide doors slid aside. They pulled themselves into the inner chamber. Joan handled the controls, removing her helmet when pressure and temperature reached normal.

Chayn opened the inner hatch.

There were ten men inside the bridge waiting for them. Seven were armed troopers, their weapons holstered, their legs hooked through rungs around the walls of the bridge. The other three were General Pak, Trenton, and Jarl. There were handholds in the low ceiling. Chayn entered the bridge with a grin.

"Chayn, it's good to see you again," Trenton said. He watched Joan enter behind him. "You've made another friend."

Joan's eyes were fixed on General Pak with an expression of dismay.

"What's happening?" Chayn said.

"The Betafax IV has been abandoned," Trenton said. "All military personnel have reported to the Jasper base by shuttle. The Blackstar aliens are massing for an attack, Chayn. Jasper doesn't care about you or the ship anymore. They abandoned the Betafax. They put General Pak in charge of double-checking for your presence, but Jasper figures you were killed during deceleration."

"Will they let me have my ship?" Chayn said.

Trenton shook his head.

General Pak spoke. "General Cornoben is Supreme Military Commander of Rashanyn. He disallows the release of your craft, Jahil."

"What's this all about, then?"

"When the Blackstar fleet moves in, billions will die," Trenton said. "There's no effective defense. In retaliation, Rashanyn's fleets will move out to attack the bases at the black hole and the two dwarf systems. It will be a war of mutual destruction. It's been considered inevitable for so long, nobody is searching for alternatives at this late hour. If we could provide you with access to your craft, Chayn, how could you affect the outcome?"

"You know the answer to that!" Chayn said in an angered explosion. "I can run a reconnaissance mission and return in hours! I can communicate with them! Damn, Trenton, you know me better than to distrust me!"

Jarl spoke. "How are you able to effect interface with the computers without the use of the equipment we provided for you?"

"Jarl, figure it out for yourself! The sublevel maintenance people!"

Jarl frowned. "Did they microminiaturize the equipment? Is that what you're saying?"

"It's inside me!" Chayn said, holding out his right palm. "I stopped the military from entering Reylaton in exchange for their help!"

Joan moved to Chayn's side. These were men who knew Chayn as she had known him, people who could ill afford to distrust him now.

"How would you go about retrieving your craft?" General Pak said. "Ultimately, it's my responsibility. Can you recover it without attracting undue attention or damaging the defense effort?"

"I can check and see," Chayn said. "I can look around and back out without being noticed.

"Will a microwave relay suffice?" Jarl said. "It's the best we can offer."

"Jarl, all I can do is try."

General Pak pointed to an exposed field plate on the console behind him. "Then be our guest, citizen Jahil. Jasper has never suspected that a radio link poses any threat to them. But Jasper's the most heavily shielded base in the system. Any sabotage at all will trigger a general alert. If that happens, I'll have you executed on the spot. Is that clear?"

Chayn glanced around at the armed guards. "You couldn't make it any clearer, General."

Chayn launched himself toward the console. He pulled himself into a seat and latched a belt across his lap. He glanced at Joan, offered her a smile of reassurance and turned around, placing his right hand across the field plate.

It took time for the microwave relay to reach Jasper. His psyche fell into a light as white as the hottest star, filtering through a lifeless structure of intelligence. His consciousness of the self he had known gave way to pure knowing and expanded into a reality of symbolism vaster than the universe he had known through his own organic brain.

Chayn entered a sublevel of reality itself.

Twenty-four

Villimy awoke, conscious without content of thought, aware without feeling. She gradually regained bodily sensation and felt uncomfortable pressure. Stirring to life, she tried to move, but discovered herself immobilized. Still naked to stifling heat, she innocently wondered what had happened to the air-conditioning unit in the apartment, running Jak's number through her thoughts to ensure she still remembered it. Something was wrong. She retraced her memory, but could find nothing to explain her inability to move.

She opened her eyes, blinded by fluorescent tubes glowing overhead. She turned her head and saw black-robed figures standing over her. Startled to full consciousness, she looked about wildly.

Both Kraken and Hadak stood beside her, another guard position near a door, all three studying her with expressionless intent. She raised her head to see why she couldn't move, but a large, rectangular device lay across most of her body. She moved her arms and legs to confirm her suspicions. Her wrists and ankles were strapped down to an examination table.

"It ends where it all began," Kraken said to her. "In case you don't recognize your surroundings, these are the laboratories of the Institute of Exobiology."

Villimy lay her head back down, staring into the lights. An overpowering depression overcame her.

"You have won a major battle, Villimy Dy. I grieve for my people. I, in turn, have won only a small victory, provided the privilege of ridding Reylaton of your influences and further harm. My people have sinned. For that they will suffer. But you will torment them no more."

Kraken walked slowly around the table. "You have the body of an angel, the soul of a devil. Your eyes are the color of Star Rashanyn, vanity that gave you away in the very beginning. Only a demon would have the audacity to haunt us by such an appearance. And your friend of such great physical strength. Where is he?"

Villimy closed her eyes, barely listening to Kraken's insanity.

"The machine above you is one of Trenton's toys," Kraken said. "It's a fully automated, computer-driven, biological systems analyzer. There is some life in this system. We discover new species each year. A specimen is fed to this machine. It dissects and analyzes, tissue layer by tissue layer, identifying organ function, tracing neural circuits. After all, a living organism is like a machine and can be defined by function and components. I am curious as to whether it is sophisticated enough to handle something as complex as a human or near human body.''

Villimy opened her eyes again. Chayn would be returning soon. Why did she give up life why she still lived?

"Where's Chayn Jahil?" Kraken said.

"He left."

"Left? How? To where? For what purpose?"

"Chayn destroyed the hub and escaped. He goes to the Blackstar system to stop the invasion."

"He's not on Reylaton?"

"No."

Kraken began pacing along the length of the table, glancing at her from time to time. "I do not expect the truth from you."

"Then examine your own motives for speaking with me at all."

Hadak stepped forward. "Kraken, this is dangerous. Kill her."

Kraken waved him aside, his brows furrowed in thought. "You imply that Chayn Jahil has power sufficient to stop the invasion. Where does he obtain such power?"

"Through the starcraft provided to him by the stargods."

"The Stargods of the Word of Rashanyn?"

"They do not exist in those terms," Villimy said. "They are not supernatural. Any form of life that evolves beyond the comprehension of another form of life is a stargod relative to it."

"And what of the Dark Stargod."

Villimy turned her head to look at the man. "There is no Dark Stargod. Evil does not exist in the universe, only ignorance and hatred born of fear."

"Kraken, do not listen to her! I beseech you! Destroy her before it is too late!"

"Hadak, be silent," Kraken said, then turned back to Villimy. "What of the Word of Rashanyn?"

"The Word of Rashanyn is a personal account of the arrival of your people into this planetary system. It is vague because it is a consensual opinion of events that transpired causing the near failure of the early colonies to survive and authoritarian because of the self-discipline required for survival. Neither are my people native to their world. No human in this galaxy can be native to its world. There was another galaxy and another alien invasion on a vast scale. We knew that many ships attempted to cross an intergalactic abyss, but did not know that other human civilizations had established themselves here just as Rashanyn does not know of other human civilizations."

"And does your people have its Word?"

"Yes. In the beginning, this galaxy was called Andromeda. And all of humanity originated in the Galaxy of Man, home of the stargods of humanity."

"How do you know that man survives in this Galaxy of Man?"

"Chayn Jahil is proof of that. It must have taken our people and yours millions of years to make such a journey. Your history goes back two thousand years since your arrival at Star Rashanyn. Ours goes back ten thousand years. Chayn Jahil arrived from outside this galaxy, travelling at at speed greater than the speed of light. He must have departed just yesterday in comparison to such lengths of time."

"And who are the Stargods of your Word?"

"They are just myths and legends of entities that protect humanity from obligeration, entities that nurture and protect us."

"They are not eternal, living outside of time and space?"

"They are now. Our legends say that they once lived on a world, that they evolved on one world from a seed of life

253

and lived as men before evolving beyond physical being millions of years ago. We would have shared such a destiny except for the millions of years we spent in suspended animation, transversing the abyss between the two galaxies.''

"What is the name of this world?''

"It was called Earth.''

"Is Chayn Jahil a Stargod?''

"Chayn Jahil thinks of himself as an orphan, a tool of the stargods. Obviously, because of the starcraft, he is close to the truth.''

"And you call yourself human?''

"Kraken, Chayn Jahil must be representative of humanity as it was in the Galaxy of Man a long time in the past. Rashanyn lives in space, shaping the environment to suit yourself. In two thousand years of animate life you have not changed, but my people adapted to the surface of an alien world and changed to fit into the environment and the biosphere. I know that now. And you know that I am no demon. Men endow demons with superhuman abilities, but you have been defeated by your use of fear to manipulate your people. I have not displayed supernatural powers. Neither has supernatural intervention played any role in recent events. Chayn Jahil destroyed the hub to aid in your downfall, not to protect you from General Pak. Chayn obtained that power from your own technology, from Reylaton Electronics and the people of the sublevels.''

Kraken nodded slowly and began pacing again. Hadak followed close behind.

"Kraken, destroy her.''

"Hadak, do you insult me by accusing me of being beguiled by the words of this creature?''

"No, Kraken.''

"Do you believe that a demon is physically invincible?''

"No, Kraken.''

"Why your impatience to destroy her? What is the power of a demon, Hadak?''

"Deception, Kraken."

"And how do you judge the behavior of men?"

"By acts rather than words, Kraken."

"Therefore, her words in themselves are futile, but she claims that Chayn Jahil will stop the Blackstar invasion which is an act of great magnitude if accomplished. Villimy Dy, when will this be accomplished?"

"Within two days," Villimy said.

"Hadak, we have defiled Rashanyn to force our people to realize that fear is a greater menace than the Blackstar aliens. Now that invasion is imminent and we are powerless to accomplish more, we can only continue the hunt for Chayn Jahil upon Reylaton. But this creature will live for two more days. Much of what she has said is truth and I do not enjoy seeing myself reflected in her words."

Kraken turned and left the room.

Hadak began pacing around the examination table. Villimy tensed, aware that the greatest hazard remained to threaten her.

"Kraken is beaten and weakening," Hadak said. "He does not carry the battle to its conclusion."

Hadak stopped, standing out of sight at the head of the table. "Why do you not speak with me as you spoke with Kraken."

"My respect for Rashanyn grows," Villimy said. "I thought Kraken to be insane, but he only lives through the figments of his own fears. Ultimately, he must use reason to escape his own nightmares."

"Blasphemy! You speak nothing but blasphemy!"

Villimy smiled. "And you, Hadak. You have been reduced to pettiness by your fears. The smaller you become, the more overpowering your fears become. You defile the worlds of Rashanyn with your pettiness. If evil exists, men like you are evil. You believe in evil to such depths, to be called ignorant and weak would be a compliment in comparison with the truth. Men are primitive entities in this galaxy, not at all like the destiny that awaited men in the

Galaxy of Man. And in this galaxy, Hadak, you are among the most primitive of men.''

''I shall destroy you, demon!''

''Try, Hadak.''

Hadak exploded in rage. He rushed to the console controlling the apparatus hanging above her. He flipped a switch.

Villimy felt the machine come alive above her. Hydraulics whined. Motors whirled. Villimy felt innumerable blunt probes tough the flesh of her torso, outlining her shape and form as they ran down the length of her body. On data screens, Villimy watched the vast amount of information the device accumulated. She didn't feel the X-rays taken or the sonic probes forming a three-dimensional image on one of the screens.

A red light flashed on the console. A computer synthesized voice spoke.

''Analysis terminated. Specimen exceeds physical parameters.''

''Override!'' Hadak cried out. The machine did not respond. Hadak searched the controls with an explosion of rage. Somehow, he managed to override the automatic termination.

Villimy tensed, her heart beating furiously. Heavier mechanical arms tested the firmness of her flesh, clamping tight on her hips. She felt pinpricks of needles entering her flesh and withdrawing at random. Her body jerked as electrical stimulation contracted muscle groupings. The pinpricks became increasingly selective, narrowing down the structure of her muscular system.

The red light flashed again. ''Biopsy analysis terminated. Specimen qualifies as aware. Anesthesia required.''

''Override, in the name of Rashanyn!'' Again, Hadak managed to reactivate the machine.

The canopy covering her torso began humming. Villimy felt a breeze of countless, whirling scalpels caressing her skin. She tensed and closed her eyes. At the first flicker of pain across her stomach, Villimy screamed.

"Stop!"

The red light flashed. "Specimen qualifies as self-aware. Biopsy priority terminated."

"Override! Override!"

Hadak fought the controls, but the console failed to respond. Even the restraint system released automatically. A slight pressure against the canopy sent it rising on a central pole. Villimy rolled off the table and stood. Hadak backed away from her, his eyes wide with terror.

"Your first lesson in humanity, Hadak. Your technology is extensive enough to prevent it from being abused. Safeguards were built into this equipment from its conception. But that never occurred to you, did it, Hadak? Kraken knew about it. That's why his threats were tacit and implied. He will murder if it serves his purpose, but not out of personal vengeance. Kraken is not a fool, but you are, Hadak. In all of Rashanyn, you're the only real enemy I've had. And you are not even a worthy opponent."

"Shoot her!" Hadak called to the confused guard standing next to the doorway. "The demon is loose! Shoot her!"

Villimy leapt forward faster than Hadak could retreat. She grabbed him by the scuff of the neck and dragged him around in the same moment the guard fired. Hadak jerked once and Villimy screamed, but enough of the laser beam dissipated in Hadak's chest to do more than to cauterize a small circle of skin high on Villimy's left breast. The pain served a useful purpose. In a strength born of rage, Villimy threw Hadak's body across the room and across the path of the guard trying to escape through the door. He fell and struggled to his knees. Villimy leapt forward, cracking his head against the wall with the heel of her foot.

Villimy looked around the lab for a communications screen. She took two steps toward it.

"It is quite useless," Kraken said.

Villimy spun around. Kraken stood in the doorway, a pistol in his hand.

"I am convinced you ar who you say you are," Kraken said, looking down at the bodies of his comrades. "We have underestimated each other severely."

Kraken pointed to the far corner of the laboratory. "Dress," he said. "I appreciate beauty, but I am not perverse."

Villimy found her pair of white coveralls draped across a table. She pulled them on and turned on the air conditioner. With the low hum of the device, she felt cool air creeping along her body. She leaned against the table, fatigue coursing through her like a fatal disease.

"Do not try to attack me," Kraken said. "I mean you no harm with this pistol, but you must stay with me for a short while. I don't want to die at your hand, but neither do I wish to shoot you. Come with me, please."

Villimy led the way out of the lab and through a short corridor to a small office. Kraken sat behind a desk inside and motioned Villimy into a chair against the wall.

"Do you have any idea of how long Rashanyn has suffered?" he asked after a moment's silence.

"Tell me what you wish to say," Villimy said.

"Rashanyn built an empire during the first thousand years of its existence. For a thousand years, Rashanyn believed it could overpower the Blackstar aliens. Until the first probe incidents began and Rashanyn became aware of the power it faced."

"Rashanyn has declined since," Villimy said. "Is that what you have to say?"

Kraken looked surprised. "So few recognize the fact. When you were in the sublevels, did you notice the unoccupied areas? Have you noticed that Reylaton's population here on the surface occupies no more than the pavilion strip that circles the torus of the city?"

"I've noticed," Villimy said. "It speaks of greater populations in the past."

"It does indeed. A thousand years ago, Reylaton had a population of one hundred million and an average of two cities a year were being built in the system to house our expanding population. One hundred billion people lived in the Empire."

"One hundred billion?"

"Does that surprise you? It's such an intimate facet of our lives, not at all apparent. Not to the civilian authorities or even to the military. We seem to function at high levels of efficiency, but the fact remains that Rashanyn has had a negative growth rate for one thousand years.

"It used to be that Rashanyn panicked over the probe incidents, rallying behind a banner of patriotism that the military could barely contain. But the military convinced the population to wait, until Rashanyn's strength increased as they believed it would, century by century. But there hasn't even been any technological innovation in over five hundred years. Rashanyn's strength does not grow, it wanes.

"Today, even more severe steps are necessary to rally Rashanyn to an attack of the Blackstar aliens before it is too late. Even if only one percent of our population survives retaliation by the Blackstar aliens, that one percent will be freed of the weight of chronic repression. That one percent will grow and thrive and perhaps leave this system altogether for richer and safer worlds upon which to grow. Do you understand what I am saying?"

"Yes."

"You and your friend arrived at an inopportune time. I am not alone in my efforts to stir the public to new heights of fear and panic. It is the only weapon left to us. There are many like me who have formed a secret organization that seeks to cure Rashanyn of the slow cancer that threatens us with extinction. I will tell you of our strategy, Villimy Dy. You deserve to know, but at the same time, it will be too late to act to stop us."

Villimy waited for Kraken to continue. He rose and stood

looking out over the city through a small window. It was daylight outside, perhaps late afternoon already. Chayn should have returned by now.

"This organization of which I speak had intended to simulate a Blackstar invasion by destroying one thousand cities throughout the Empire with thermonuclear warheads."

"What!" Villimy gasp of astonishment sounded as a whisper.

"There are fusion devices planted in one thousand cities. None have substantial military bases in the area. We would not think of damaging our military capacity. For when the cities were to have been simultaneously destroyed, the military mind would never have conceived of such a monstrous plot within the civilian population of Rashanyn. Automatically, the military would have launched its attack upon the Blackstar aliens.

"The journey to the Blackstar and its colonies would have taken a decade. Once the first fleet was launched, it would have been too late to back down from the attack, even if later, the military had learned of the nature of the mysterious destruction that would have taken the lives of one half billion people. All of Rashanyn would have been put on a war footing. At one year intervals, other fleets would have been launched behind the previous one. And the population would have had at least two decades to prepare for civilian defense."

"That's unbelievable!" Villimy said.

"When you arrived, we simply included you in our strategy. We tried to use you to add to the fear and panic of alien invasion. It was an unfortunate, but necessary decision. Rashanyn is so seriously ill that it could not even respond to news of aliens from space in the manner that a mentally healthy civilization would have responded."

"You speak in past tense," Villimy said. "You called off the destruction. Why? Because of Chayn Jahil?"

"Of course not. We cannot rely upon one man to solve a dilemma that has taken twenty centuries to accumulate. We cancelled the destruction because of recent news. The Blackstar aliens are massing for an attack outside of the planetary system of Star Rashanyn at this very moment."

Villimy all but leapt from her seat in shock. Kraken's pistol leveled on her, an expression of fear appearing and passing from his face.

"We assumed that the massing forces would galvanize the civilian populations to action, a massive campaign of survival. We would have preferred to see Rashanyn take the initiative in the inevitable war, but we waited too long. We thought that events would run their course without our intervention and that some part of Rashanyn would still survive to flourish again."

Villimy stood, a confused and frightened expression on her face. Kraken backed away from the window and gestured for her to look. It was what she wanted. She could sense no activity in the city. Villimy moved to the window and looked out. In the bright gold light she saw no movement. The pavilion looked deserted.

"How much panic do you see in Reylaton? The apathy, the lethargy, the malaise is so deeply ingrained, that even facing annihilation, Rashanyn still does not respond. The military will fight the Blackstar fleet as well as it can, but the civilian populations do not move to defend themselves."

"So you're going to still do it," Villimy said. "You're still going to destroy the cities."

"The shock will break through the malaise. The populations will respond. One half billion will die, but of the remaining nineteen and a half billion, even more will survive the attack. There is so much that can be done. If Rashanyn doesn't move soon, we fear total annihilation. No survivors at all."

"When?"

"Minutes, hours." Kraken smiled. "The plan is automated. No one can stop it from happening now. Even a warning in this last minute would be lost from memory during the cataclysm.''

''Reylaton?''

''Reylaton will not exist tomorrow.''

Twenty-five

Chayn Jahil's identity reassembled before the cold intent of the Watcher. Memories, beliefs, expectations, ideas and attitudes that were his restructured to self-knowledge. Recovering from the psychic shock of dissolution, Chayn spent a few moments basking in the security of the magnetic presence of the Watcher before attempting to explore the nearly infinite data processing structure of the military base for evidence of the presence of the starcraft.

He found it stored in the vacuum of a small cargo bay and explored different approaches to freeing the craft without triggering security alarms and risking his own life. On impulse, Chayn tried to interface with the starcraft through the microwave relay.

His consciousness spread through the starfields. Elated by the unexpected, indirect interface, Chayn discovered the means of escape. He systematically neutralized the security systems of the bay, then opened the bay door through the Jasper base computers. The starcraft went hyperlight and, within fractions of a second, appeared alongside the Betafax IV. Chayn gradually disengaged from the complex interface. More than ever before, he recognized the limitations of his physical senses. Back on the bridge of the Betafax IV, he looked around at the human figures clustered around him.

Chayn unbuckled the seat belt. "Am I free to leave?"

General Pak stared out through a three-dimensional screen at the black oval of the starcraft hanging in space alongside the Betafax IV. "How can we be certain you won't abandon us?"

"Do I owe you anything?"

General Pak refused to take his eyes from the screen. "No."

"I'll do what I said I'd do," Chayn said. "Then I'll go back for Villimy Dy."

Chayn glanced at Trenton and Jarl. "Whatever I might accomplish, be sure you two take your share of the credit."

And to Joan: "Accompany me to the airlock?"

Joan smiled and donned her helmet. Chayn slipped on his own and sealed it in place. Together, they cycled through the airlock and drifted through the airless corridors, hand in hand.

Stopping before the main airlocks, Chayn swung around and touched the forehead of his helmet to Joan's, looking through the reflections of their faceplates to her dark eyes.

"I may not be able to return."

"A part of you does not leave."

Joan backed away and opened the inner airlock. She joined him in the chamber. When the outer lock opened, the bulk of the starcraft blotted out most of the starfield. Joan squeezed Chayn's hand in a final farewell.

Chayn turned to the starcraft, hoping he could make an accurate freefall dive between the two airlocks. It would be embarrassing to miss and go spinning off into space. He jumped off, the blackness of the hull field rushing toward him. Entering the interior of the alien craft, he skidded across the deck in its inexplicable, artificial gravity, the most graceful entrance he could make under the circumstances.

He stripped off the pressure suit and helmet and with a growing anxiety, climbed into the contoured crypt on the dais centered in the chamber.

The universe sprang into existence around him, including the transparent detail of the Betafax IV and its crew of eleven. The mind field of the civilization of Rashanyn glowed like a bright aura throughout the planetary system of Star Rashanyn.

Chayn focused on distant Reylaton and confirmed only that Villimy still lived. He allowed nothing else to distract him from the challenge of the Blackstar fleets massing in an arc outside of the Rashanyn system. He sensed a strange kind of life aboard those craft, but could not be sure he could communicate without an actual attempt. And that would best take place in their home system, the civilization built upon the debris of the nearby black hole.

Chayn moved there. The background of the stars barely shifted in the short distance of three light years. He gazed upon the gravitational vortex of the black hole radiating a sphere of light in the high end of the spectrum as matter spiraled and converted to energy before siphoning at the speed of light through a pinhole in space-time.

Chayn turned his attention to the debris orbiting the black hole, much of it in semi-stable, but eccentric orbits. Somewhere in the past, the black hole must have torn apart a small star and its planetary system. The massive belts of asteroids, dust, and gases couldn't have been retained from its own past history.

Evidence of the technology of the Blackstar aliens wasn't hard to detect. Several hundred kilometers out, a symmetrical, orbiting band of civilization glowed with the ruddy heat of industrial waste. The largest structures Chayn could find were less than a hundred meters across, but there were uncountable numbers of them. The densest regions of the asteroid belt were crawling with insect like machines burning and crushing their way through the debris for useful elements, vast, open-structured factories functioning like living organisms, serviced by the same machinery they produced.

Chayn found the aliens. They lived inside their machines. They were an archaic, ancient life form that couldn't have evolved much over the eons, blobs of protoplasm with complex neural systems interfaced with electronic and mechanical systems of their technology. Chayn couldn't detect where organic life ended and mechanical life began. Isolated from their technology, the Blackstar aliens would be blind, deaf, dumb, isolated from physical reality. Even their intelligence appeared to be augmented by electronics. They were a simple life form evolved to its absolute potential.

Chayn moved to a densely populated region. Swarms of craft detected him, altered trajectory and began converging upon him. Within minutes, the starcraft became the dark core of an artificial star burning so bright it would be visible in the Rashanyn system within three years. The mindless, vicious attack lasted for what seemed like days. Chayn withdrew into himself, sending out tendrils of his senses occasionally to check on the progress of the attack.

When it ended, Chayn checked out the most common forms of communication in use between individual components of the fleet surrounding him. Chayn began radioing on the same frequency, wondering if the intelligence of the starcraft standing behind him would have any difficulty translating communications from a life form that had little in common with humanity.

"We are people of the Blackstar," the translation began. "You have invaded our realm. We cannot destroy you, but we demand that you depart and leave us in peace. We have no desire for communication or commerce with you."

"I visit your realm, respecting your dominion over this system of the Blackstar," Chayn responded. "I come in peace to ensure peace. I am from the distant stars, but I come as representative of the people of Rashanyn, the intelligence inhabiting the realm of the gold star which you prepare to attack."

Chayn sensed the excitement and sudden anger. "Invaders! Aliens! The contamination must be sterilized! It spreads and threatens our destruction!''

"Mutual destruction is threatened. You cannot destroy Rashanyn without facing destruction yourselves. Violence on such a scale satiates no anger, neutralizes no fear, solves no problem nor does it ensure future peace and prosperity.''

"Rashanyn is alien. Rashnyn is the unknown. The unknown is to be feared. Chronic fear debilitates. Circumstances are intolerable. Rashanyn must be destroyed at all costs.''

"Your logic is unfortunately correct. Perhaps it never occurred to you as it did not occur to Rashanyn, that the dilemma is a mutual one. Neither is there a viable solution to the dilemma if neither life form can communicate with the other. Unless, of course, an objective third party cares to mediate. I am such an agent if you wish me to be. I can communicate with the people of the black hole and with Rashanyn. I am known. With communication, the unknown becomes known. With my help, you and Rashanyn can communicate, form agreements, and cooperate. You are alien to one another, but there is value in differences. You have needs that Rashanyn could provide. Rashanyn has needs that you can provide. Commerce is infinitely preferable to death.''

"Agreed. In principle,'' the voice said.

"Before armed conflict commences, you must construct devices of communication. It must be your responsibility.''

"How is that to be done?''

"Translation is now being accomplished by a technology far in advance of what your people or Rashanyn possess. Arrange to broadcast your language and its structure to me and I will arrange for you to receive a simultaneous equivalent, the language of Rashanyn and its structure. Despite the vast amount of data that must be processed, I perceive that your data processing technology is sufficient to the task in a relatively short period of time.''

"We will comply in one rotation about Blackstar."

That amounted to one day. Despite Chayn's impatience, he couldn't help but be impressed by the tight communications grid that connected the system into a single web of intelligence. Swept along on the outer rim of a whirlpool of violence, Chayn provided the Blackstar aliens with information on himself, his experiences, detailing the science and the biology of Rashanyn as best he could. He forced himself to speak of relevant matters for hours, knowing the Blackstar aliens would need a vast amount of information to work with as a foundation of understanding of their neighbors in space.

The Watcher functioned in conjunction with the consciousless intelligence of the starcraft to effect the enormous challenge of communication. As Chayn probed the system, he learned that the Blackstar aliens were not individuals but gestalts of individual organisms that in themselves had no respectable levels of intelligence. Chayn spoke to the collective intelligence of a species rather than to an organization of individuals. They perceived space and time in strange ways. Their senses were completely beyond his comprehension. They perceived magnetic fields and spoke with neutrinos.

After the mass, high-speed transmission of data, the Blackstar aliens checked out their computer-processed translation, speaking directly to him, bypassing the Watcher and the starcraft.

"Do you understand these words?"

"Clearly. How about mine?"

"Adequately. One problem remains. Our fleets prepare to destroy the aliens of the gold star. This task force functions as an independent entity. It would take three years to reestablish communication with our brother. You must stop them, but you must not harm them."

"How?"

"We do not know. You cannot reason with them. They

267

will destroy Rashanyn or die in the process."

"I will find a means to turn them aside peacefully," Chayn said. "But your next fleet of probes must be devices of communication. I will stop Rashanyn from initiating hostilities during the spans of time necessary to travel the distances between your civilizations. You will, in return, receive communication from Rashanyn. I guarantee that Rashanyn will respond in a rational and intelligent manner to your suit for peace. I firmly believe that you will respond in a similar manner. You are alien to one another, but you share the same physical universe. Alternatives to peace are limited to mutual destruction. Do you agree with my proposition and my analysis of the situation?"

"We fully agree."

"Then I depart your system in peace. I am proud to have known a people as great as yours."

Chayn left for Rashanyn, trailing a shimmering blue radiation that would crawl across the void at the speed of light. But within moment, he probed the void ahead, located the Blackstar fleet moving in on Star Rashanyn and appeared in space before it.

Chayn knew that interface with the starcraft took place on a subconscious level. He knew what he could accomplish and what he could not accomplish with the starcraft, but only on an intuitive level, never with a clear, conscious knowing. Neither could he comprehend how he accomplished what he did.

He anchored the starcraft in another dimension and unleashed the space-warping drive of the craft. Chayn sensed the distortion of space and time into which the alien fleet fell headlong. Individual vehicles elongated and fled down the fields of distortion, shifting at right angles back into interstellar space. From their perspective, the gold star ahead became a bar of light, the universe itself distorting off to one side. Without altering velocity or trajectory, the alien fleet found itself heading back into space at vastly increased speeds.

Chayn followed the fleet. Within hours they began the tedious process of decelerating and swinging back toward Star Rashanyn. Again, Chayn used the distorting fields to send them swinging back at ever increasing velocities. After the second incident, from what he could interpret of the alien mindfield, he felt certain that they had shifted the focus of their attention to a return to home ports.

Chayn sped back toward the gold star, narrowing down his journey to a torus of metal circling the fourth world. Elated by his success, Chayn wanted to broadcast to the entire system his success in turning aside the threat to Rashanyn, but at the sublight speeds the two technologies were limited to, time was of no importance. Chayn reached out to touch the mind of Villimy Dy, hoping with a quiet, suppressed desperation that she had survived the turmoil of events upon Reylaton.

Chayn pulled in close to the hub of Reylaton, recoiling in horror at the contents of Villimy Dy's mind. She would survive. Chayn would see to that immediately. But soon, in some indeterminate amount of time, a half billion other human beings would die.

Twenty-six

Chayn Jahil overpowered every radio receiver on Reylaton. "This is Chayn Jahil. Do I have authorization to dock?"

Two minutes later, he received his reply. "Citizen Jahil, this is Reylaton Traffic Control. You have authorization to dock in bay forty, berth fifteen. An escort is being sent up to take you before the Reylaton Council. Please wait in the reception terminal."

Chayn located the small docking bay off to the side of

the construction work under way on the damage he had caused to the trio of giant bays for the transporters clustered around the hub, craft pulled from local service from every available source to aid in Reylaton's evacuation. The dark side of planet Gilderif glowed with the light of thousands of fusion engines burning, spacecraft and even orbital colonies themselves accelerating slowly into higher orbits about the planet. Warnings of the thermonuclear warheads planted in one thousand Rashanyn cities were spreading throughout the system. The colonies were dispersing, assuming by order of the Supreme Council that the nearest neighbor of every colony would soon vanish in the fireball of a three-hundred-megaton thermonuclear explosion. On Reylaton, the only city known to harbor a warhead, hours, perhaps only minutes, remained to evacuate fifty million people, in itself, an impossible task. Blind searches for hidden warheads were under way within every other city within the Rashanyn system.

Chayn docked, matching airlocks as closely as possible and locking the starcraft in position. He donned his pressure suit and stepped into an airlock, cycling himself through into a prep chamber where he changed into coveralls. Guards were waiting in the reception terminal, a group of four men in gold and blue military uniform with one leg tucked through rungs in the wall in the weightless room. They escorted him to a personnel elevator for the trip to the torus.

Reylaton appeared normal to Chayn, the streets busy with crowds moving with purpose toward the spoke terminals. But in comparison to their usual, subdued behavior, they moved in quiet panic. A monorail bus delivered him and his armed escort to an impressive-looking piece of architecture, Reylaton City Hall. The Council occupied a small, dark chamber. Three men sat behind a curved bench at the end of the room. They motioned Chayn to take a seat before them. The guards filed from the room.

"Where's Villimy?" Chayn said.

"She's with a sublevel foreman, a man named Jaklin Tellord," the central figure behind the bench said. They didn't seem to be interested in adhering to formalities.

"And Kraken?"

"He has been arrested."

"How did you learn about the warheads?"

"From Villimy Dy," the man said. "We do not know what to make of her warning. However, Kraken will not speak and we do not have the time for procedures which would reveal the truth. We are operating under the assumption that Reylaton is in critical danger."

"What can be done about the situation?" Chayn said.

"Very little. Every colony is conducting searches, including Reylaton. It is, however, a hopeless task. Even Reylaton cannot evacuate its population within the general time limit we have to work with. Some of our topside personnel may be evacuated in time, but sublevel personnel have elected to search for the device."

"Am I free to move about as I please?"

The elderly man nodded solemnly. "You are."

"I have a report to make to Jasper and to the Supreme Council."

The Council member looked doubtful of the potential usefulness of Chayn's information. "We will have our interplanteray broadcasting facilities standing by."

"Can you provide me with an escort to get me down to Jak Tellord's section as fast as possible?"

"That will be arranged immediately."

Chayn stood, but hesitated before leaving. The three men gazed at him without expression, whether paralyzed by the shock of current events or merely stoic to their fate, Chayn couldn't tell. As he left, one of the men picked up a communicator. A grim-faced, armed guard met him in the outer offices of the Council and led the way to the nearest elevators within the building complex.

In the sublevels, an electric cart awaited them. The guard drove, using a dash communicator to locate Jak Tellord and arrange for a meeting. They parked alongside a cluster of small buildings in an open area along the main aisle. They entered an office and silence fell. Villimy Dy turned, her eyes locking onto his. She ran to him, slipping quietly into his arms. She held him tightly, her body shuddering, her hot cheek pressed against Chayn's broad chest.

"Obrian's assigned me to this area for the search," Jak said to Chayn. "If there's a bomb, I don't think Kraken's people would have planted it in the sublevels. Chayn, without some idea of where to look, this whole search is futile."

Chayn slipped an arm around Villimy's shoulders and held her tight, intuitively knowing that he couldn't let her go again without an emotional catastrophe.

"I have a way to help," Chayn said. "Right at the moment, I must use a wallscreen."

Jak assigned one of his men to escort them. Chayn and Villimy followed across an expanse of open pavement to a corridor and the first apartment within it. Chayn keyed for the Council and worked his way through three secretaries to one assigned his request.

"Citizen Jahil, we have opened a channel to Jasper, but we've been put on automatic hold. And we can't obtain an audience with the Supreme Council. The emergency has backlogged even priority calls."

Chayn started to protest, then closed his mouth. He shut off the screen. "The starcraft is faster. I have to talk with General Cornoben or the Supreme Council," Chayn said to Villimy. "We can't risk getting killed here."

Chayn returned to Jak's office, walking in step with Villimy Dy. "I have a way of locating the warhead," Chayn said to Jak Tellord. "I need to know what one might look like."

Jak turned to a small screen nearby and tapped a key. A schematic appeared on the screen. "It's basically just a container of tritium that's detonated by raising its temper-

272

ature high enough to sustain fusion by a high powered laser. We have ten year olds down here who could both design and construct a weapon of this type. The only problem would be a power source. The laser would have to tap into a high voltage line and too sudden of an unexpected drain would trip circuit breakers.''

Chayn studied the schematic. ''I think I could recognize something like this if I saw it. Jak, I'll work through you. If I find something, get the information through channels fast.''

Chayn picked up his escort outside the office. ''Back to the hub. Fast.''

Once back in the weightless environment of the hub, Chayn passed a computer terminal near the prep chamber, Villimy noticed the skill with which Chayn handled himself in the weightlessness. Chayn broke their forward momentum and stopped, looking into the deserted room with its wall of computer terminals. ''Villimy, go on ahead and stay aboard the starcraft. I can interface through the starcraft for the search if I can arrange a microwave relay, but I can communicate better with Jak through a direct channel.''

Villimy balked at the idea of leaving Chayn's side.

''We won't be returning to the torus,'' Chayn explained. ''We'll be leaving for Jasper immediately. They have to know what happened at the black hole.''

Villimy complied, knowing Chayn would function better without distractions. She could accomplish nothing further. Only Chayn stood a chance of saving fifty million human beings from imminent destruction.

''You risk your life here,'' Villimy reminded him.

''I'll find the damned thing before you get a pressure suit on. Be sure you do. There's a meter's worth of vacuum between the outer airlock and the starcraft. If I run out of time, I don't intend getting blown up with Reylaton. The rest of Rashanyn is depending upon what I've learned of the Blackstar aliens.''

''Will the starcraft survive if the warhead detonates?''

273

Chayn grinned. "Yes, it will. Believe it or not."

"I prefer to believe."

Chayn chose a terminal at random, sat down and pulled the field plate alongside the device free. He placed his right hand over the plate and dived into the crisp, mathematical structure of the computer network. He located access to microwave communication equipment, but no line of sight between the antenna dish and the starcraft nestled in the docking bay. Chayn used navigation to locate a transporter he had noticed hovering off the hub. Without arousing anyone to his activities, Chayn established a link with the transporter.

Interfacing through the starcraft by way of the microwave relay, Chayn turned the focus of his consciousness upon the city. His enlarged consciousness could sweep through large areas of the city in seconds, but it took several minutes to locate the suspicious-looking equipment at the base of a spoke hull in the sublevels.

Chayn established direct voice link with Jak through the man's personal communicator. "I've found it, Jak. It's disguised as a generator, the center one of a cluster of three. There's a support beam number 8867 almost directly overhead."

"We're headed there now," Jak said.

Chayn watched Jak proceed to the location. From other parts of the sublevel, Obrian and his best technicians converged on the area.

"Jak, be careful," Chayn said. "The thing is booby-trapped. The access panel will short-circuit a high voltage through the triggering laser if it's removed."

"Chayn, where are you? How are you obtaining this information?"

"I can't explain now. Don't let them go through the access panel. Cut through the sides of the generator housing. There's enough insulation to protect the tritium container."

Obrian and his technicians were close enough to overhear

the conversation. They proceeded as Chayn directed.

"Something's happening," Chayn said. "Cut off the power to the cable running in the six-inch conduit directly behind the generator housing."

"Chayn, that's a main power cable to the hub. We can't cut off power until we provide alternate sources of current."

"You can and you'd damned well better. I saw a relay trip. There's a power drain in progress. What does that mean?"

"That's how they avoided tripping a circuit breaker. A condenser is building up a charge. It'll short circuit through the triggering laser."

"How much time do you have?" Chayn asked.

"Enough time, Chayn. We're going to go directly through the access panel and destroy the laser. We won't be any worse off than we are now."

"Jak, that's not the way it's designed. Don't . . ."

It was too late. Chayn saw the short circuit. A laser beam glared bright for an infinitesimal fraction of a second. A fireball blossomed.

Whiteness obliterated the universe.

Twenty-seven_____

"Villimy?"

Villimy looked around the empty chamber of the starcraft. "Chayn, where are you?"

"Do as I say, Villimy. I've readjusted the life support parameters of the starcraft. The temperature is dropping. Take off your coveralls and lie in the contoured crypt. The contour will readjust to your shape. I have something to show you."

"Chayn! Where are you! What's happening!"

"I'm here with you. Do as I tell you so that I can show you that everything is okay."

"But where are you?"

"I'm still interfaced with the ship. I can't explain now."

With her hands shaking so badly she could hardly hold onto the zipper clasp, Villimy stripped off the coveralls. The air cooled rapidly. It thinned, smelling fresh and clean, triggering old memories of the face of a bright world. She stepped onto the dais with caution, running her hand inside the soft lining of the crypt. It was Chayn's shape. It belonged to him.

"It belongs to you, Villimy. Lie inside. I have something to show you."

Chayn sounded cheerful. He didn't sound as if anything was wrong. Villimy could hear the gentle, compassionate coaxing in his voice. She stretched out inside the contour. For an instant, she lay awkwardly, the contour pressing in all the wrong places. Suddenly, it softened and reformed. She sank into its embrace. It firmed up about her hips and the small of her back, gently grasping her limbs and each individual finger.

A shock passed through her. It felt like she pivoted over backwards. She tumbled off into momentary darkness. Then, there were lights.

Stars.

She could see all around her, an awesome spectacle of the universe from an omniscient perspective. Star Rashanyn glowed warmly in the distance. The dark face of a world turned slowly beside her. She could feel the texture of the world and perceive its hidden side. Too awed to panic, Villimy lost herself in the titillating task of trying to discern how she could see in so many different ways.

"There are more than three dimensions here," Chayn

explained. "The human mind can't perceive them. You'll never understand how it's all accomplished."

Chayn drew close to her. In a way not quite physical, he pressed up against her, merging with her so that the essence of his being became hers as well. Villimy sighed, more satisfied by his presence than she could have imagined, the biological pairing instinct quieted and fulfilled.

"It's not so bad out here like this," he said, his thoughts clear to her in all their subtle nuances. "We have to go to Jasper now."

But neither could he hide anything from her.

"Chayn, where is Reylaton?"

"Not now, Villimy. One thing at a time."

The stars brightened in one direction, shifted into the ultraviolet. Behind her, stars blackened in the depths of infrared. A starbow formed around the craft, a halo of colored light. Then the universe snapped back to its normal perspective. They moved faster than the speed of light, but only for a moment. Star Rashanyn dwindled. A world shot into view and stopped dead in space beside them, a huge, banded, monster of a world.

"Jasper," Chayn said. In some familiar manner, he indicated a bright sphere of metal off to one side. "That's the military base."

Villimy could see inside it. She could feel the people.

Chayn spoke, his voice translated across the entire radio spectrum. "Commander Cornoben, this is Chayn Jahil speaking. I have a message for you. Pay close attention to what I say. The invading fleet of the Blackstar aliens has been turned aside. They return unharmed to the black hole. When they arrive, they will learn of my visit to their system. The next probe incident you experience will consist of communications devices. The Blackstar aliens will speak to you. I have provided them with the means of communications. They, in turn, will provide it for you. Rashanyn and the Blackstar aliens have no further cause for waging war. The Blackstar aliens are peaceful, rational entities. They are alien, but have much of value to offer Rashanyn and much of value to gain.

"General Pak, Trenton, Jarl— thanks for your trust and friendship. Villimy Dy and I encountered no real enemies within the Empire of Rashanyn, only the mutual enemies of fear and distrust which we have conquered. Now is the time to grieve and afterward, to plan for the future. I would like to stay. I cannot."

Jasper moved away. The starbow formed. Villimy waited. When the stars returned to their normal perspective, they moved. Against a stable background of the universe, the nearer stars slipped past the starcraft on all sides. Villimy estimated their velocity at four or five light-years per second.

"Where are you, Chayn?"

"I've been worrying about that myself, Villimy. Obviously, I'm here with you. There's no doubt about it."

"Your *body*, Chayn. Where is your *body*?"

"I forgot, Villimy. I forgot where I was. Reylaton died. The warhead detonated. That's why I said what I had to say and left Rashanyn. The Empire suffers and we can't alleviate the hurt. A thousand cities died, a half billion people. The explosion engulfed the starcraft, but it couldn't have damaged it. You never felt the blast, did you? And you were only a few kilometers from the center of it."

"Chayn, you were outside the ship!"

"In conventional terms, I guess I got killed. But I was interfaced with the starcraft. Evidently, that counted for something. I don't feel less than I was. I feel much more. My interface with the starcraft is much deeper now. Just as you do not feel your body, I do not feel mine."

"That makes me feel strange, Chayn."

"When you are interfaced like this, you don't feel emotion as deeply as when you are in your body. Most emotions are based on physiological reactions anyhow."

Villimy remained silent, aware of herself as a center of consciousness among the onrush of stars.

"Out here like this," Chayn said, "there's not much to be said about corporeal life. Going back is almost like having the largest part of yourself die. I guess I don't have to go back anymore."

"Then I'd better stay with you," Villimy said. "I don't like knowing what I should be feeling, though. But it is so peaceful and beautiful out here."

The infinite panorama of the galaxy slid slowly by.

"There's darkness ahead," Villimy said.

"The space between two arms of this galaxy. That's where your ship died. We'll pass near, but we won't stop. I can do a few things that I couldn't before. Your navigational computers might give us a location of your home sun. It will be badly dated information, but I have ways to project it forward."

Chayn didn't let Villimy know as they passed the derelict. Villimy didn't notice the microscopic bit of metal trapped in the invisible web. Chayn gathered the data he needed and let his new unconscious, the enormous intelligence of the starcraft, process and analyze it for him. A few tens of thousands of years made a vast difference in the position of the stars within the galaxy, but the location of Villimy's home sun arrived as a knowing. Chayn altered trajectory a little and accelerated, the transdimensional engine of the starcraft pulling in foreshortened space.

Long before Villimy grew concerned about the length of their journey, Chayn narrowed in on a orange-yellow star. He spiraled into the system, passing as many of the planets as he could in one, smooth trajectory. Villimy silently observed one deserted world after another.

The third world looked like Chayn's ancient memories of Earth, a green, blue, and white world, swirled with clouds and dusted with the rusty colors of deserts. A band of light circled the equator of the planet. Approaching,

Chayn reached out to discern spaceships, countless thousands upon thousands of them, the transportation facilities of the entire system gathered in one place. But they were deserted, empty of life. Chayn probed the surface of the world. It teemed with life, but not with the civilization it had once known.

At the same time, Chayn heard the beacon emitted from a satellite far out on the edge of the system. Chayn amplified the beacon signal and allowed Villimy to listen.

"The stargods arrived," Villimy said. "The Galaxy of Man is safe for humanity once more. The Empire of Man thrives and extends its warmest invitation to the refugees of Andromeda to return if and when they so desire."

"They went home," Chayn said. "While you were gone, someone like me arrived with a message. That's what I am. A messenger of the stargods."

Villimy looked down upon the lonely and deserted world of blue skies and green forests. "I don't want to be the last one," she said.

"Come with me?"

"Where else is there to go?" Villimy said in a dreamlike state. She would need time to recuperate, to assimilate all that she had experienced.

Chayn took Villimy toward the edge of the galaxy. In time, they arrived. Chayn edged the starcraft forward into intergalactic space, but sensed that he could not return so soon. He oriented Villimy so that the starfields of Andromeda spread before them.

"Even if I could travel fast enough to span the galaxy in hour hour," Chayn said, "there are so many stars that by the time we finished exploring the last of them, the earliest would have died and new ones brought to life. There are human refugees here, Villimy, worlds and people like yours and Rashanyn. Man can adapt to anything, but he can't go back if he has forgotten his origin. Let's look around first and see how many of them we can find.''

Chayn felt her curiosity and her concern. She nudged against him in acquiescence, deriving security from his presence. Chayn rushed forward toward the wall of light. Reentry triggered an ancient, associative memory.

The stars fell around him like luminous snow falling from a black sky.

In the far future,
an interstellar pleasure ship
is launched on a voyage of death!

There are fun and games on board for
mid-flight entertainment. And suddenly,
there is a horrible accident. And blood.
And death. And then the alien armies
strike.

SCIENCE FICTION

0-8439-2058-0

$2.50

THE SCORPIO CIPHER

RALPH HAYES

Rosenfeld was the man who invented America's greatest weapon—the deadly laser cannon.

Now Rosenfeld was the captive of Iranian zealots who were determined to learn the secret of his design.

Gage was the man the President sent into Iran to get Rosenfeld out.

It wasn't routine—even for Gage, whose assignments were never routine. Rosenfeld was held under heavy guard. Rosenfeld was being tortured by a twisted master of pain.

And Gage was supposed to take Rosenfeld's place!

LEISURE BOOKS   **1060-7/$3.25**

THE MICROWAVE FACTOR

Aaron Fletcher
Bestselling author of *OUTBACK*

DEADLY STAND-OFF

As relations between two international super-powers hang in the balance, it becomes clear that two innocent children hold the key to the fate of the world. Their stepfather must keep their deadly secret to save his career—even if it means he must sacrifice them both!

Price: $3.25
0-8439-2010-6
pp. 304

Category: Adventure